# THIRSTY

## C. ALLISON DEVESLY

*C. Allison Devesly*

LUMINARE PRESS
WWW.LUMINAREPRESS.COM

Thirsty
Copyright © 2019 C. Allison Devesly

All rights reserved. This book or any portion thereof may not be reproduced or used in any manner whatsoever without the express written permission of the publisher, except for the use of brief quotations in a book review.

Printed in the United States of America

Cover Design: Melissa K. Thomas

Luminare Press
442 Charnelton
Eugene, OR 97401
www.luminarepress.com

LCCN:
ISBN: 978-1-64388-162-1

*To my husband and twin daughters.*

*Thank you for your support and patience during this endeavor.*

Daniel Branovitch was once a man with a home, a family, a wonderful life. He wasn't a rich man, but he did well enough as a police officer. He still wore a uniform after ten years, but he didn't care. Daniel never worried about moving up, making detective. He wanted to spend his free time with his wife and children, not studying for the detective's exam and not playing the politics that comes with moving up in the ranks.

He loved spending his time off going to baseball games, tailgating at football games, or barbecuing with friends and family. Daniel truly loved his life.

He could vividly remember the day he met his wife. She was sitting in a coffee shop, drinking tea while reading a book, her long black hair tied up in a knot on top of her head. She was wearing a yellow dress, imprinted with small daisies. One sandal was dangling off her toes as she gently moved her foot to the rhythm of the piped-in music, an acoustic version of "Sweet Dreams." As he moved closer to her, he noticed how worn the book cover was, as if it had been read many times and was well-loved by its owner. He walked toward her as if compelled.

"Ahem. Is this seat available?"

Darla glanced up from her book and nodded. Daniel placed his coffee cup on the table and sat down. And thus, one of the great romances began. Darla introduced Daniel to the world of novels. They would lie in bed together, reading novels to each other, taking turns reading aloud by page. She even persuaded him to join a book club with her. And although he liked mysteries best, he found pleasure in any book they read together.

On Sundays, they would go to a local bar and watch football in the fall and baseball in the spring, sitting side by side at the bar, eating wings—the spicier the better—and drinking whatever was on tap.

Daniel loved that Darla had more than a rudimentary understanding of the games. She loved sports as much as he did. And fortunately, they both cheered for the same teams.

Daniel and Darla married six months later. A small wedding in a garden populated by a plethora of colorful flowers. They honeymooned in the Caribbean for only a weekend, saving their money so they could purchase a small house. Their first child was born a year later, followed closely by the second. After a few miscarriages and many tearful nights, they welcomed a third child into the world. Daniel was thrilled. He was happier than he had ever imagined.

He and Darla found their dream house, a small cape cod on a half-acre of land. They filled their home with photos of family and friends. Books lined the walls, interspersed with mementos of times past—snow globes of the places they'd visited together, as a couple or family. The most important one was on the middle shelf, a snow globe from Disney with their family picture inside, the glittery snow cascading around their faces as they stood in front of Cinderella's castle.

He loved to play with his three children, pushing them on swings, making them go higher until they felt like their feet touched the clouds above. One night each week, the family played board games and ate popcorn, laughing together.

Daniel never missed back-to-school nights or student conferences. When he was home in the evenings, he would help the kids with homework. Nothing made him happier than spending his time with Darla and the children. Each night as he went to sleep, he thought to himself, a smile playing on his lips, how perfect his life had become—a Norman Rockwell painting.

But then the life he had so lovingly cultivated changed drastically. He was on duty that night, driving his patrol route, waiting for a call—any call—to come and break up the evening's monotony. In retrospect, he wished the night had stayed boring. He wished he had never responded to the call. Some things could never be unseen.

Daniel had just reentered his squad car, half a cup of hot coffee in one hand, when his radio buzzed to life. There was a two-car accident only a few blocks from where he was currently parked. Officers were needed, and Daniel grabbed the chance to go and do something.

He arrived at the scene and stretched himself out of his car, walking briskly toward the crushed metal that once, just minutes before, had been recognizable cars.

He could picture the people in the cars, singing along with the radio, maybe off-key like Darla, the kids in the back seat groaning for her to stop. Maybe they were out celebrating a life event, or maybe they were just quickly running out to the store to pick up something they had forgotten earlier in the day. It didn't really matter because now their bodies lay wrecked, maybe even dead.

The closer he got to the cars, the more the coffee burned in his stomach. The cobalt blue color of one of the cars matched Darla's, as did the make and model. But it couldn't be her; she was staying in that night. They had just spoken an hour earlier. She was already in her pajamas, curled up in bed with a book. The kids were tucked into their beds, sleeping. She was not going out.

As he walked toward the first car, he heard the crunch of metal under his foot. Shining his flashlight toward the ground, he saw a license plate from one of the cars. Moving his foot aside, he recognized Darla's license plate number on the piece of banged-up metal. He ran toward the wreckage as his fellow officers reached out to grab him, to stop him from seeing the carnage ahead. But Daniel got through and made it to Darla's car. He stopped, standing in a puddle of blood; four shapes lay by the car's bent frame.

He saw their mangled bodies, lying lifeless on the asphalt. Their glazed eyes staring up at the starlit night. He never knew why they were out and not in bed sleeping; what Darla had forgotten that was so important that she woke up the children and left the house. That night he had his first whiskey, one of the hundreds or thousands he would soon consume. He started with some Jack Daniel Blue, but over the next months he switched to a ten-dollar bottle of blended whiskey. Daniel was soon never without alcohol. He carried a secret flask at first, making sure that no one would be able to tell how much he was drinking, but it soon became a thermos and then just a brown paper bag.

He spent his time looking through photos, trying to remember each detail of his family. He didn't want to forget the small freckles that played over his youngest daughter's nose or the way his son's hair flopped over his eyes. He wanted to be able to vividly hear his firstborn daughter's laugh and see Darla's smile. He was plagued with the fear of forgetting the small details of them; for those details helped to keep them alive.

His home's walls became a memorial to his lost family, as he taped pictures over every inch. He scoured the house looking for every photo—even the blurry ones that Darla had placed in a rejection drawer. Each time he looked at one of them, he chuckled to himself, remembering how even if the photo was heinous, Darla still would not throw it away—each picture carefully placed in the discard drawer as a representation of a moment in their family's life. He fell asleep, each night, to the sounds of them talking in family videos or to messages left on the answering machine. The sound of their voices lulled his alcohol-soaked brain into believing that they were still alive.

As the months moved on, so did his friends. Those who initially stayed by him, who took care of him in his first lost weeks, slowly began to return to their lives. As much as their lives moved on, his had stalled in that moment. The more time he spent alone, the more he drank, numbing the pain. As memories began to fade, as much due to time as to alcohol, panic set in and he would begin to study the memories again. He slept in their beds in hope of catching their individual scents; he held their clothes close to his skin so he could feel them. He ate their favorite foods, even if he, himself, hated them. He had to keep them with him. His entire focus was on recreating his family; on keeping them alive within himself.

He was put on administrative leave and referred to counseling, but he slept through his appointment times. Although the therapist tried to get Daniel to talk to him for several months, eventually he had to report Daniel as noncompliant. The police department let him go. Too soon to collect a pension.

Friends stopped calling, unsure of how to handle the new Daniel, the constantly morose and drunk Daniel. Some of them would drive by his house, only to see darkness, not knowing that Daniel sat inside. His bills unpaid, his yard unmowed.

Within a couple of years, he had lost his family, then his job, and finally his home. He was sleeping on the streets, fighting for spots near heating grates. He had been arrested for vagrancy a few times, unrecognizable to his former colleagues. His hair, once kept short and clean, hung down to his shoulders in greasy strands. His eyes, which once were blue and filled with joy, were now bloodshot and half closed, filled with grief.

Once they realized who he was, they would hand him a few dollars and a cup of coffee and then send him back to the streets and the cold. In the beginning, they would bring him to a shelter, but as soon as they drove away, he would leave and head back to his favorite heating grate. He didn't want their help; he wanted that night to have never happened.

Then one night, in a drunken stupor, he saw Darla. She was standing before him on the sidewalk. She wore the dress he had chosen to bury her in, his favorite dress. It was yellow with small red flowers; he loved how it clung to her curves in just the right way. She looked upon what had become of her husband with a great sadness in her eyes. And he knew it was time to straighten out his life; he just needed to figure out how to begin.

He went to his first AA meeting, finding a sponsor to help him fight his need. As he moved away from drinking, he knew he had to clean up his appearance; he had to make Darla proud of him again. He found a barber who volunteered to clean and cut his hair, plus shave his face. Daniel began to look more like the Daniel of before. Only he hadn't aged just a couple of years; the lines in his face were etched more deeply than that. He looked and smelled better than he had in years, but he knew that he would have to do more if he was to truly make his family proud of him again.

Dr. Susan Andres first met Daniel by tripping over him on the streets. She had tried to step over what she thought were old clothes piled on the sidewalk, only to discover a man inside. A man with grey teeth and darkening gums. The night was cold, and no matter how much Daniel had done to improve himself, he still slept on the street, covered in old rags for warmth.

She brought him his first hot meal in days and sat with him while he ate. She was the first person to treat him as a human, an equal, in a long time. She gave him her card, promising him free dental work. All he had to do was come to her practice after hours. She wasn't sure if she would see him again, but there he was the next evening, knocking on the back door.

Daniel wasn't the first desperate person Susan had offered to help; he was just one of the many invisible people to whom she had offered "free" dental work.

# SUSAN

SHE WAS FINALLY alone in the building. The overhead lights had turned off, their soft humming quieted. She slowly inhaled, filling her lungs with as much oxygen as they could possibly absorb.

Reaching into the back of the mahogany desk's top drawer, her fingers wrapped around the ancient key. The key was made of a silver alloy that had the tarnished appearance of age. The top was curved into the shape of a fleur-de-lis. The part that would be inserted into the lock had three prongs of varying lengths, the middle one being the longest. It was obvious to anyone who saw the key that it belonged to an ancient lock. She slowly drew it out of the drawer.

As she pushed away from the desk and stood, she dropped the key into the pocket of her white lab coat, changed her red stilettos for sneakers, and exited her office.

Walking down the stark white hallway, she began to feel the familiar pangs of guilt and remorse. Part of her mind chanted, "This is wrong, this is wrong," as she moved toward the door. She knew she had to shut the phrase out of her mind or she wouldn't be able to finish. She had to enter room 5.

Room 5 was located at the end of the corridor, around a corner and down six stairs, away from the other examination rooms. It was inconveniently located and therefore never used. The staff often forgot about the room and didn't check it at night or open it the next morning. It remained an anonymous hideaway and served her purposes well.

She stood in front of the door to room 5, her fingers playing with the keys in her pocket. Outlining its shape, slowly tracing each groove into her mind, she located the key that she needed. It was a newer key, one that could be duplicated in any hardware store. She would use the antique key later, for the hidden door, her secret entranceway into its chamber.

She could hear the hum of the machine through the door. It was a low-pitched hum, inaudible during the busy, noisy day. But now, at night, when she was alone in the building, the machine seemed to echo out of the room and send a throbbing rhythm throughout the building. She was once again thankful that no one else bothered to come to this room.

As she slipped the key into the lock, her mind flashed an image of what would be on the other side. Her body trembled uncontrollably at the initial thought, but as before, she shook her repulsion and fear aside and opened the door.

The faded mint-green dental chair was still in the reclined position, the patient's head angled slightly above his feet. The chair faced the far wall, overlooking the outside garden, so the doctor could only see the top of the patient's brown hair. He appeared to be waiting patiently for the doctor to finish an exam. She walked around the chair, playing the doctor game. "How are you doing, Mr. Branovitch? Are you ready to rinse and spit?" She smiled to herself as she looked at what was left of her patient. She examined Daniel Branovitch, making a note of the jaundiced appearance of his skin. As she strolled around the chair, she tripped over Daniel's shoes, which lay where they had fallen under his yellowed, curled feet.

"Excellent," she exhaled. "He is finished." She removed the dental bib from around his neck, lifted the chair's arm, and carried Daniel Branovitch down into the basement. His weight had dropped noticeably since entering the building; she had discovered early on in her experiments that she was able to carry even the heaviest of patients after the procedure was finished.

The basement entrance was near the small kitchenette. Its door was always locked, so no one besides the doctor could enter its darkness. At first, Susan thought that she would move a file cabinet in front of the door, so no one would know it was there, but she quickly realized that that would be too cumbersome to move nightly. So, she told the staff it was more of a root cellar than a basement, with dirt floors and cobwebs hanging from the ceiling. No one ever expressed a desire to go through the door or down into the space.

. . .

WHEN SUSAN HAD FOUND THE OFFICE SUITE FOR LEASE, located in an old Victorian mansion on a residential street near downtown, she had diligently explored all areas, including the basement. She originally planned on filling the basement with file cabinets holding the many dental x-rays and patient files they hoped to have.

Those plans changed quickly. When she walked down into the basement, she found antique dental tools—a drill, a chair, even a suction straw. They were in a back corner covered with a dust-covered tarp. She wondered if the suction straw was an original—it resembled the first-generation suction straws she had seen in textbooks. She examined each antique, gently blowing years of dust and cobwebs off them. The drill bit was covered in dirt and rust; the chair had a hand crank to raise and lower it. She thought that these two pieces could be used as décor in her partners' offices. She would surprise Keith and David with the tools when they moved into the suite officially. The suction straw was not nearly as old, but there was something about it that drew her in. This piece would be hers. She didn't know why; she just knew it would.

"These would be great in the offices. Do they come with the lease?" she asked the real estate office.

"Yes, I'm sure they do. And if not, I'm sure we can make a deal for them. But you may want to put them in the back offices. Patients may not want to see torture devices. Many people are afraid of the dentist as it is," the real estate agent said, smiling awkwardly.

Susan smiled, deciding that this office would work. They would lease the entire first floor along with the basement, with the hope that maybe their practice would expand enough to eventually lease the entire house. All she had to do was convince her partners. This, she also knew, would be easy. She had been entrusted with the responsibility of finding the office space. They just had to sign on the lines, initial the appropriate boxes, and their offices would be officially opened.

They moved in shortly after signing the lease and began to advertise their new dental practice. Each of them had excelled in school, graduating near the top of their respective universities. They all continued to learn the latest techniques in dentistry by reading journals, taking workshops, and attending seminars and conventions. Their work ethics went together perfectly.

That was how they met, at a dental seminar on teeth whitening. They sat together at the bar, after the Keynote Speaker's address, complaining about the high cost of overhead—rent, updating equipment, maintaining a good staff, advertisements. They barely made enough to pay back their student loans; forget about saving for the future. They had to work so many hours, there was no time for fun, no time for a social life.

The partnership brainstorm occurred over their third or fourth scotch. They could split overhead costs, have more time off, and split profits. It would be perfect, if only they lived near each other. The best-laid plans...

The three of them exchanged numbers at the end of the seminar and stayed in touch for a year. The following January found them all attending that year's seminar on tooth implants. On the morning of the seminar's last day, Keith lazily rolled over in the king-size hotel bed, wrapped his arm around Susan's naked body, and whispered, "Let's find David and do this partnership thing."

Susan smiled, saying "Okay," as she rolled into Keith's embrace. Two hours later, they found David sitting in the hotel's breakfast room. The three of them agreed that they were ready to make the move. They found a map of the lower forty-eight, marked where they each currently resided, and drew three lines toward each other. Where the lines crossed, a college town called Philipsburg, they would move and open a new practice. They decided that Susan would go first and find a suitable office space. Once Susan had located the office, David and Keith would follow. And they did.

It was after they had moved into the offices that she discovered, or was led to, the key and then to the door it opened. She had been carrying the suction straw up the basement stairs when she heard a slight metallic ping. Looking down she saw an old key, which must have fallen out of the suction straw's base. She felt a compulsion to search for the lock and spent her after-hours time in the office trying various locations. When she finally found the lock in a small four-foot door in a dark corner of the basement, relief overcame her. She unlocked the small room, ducked down, and entered the darkness. She didn't immediately notice the change in her heartbeat; curiosity had taken her over as she searched for and found a chain hanging from the ceiling. Pulling on the chain illuminated the deceptively large chamber in the flood of a naked light bulb. It was then that she noticed her pulse had slowed down, so slightly it was barely perceivable.

She suddenly felt a need to go back upstairs to her office, a need to touch the suction straw. She locked the door, pocketed the key, and quickly made her way to it. As she ran her hand over the machine, she knew what she had to do. She carried the device into room 5, set It up, and then locked the door. She would tell Keith, David, and the rest of the staff that the room needed work; that she would be fixing it up, modernizing it.

When Susan was exploring, she had found the original and subsequent blueprints for the house. She had noticed that room 5 had been made into a dental office during the 1950s. She knew somehow that it was the only room in which the suction straw belonged. She locked her office and left the building.

She then drove home to rest—the last good night's sleep she would experience for a long time.

. . .

THEY ADVERTISED THEIR NEW PRACTICE IN LOCAL PAPERS and Pennywise. Patients began to make appointments and then referred friends. Their practice grew, and David and Keith found themselves able to take time off, to live beyond the world of teeth. They were finally making enough money to not only pay off student loans, but to be able to go to nice restaurants, to see shows, to live the life they imagined a doctor would have. Keith repeatedly asked Susan to have dinner with him or to catch a movie—he had assumed that once they had moved to the same location, their relationship would move forward. But Susan continued to make excuses about why she could not go until he quit asking and began to date other woman. He dated as many different women as possible, desperately trying to replace Susan.

But Susan did not begin to live her life after they became a successful practice. Susan chose to stay at the practice; keeping long hours, well past closing time. Unbeknownst to her partners, she even began to sleep in the office.

Over the ensuing months, Susan's obsession with the office had become more apparent to those who knew her. She rarely left, if ever. Her face showed the signs of insomnia—dark circles wrapped around her brown, bloodshot eyes. Her appearance was disheveled, her clothes mismatched, her hair pulled back into a perpetual, half-made ponytail, strands of oily hair hanging limply around her face. Of course, no one even began to suspect the truth; no one ever could.

And now, here she was, the dehydrated shell that once was Daniel Branovitch stiff in her arms as she carried him down the stairs into the basement's abyss. She lay the body onto a waist-high slab of cement, stretched above her head, and pulled an antiquated chain. She marveled frequently how a chain so old, so covered in rust, never broke as she tugged on it until it clicked the light on. As the bare bulb flickered to illuminate the area, the doctor inhaled the musty air, drawing it deeply into her, its acrid undertones scorching her lungs.

She glanced around the room as she slowly walked around, stepping gingerly over the uneven dirt floor. She began to recall where she had interred the others, as she reached for her shovel, which was kept hidden in a dark corner of the room, absorbed by shadows.

"Now, where can I bury this one?" She continued to pace around the cellar, feeling the hillocks of bodies. She finally came to flat ground and forcefully pushed the blade of the shovel into the dirt.

As she rhythmically lifted the dirt out of the ground, a song from her childhood crept from her subconscious onto her lips.

> *"After the ball was over, Sally took out her glass eye. She took off her false teeth and carefully laid them by. Stuck her wooden leg in the corner, hung up her wig on the wall. There wasn't much left of poor Sally, after the ball."*

She could hear her mother's tinny voice singing her this song; she wasn't sure how young she was when she first heard it, but she had understood the lyrics, had understood how the frailty of life could in fact be comical. She struggled not to laugh as she dug deeper into the basement chamber's floor.

As soon as the hole was deep enough, Daniel Branovitch found himself shoved into his new home. She covered him with dirt, spreading the extra dirt carefully around, so there wouldn't any signs that someone had been here just in case someone, for some unknown reason, entered this part of the basement.

Then she replaced the shovel, turned off the light, and headed back up the stairs. After carefully locking the cellar door, she walked down the hall to her office and replaced the key in its place in her desk drawer.

Only then did she let out a sigh of relief. "It's done now. Maybe It will let me rest for a while. Maybe It won't call me, at least not any time soon." She could feel the exhaustion in her limbs; her body ached and cried out for relief, for rest.

But she knew she wouldn't get the necessary time to recuperate. She knew It would call her again. Louder next time, more urgently. The machine was becoming, or had already become, insatiable. The more she obliged Its demands, the more It demanded. She toyed with the idea of ignoring Its pleas, or even of destroying It.

She often fantasized about taking It out of the office, throwing It in a junkyard crusher or burning It on a bonfire. Sometimes the fantasies became more elaborate and she imagined driving down to the ocean, jumping aboard a ship, and hurling It into the deepest parts of the sea. She would picture barnacles growing on Its base, fish swimming around It, nibbling on Its tubing.

But as always, she would do nothing until It called again, and then try as she might, she would not, could not, resist. She would follow Its orders; she would heed Its beckoning call. She knew it would happen; she just didn't know how soon. She laid down on her couch and tried to get some sleep.

. . .

In the beginning, when she first heard Its call, It took Its time. It started as a slight irritation, like a gnat, in the back of her mind. Slowly gnawing away at her. The more It gnawed, the louder It grew, the more difficult It became to resist. Until she felt that she had no choice but to listen to It; to obey Its siren's call. She didn't know what It wanted from her; what It was demanding that she do. She only knew that she had to obey.

Her first victim was an elderly man, easily in his late eighties or early nineties. She was able to rationalize it that way. It really wasn't *that* wrong to do; by the condition of his teeth and gums, she knew that he didn't have much longer to live. She was just helping him die faster, maybe even with less pain and suffering.

She was amazed at how easy it was to do, once she gave herself over to it. All she had to do was have the patient sit in the examination chair and then she would turn on the machine. The machine did the rest. She never stayed in the room while It worked. She didn't think she could stand to watch the victims. She was afraid to see if they writhed in pain. If she caused them pain. She could still sometimes remember her training; she recalled the promise she made to herself: she would never cause a patient pain. Part of her couldn't bear to know if she had broken that promise.

She wondered why the patients didn't struggle; why they didn't pull the curved straw out of their mouths and run from the room, complaining about the machine. She had a sick feeling that one day she would know, firsthand. But not tonight. Tonight, she would rest.

Even though she had signed a two-year lease for her apartment, eventually she moved out. Leaving her apartment vacant, in case she ever needed to use it again. It was easier this way. The farther away she was from It, the worse she felt. It had a connection to her. It fed her as much as she fed it. Whenever she went home, she found herself needing to head back to the office. At first, she tried to resist the call, but by three in the morning, there she would be, driving back to the office. She would curl up on her office couch and try to sleep.

Sometimes, not often, she would sleep and then dream. Those dreams, the ones where you wake up drenched with your own sweat, on the verge of screaming. She dreaded those dreams; she dreaded going to sleep. So she didn't; instead she would sit, knees drawn up under her chin, on the carpeted floor.

She would sit, trying not to think, not to visualize the torment she forced on her patients. Images sometimes crept into her mind. She would see faces contorted with pain and suffering. Susan tried to block these images, but they would surge into her consciousness, making her squirm. She saw the fear in their eyes as they realized that their lives were being drained away; that they were dying. She imagined what they felt when they realized that they would never see family and friends again. Or that friends and family would always wonder what happened to them, where they had disappeared.

So, she chose her victims carefully. She read the folder before putting them in that room. She made sure her victims had no family listed, no emergency contact person. She chose those who arrived alone, so no one would notice that they never left. And if the receptionist noticed that she never saw them leave, which rarely happened, Susan would calmly, rationally explain, "They left through the back entrance, so they wouldn't have to walk all the way around the building." But most likely, they were like Daniel; she found them homeless, nameless, faceless on the streets. She knew that the machine must be kept secret; It could never be found out; Its existence must never be discovered.

# NATHAN

JULIE RUSHED OUT of the bathroom that morning, yelling, "Steven, Steven. Come here quickly."

Steven ran up the steps, two at a time, hurrying toward his wife's yells. "What is it? What's wrong?" he sputtered as he ran into their bedroom.

Julie stood looking at her side profile in the long mirror that hung on their bedroom wall. She gingerly ran her fingers over her flat stomach, trying to imagine it swollen.

She turned to her husband of ten years, smiling. "It's positive. I'm pregnant. We're having a baby!"

She threw her arms around Steven's neck as he picked her up, spinning gleefully around the room.

For just that moment she forgot about work, about fighting for partnership, about the hours she put into her career, the years of law school. She just felt the overwhelming joy of impending motherhood, plus the need to protect her new child. But by the time she was dressed, it all started to come back.

She had dressed in her best suit, a navy summer wool. She grabbed her briefcase and reached for her coffee. It wasn't in its usual place on the counter.

"No caffeine," Steven sang out.

"Oh, yeah." She would pick up a decaf on the way to work. She had to keep up normal appearances; no one at her firm could know the truth.

The rumor mill at work was that a new partner would be named that week. No matter what the law stated, being pregnant would hurt her chances of being named. She had worked so hard for this; she couldn't lose it now.

When she arrived at her desk, the executive assistant came in. "Mr. Wilcox would like to meet with you at eleven today."

"Oh, okay," Julie said. She exhaled slowly and began to review the files on her desk. At eleven o'clock precisely, she went to Mr. Wilcox's office.

When Steven came home from the office that night, they had a double celebration.

. . .

WHEN NATHAN, THEIR SON, WAS SIX WEEKS OLD, HE entered daycare. They had spent the past eight months interviewing nannies, trying to find someone who could bring their baby to school and then home afterwards. They set up a suite in their garage where the nanny could live. They had decided to hire a college student, someone who was studying early childhood development, someone with a flexible schedule. They needed someone who could pick up Nathan in an emergency, at a moment's notice. They knew that with their busy schedules, they would need someone responsible to help with the baby and of course with the child once he grew.

Julie continued working long hours as the youngest partner in her firm, while Steven's consultant firm prospered.

They hired many different nannies to take care of their son over the years, from potty training to helping him with his homework and bringing him to various lessons and games. They did not spend much time with him, but they were assured that he had everything he could materially want or desire.

. . .

THE DAY STARTED OUT GLOOMY; GREY CLOUDS HUNG LOW in the morning sky. Nathan slowly opened his bloodshot eyes and looked at the digital clock on his nightstand. As his eyes focused on the numbers, his mind jolted at what it read.

*Eight thirty? How is it eight thirty? Shit. I'm missing first period. The test is second period.* His body, reacting slower than his mind, suddenly awakened with shock as he threw himself out of the warm comfort of his bed and planted his feet on the cold wood floor. Nathan raced through his morning routine, skipped breakfast, and ran out his front door.

He had missed the bus, and his parents had left for work already, forcing him to run to the school. Thanks to cross-country practice and interval training, his lungs were still effortlessly filling with oxygen as he rounded the corner near the school's entrance.

His concentration was so focused on reaching the school doors that he never saw the small dog. As his stride stretched into a final push, he felt a slight resistance; his left foot had caught on something and he was falling. Instinctively, his arms reached outward as his body met with the concrete sidewalk. He heard a yip of shock or pain (he wasn't sure if he cared which it was at that moment) from the dog as it ran home, glancing furtively over its back. Nathan lay on the sidewalk, breathing hard, wondering why he hadn't just stayed in his warm bed. He realized now that he could have made the test up, rescheduled it for another day. He could have just stayed home. His parents would never have known; he doubted they would have cared unless his grades slipped.

He heard the school's bell ring and tried to push himself up. His left wrist sent waves of daggers through his arm and into his shoulder. He looked at the wrist and saw it was bent at a strange angle; a lump jutting outward where just moments ago, the skin had lain flat. *Shit*, his mind said for the second time that morning.

He rolled onto his back, pulled himself up, and stumbled toward the school, cradling his arm against his stomach. His books lay on the sidewalk, deserted where they had fallen.

He made it through the front glass doors and stood, swaying, in the school's foyer. The receptionist looked at him, jumped up, and ran toward him, just as he fell forward again. Yelling for help, she lifted his head from the floor and waited for the nurse to arrive.

. . .

HE HAD LAIN ON THE COT IN THE SCHOOL NURSE'S OFFICE, waiting for one of his parents to come pick him up. The nurse had left messages for both, but neither had returned the call or shown up at the school. Nathan knew that once they arrived at the school they would say that they had been in a meeting and came as soon as they received the message.

The nurse called an ambulance to take Nathan to the nearest emergency room; the school's principal followed the ambulance to the hospital, paperwork giving him the authority to allow any medical procedure deemed necessary laying on the car seat next to him. Nathan's arm was quickly x-rayed. As the doctor manipulated the bone back into place, Nathan did his best to breathe through the pain. His stomach turned and rolled each time he heard his bones scraping together. After the cast was set on his arm, the principal drove Nathan back to the school. Nathan climbed out of the principal's car just as his mother's Lexus pulled up.

She got out of her car and stood, looking at Nathan climbing out of the beat-up Chevy. A white cast enveloped his arm. Her mouth dropped as she moved quickly to her child.

"Thank you," she quickly said to the principal, "Thank you for helping Nathan. Come on, honey. Let's get you home." The principal handed Julie the paperwork from the hospital and headed back into the school, saying over his shoulder, "I'll let the receptionist know that you took Nathan home. Get some rest, Nathan. We'll see you next week."

Nathan climbed into his mom's Lexus, closed his eyes, and slept on the ride home.

. . .

LATER THAT NIGHT, HE LAY IN BED, HIS LEFT HAND AND wrist in a cast, dreaming. His parents were downstairs in the kitchen, talking over coffee about what had happened. How the school had tried to call them both that day; how neither one had heard the messages in time; they had been too busy. Nathan had had to go to the hospital in an ambulance with the school's principal playing their role as guardian. Their son had gone through a traumatic experience and they had not been there to help him through it.

Now, their only son was upstairs, asleep on pain pills, with a fractured ulna, and they hadn't been there. They had failed him as parents again. He was fifteen years old and knew all too well how disappointing parents could be. He hadn't been surprised that his mother had shown up so late. He'd expected it. They couldn't remember the last time they had attended a school event or game. They hadn't done back-to-school night since he was in first grade, nor had they ever scheduled a conference with his teachers. They weren't *those* parents, were they? They began to fear that they were. And they knew they had to change, had to become the parents they had dreamed they would be.

They looked at their workloads, when meetings were scheduled, trying desperately to find a solution. Nathan would be going to college soon; he would be leaving them in just a few years. They wanted to be certain that he would go off into the world knowing he was loved. They knew they had to change their priorities. They just didn't know how. They decided to each pick only two days to work late, so one of them would be home for Nathan each night, and they would only work ten hours on the weekends. Nathan would become more of a priority.

They began spending more time with him. They made sure to have dinner together at least three nights a week. They checked his homework and attended his cross-country meets, when they could, to cheer him on. Nathan realized that he was probably the only person he knew who was grateful for a broken bone. But he still was aware of how this could all quickly change back. He never truly believed in an absolute change in his parents; he still knew that he had to be self-sufficient. He could not completely rely on his parents. They could change back at any time.

When the time came to choose a college, Nathan chose a state school. One that was only a few hours from his parents, his home. He loved college, its sprawling campus with tall oak trees seeming to reach into the endless sky. Although his classes were challenging and his course load heavy, he felt comfortable there and quickly made friends. He had to admit that his parents had raised him to be self-reliant and independent. He never suffered from home sickness, since he was used to being on his own from a young age.

His junior year, he moved into off-site campus housing, a two-bedroom apartment with the friend he had lived with since freshman year. He loved the quiet, when he needed to study. He would sometimes remember the constant dissonance of dorm life, the blast of various musical styles not blending together. The sound of voices—laughing, screaming—echoing off the tiled walls. The hours spent in the musty library trying to find some peace in which to concentrate. He was happy to live off campus, so he could have quiet.

And yet, he was still close enough to the campus that he could walk or bike to classes and of course enjoy the social aspects of college—spending time with his girlfriend Annie in her dorm, the parties and study groups that seemed to happen every night. He even liked most of his classes, professors, and teaching assistants. He went to his classes regularly, diligently taking notes, completing all the reading assignments. He joined as many study groups as possible and enjoyed talking about the issues brought up in class. Nathan was happy.

. . .

Nathan lounged in the hard plastic chair, his legs sticking out from beneath the desk. He held a pen in his left hand, trying to focus on the equations written on the board. As he copied the problems and their solutions into his notebook, his right hand absentmindedly rubbed his jaw. The dull, constant pain he had felt last night was becoming jarring. Pain seared through his tooth, shooting upward through his sinus, his eye, and right into the center of his skull. He imagined this was what it would be like to have a knife pushed up through your chin, right into your brain.

He lost focus, again, as another wave of pain hit. Nausea filled him. He knew that this day was going to be useless for learning, so as soon as the class ended, he headed off campus, unsure if he would return for his evening classes.

As he walked home, he passed a dental practice and decided to see if there were any available appointments.

He walked up the stairs that led into the building's interior, pushed open the heavy wooden door, and entered the waiting room. Across from the entrance sat the receptionist, her name plate reading Charlotte Grappe. As Nathan tentatively crossed the room, he noticed the telltale odor of dentist's office: that strange mixture of mint, chemicals, and sour, dry breath. The receptionist glanced up at Nathan.

"How can I help you?" she inquired, smiling a tired, lopsided smile.

Nathan, now holding his right hand gingerly to his right cheek, replied sheepishly, "I, um, have a really bad ache, er, pain in my tooth. Is there any way I can see a doctor?"

"Have you been here before?"

"No, I was walking by, I'm a student at the college, and thought I would just stop in to see if anyone was available."

"Well," she clicked her pen against the front of her teeth, a nervous habit she had acquired when she was a young child. "There don't seem to be any spots available today … " she began, noticing Nathan wincing in pain, "but let me see what I can do. Have a seat and fill out these forms, please." She stood up, handing Nathan a clipboard and pen, and quietly walked through a door and into the back offices.

Nathan sat on the avocado-green couch and began to fill in the necessary forms, calling his parents for the necessary dental insurance information. The sounds of electric toothbrushes, drills, and canned music blended together in a cacophony of noises, causing Nathan's stomach to begin to turn. Just as he finished the forms, the receptionist came back.

"Looks like Dr. Andres will be able to squeeze you into her schedule today. You're very lucky; she's usually booked solid for weeks."

"Thanks," Nathan said, handing her the completed forms. He followed her through the door and into the back offices.

"All the main examination rooms are being used, so I'm putting you in the room off toward the back. But don't worry; we won't forget about you," Charlotte smiled.

Nathan stood in the exam room, waiting for the doctor. As he waited, he began to look around the room. *This room is definitely not used often*, he thought, noticing a slight agedness to the dental paraphernalia, as if it had a layer of dust entombing it. The posters had a worn look, as if they had hung on these walls for a long time. He stood and read the poster featuring two sun-faded children, encouraging the patient to eat more apples. He began to move toward a poster of a ship loaded with vegetables when he felt a strange pull toward one side of the room. A need began to creep into Nathan, a deep-seated desire to lie down on the yellowed leather chair. The pull intensified until Nathan could no longer stop himself; he climbed into the examination chair, swung his legs up, and adjusted the neck rest behind his head.

The pull began to ease at first. Nathan sighed with relief; never had he felt a sensation like that before. He closed his eyes against the pain in his tooth, rubbing his left wrist methodically. He traced the outline of old pain he still carried from the fall years ago, as he tried to breathe the pain in his tooth away. He had discovered years ago that whenever he felt stress, or the weather was turning bad, or he felt pain elsewhere in his body, his wrist would hurt again. It was as if the bones in his wrist felt empathy for the new pain. His wrist had become a barometer of bad tidings to him, one to which he had learned to pay attention.

The pull came back, stronger than before. Absently, his left hand began reaching out, stretching toward the spit sink, feeling for the desired apparatus. He gently closed his fingers around the base of the apparatus and began to move it toward his mouth. He could not stop himself, though he knew something was wrong—terribly wrong. His mind screamed for him to stop, but he didn't, he couldn't, stop. As the hook of the straw grazed past his lower lip, bumping into his upper lip, his mouth involuntarily began to open wider. He suddenly felt himself recoil from the straw and quickly replaced it in its holder.

"Wait, no, stop!" a woman's voice yelled. A dentist ran toward Nathan, grabbed the straw, and pulled it away from him. "Another room has opened up," she panted, moving the arm of the chair up and helping Nathan out of it. "We're going to move you into there. Let's get you into a more modern room; this one is still waiting to be updated."

Nathan sat, frozen, unable to find it within himself to move. He didn't want to leave the room; he didn't know why, just that he didn't. Susan reached out and touched his shoulder. She slowly guided him up and out of the room. As first, he resisted, but the closer to the door he got, the easier it was to leave.

Hesitantly at first, and then willingly, he followed Susan down the hall and into a different examination room. This one was obviously used regularly. The equipment was new, the posters encased in glass. Nathan was thankful to be out of that other room, yet part of him—a primal part—wanted to go back. Wanted to finish what he had started.

. . .

Susan examined Nathan, her quickened pulse easing with each passing moment. She found why the tooth hurt so much, as her mind tried to figure out how to prevent such a near disaster from ever happening again.

"Okay, so here's the problem. One of your wisdom teeth is impacted. We will have to remove it soon. We don't want the infection to spread to your other teeth. Do you have time tomorrow?"

Nathan thought about his schedule, and as another wave of pain shot through him, he decided that he would come in tomorrow. He set up the appointment for the next morning and arranged for his housemate, Kevin, to drive him home after the surgery.

When he called his parents to tell them, they immediately offered to come down and stay with him after the surgery—or, they said, they could make an appointment with their dentist and Nathan could come home. But Nathan said no. He was an adult; he would be fine.

. . .

THAT NIGHT, NATHAN BARELY SLEPT. HIS TOOTH WAS sending sharp, gasping pain through him. He spent most of the night sitting in his favorite chair, his face cradled in his hands. By the time the sun rose the next morning, he was ready to pull the tooth himself.

Kevin dropped Nathan off at the dentist's office, promising to be back in two hours, after his morning classes. Nathan slowly walked up the front steps, pushed open the door, and waved hello to the receptionist.

As Charlotte led him down the hall to the procedure room, he felt an odd sensation; he yearned to turn around, to go down the other hall, the one from yesterday. He wanted to enter the old, rarely used exam room, to once again hold the suction straw in his hand, to guide it into his mouth and turn it on. He followed Charlotte into the room, glancing over his shoulder toward the pull, and sat in the dental chair. He wasn't there long before Susan walked in.

"Are we ready? This shouldn't take too long. Did you remember to make arrangements for someone to pick you up, or should I have Charlotte call a cab for you?"

"Um, no, I mean, my friend Kevin is coming by to pick me up."

"Great. Then let's get started."

When Nathan woke up, he was groggy, his head fuzzy. He tried to sit up but felt an overwhelming need to put his head down again. He closed his eyes and went back to sleep.

"Nathan. Nathan," he heard his name being whispered, as if the caller was speaking through fog. Charlotte and Susan each held one of his arms. "Nathan, where are you going?"

Nathan's eyes opened, and he saw that he was standing in the hallway, his hand on the doorknob of the room. It had been haunting him since yesterday, and now he found himself trying to enter the room, to hold the suction straw again. He vaguely remembered his dreams involving the straw. It beckoned him through his fog-addled mind.

"Your friend is here to take you home," Charlotte told him.

Nathan slowly let go of the doorknob and allowed himself to be escorted out of the hallway. As he left the building, he hoped to never enter the place again. But he knew it wasn't over; he knew he would be back here, probably soon—the pull was getting stronger. He wasn't sure if he could resist for too long. But for now, he would go home and sleep, and hopefully he would not dream.

# CHARLOTTE

VICTORIA HAD NEVER wanted children. They were noisy, dirty, and just plain undesirable. She never played with dolls as a young girl, finding the notion of even pretend motherhood stifling and unattractive. She knew she would not only never have children, but would never take the risk of becoming pregnant; she decided to never date. *Why be with a man, if I never want children?* she would ask herself. *Men only bring messiness and degradation with them.* She was satisfied to live alone. Her home, her own. No one else's stuff taking up space, everything put away just where she wanted it. She kept to herself, preferring to keep her life simple and clean.

    One night, after a particularly difficult day as the main secretary at the local mill, she decided to go out for drinks with some of the other single female employees. Victoria had been invited on these girls' nights before but had always found reasons to decline. But this had been a particularly stressful day, so Victoria acquiesced this one time. The other women decided that Victoria needed to make herself more appealing, more attractive, so they worked hard to convince her to take her auburn hair out of the tight chignon she always wore it in and put some lipstick on her pale lips. They convinced her to unbutton the top two buttons on her blouse and to smile more. Against her instincts, she listened to them and decided that she would just stop in for a quick drink and then head back to her small house for dinner. But one drink led to another, one story following another, and Victoria soon found herself out later than expected and more drunk than ever before.

Victoria had been saying good night to the women when a tall, dark stranger had offered to buy her just one more drink. She uncharacteristically agreed to have a drink, and to be polite, she spoke to the stranger while she sipped her last vodka martini of the night. She soon found herself stumbling out of the bar, clinging to his arm. The other secretaries smiled to each other as they watched Victoria leave on the arm of a handsome man.

They went to his hotel room, where she stayed the night. She never bothered to learn his name or even where he lived, nor did she tell him hers. She was glad that she had thought to use a fake name the night before. She wanted to have no way of ever seeing or hearing from him again. There was no point. She would never need to see this man again as she never wanted a relationship, never wanted to be tied to any person.

She called a doctor two months later, in a panic, for her period had never been late before. She was pregnant. One night of drunken irresponsibility had sentenced her to a lifetime of dirty, noisy hell. She had to admit to herself that she did not know the father's name or where he could be found. She would need to invent a story for the rest of society; the truth could never be known. Her reputation was at risk, her job possibly lost.

Now what she had thought of as a positive had become a detriment. If she couldn't find him, she couldn't leave the child with him to raise. She couldn't force that responsibility onto him. Or at the very least, force him to help pay for the child's expenses. But Victoria, being punitive by nature, would take her punishment for that night; she would suffer through childbearing and child-rearing. She was, if nothing else, responsible and owned up to her mistakes. She would have to face this on her own, including the fact that all would know of her lapse in judgment, all would know that she had chosen poorly, she had made a grave error.

Her months of pregnancy went by without much drama. She never felt morning sickness, experienced strange cravings, or had trouble sleeping. She couldn't understand why other women complained about pregnancy—maybe they craved attention, she thought. In fact, she would have been happy to keep the baby inside her forever, to not give birth, to not raise a child.

She approached labor in much the same way as everything else in her life. She refused to scream out from the pain, for she saw it as penance for the sin she had committed. She believed that penance was to be born down on and never reacted to. The pain of childbirth was welcome to Victoria, for now her initial sin was paid for.

The first time she saw her daughter, she knew her name was Charlotte and that she would be a very well-behaved child. Victoria had been raised feral by parents who did not take the responsibility of parenting seriously. But Victoria believed in the ideal of not "sparing the rod ... " and firmly believed in corporal punishment for even the smallest of infractions. Nevertheless, she also knew that it must be doled out carefully, ever mindful of the line between discipline and abuse. She bottle-fed Charlotte from the beginning; she had read that for many women breastfeeding was in some ways akin to having sexual relations. Just the thought that her daughter could possibly arouse such feelings repelled her, not to mention that the idea of a child suckling from her body seemed repulsive and unclean. She had Charlotte out of diapers by the time she was one and a half years old, and by three Charlotte knew that all her toys must be put back in their proper places by bedtime or she would fall asleep with a tear-stained face and a sore bottom, and that she would awaken with fewer toys than the morning before. Her mother taught her that if things were not put away in their proper places, arranged in a display as if they were on a shelf in a toy store, then they would be judged as not important, worthy of the garbage dump.

Victoria withheld physical affection from her daughter, fearing that it would teach her that love is physical. Once Charlotte was able to sit on her own, Victoria rarely held her daughter, doting only on accomplishments, not the child.

At the age of five, Charlotte started Kindergarten knowing her letters and numbers. She also knew how important it was to write them just right, to follow the lines carefully and precisely. She knew how to pass a white-glove test at home and brought this fastidiousness to school with her. Her teachers would comment on her politeness and neatness with her work. When the other students were playing with toys, enjoying some free time from work, Charlotte would reorganize her cubby and school bag, making sure everything was not only in its proper place but also completely dust-free. Anything less would cause her to become distracted during lessons. They knew she would never be a star student but that her work would always be the prettiest in the class, even the school.

Over time, her teachers noticed that Charlotte's perfectionism was becoming a problem. By the time she was in the third grade, they were concerned for her future well-being. They had noticed a nervous tic whenever Charlotte felt overwhelmed or confused—Charlotte would tap her front teeth with her pen, pencil, or even her finger. Each letter on her papers had to be written just so; no erasure marks allowable. She didn't worry if her answers were correct, only that the paper looked perfect. She would throw out artwork that she had spent days or even weeks on for one small imperfection, if one line was out of perspective. Her teachers began to think that perhaps it was Charlotte, or maybe Victoria, who lacked the proper perspective.

Victoria smiled when they told her their concerns. She thanked them for caring about her Charlotte so much and nodded in agreement over the "distressing" news. "But she is polite? Is she a disturbance to others around her?"

When her teachers replied that she was very polite—"A disturbance? Never!"—Victoria smiled and left the conference satisfied. Her daughter was well-behaved and obedient. Being concerned over the girl's neatness, which seemed like a positive trait to possess, made Victoria shake her head in disbelief. Victoria knew that the teachers were overly preoccupied with psychology nonsense, but it wasn't their fault. College did that to them. They should be more concerned with the lack of discipline in children instead of worrying about whether a child was "happy." Victoria was pleased that she knew what was truly important. She was doing a good job.

As Charlotte grew and progressed through school, her perfectionism became more and more apparent. Her nervous tic had become a trait for which Charlotte was known. Whenever she had a task at hand, she would start to click on her front teeth without rhythm. Her guidance counselor pushed her to become a receptionist or secretary; her need for perfection and organization would be an asset to any office, while her lack of decent grades would surely keep her out of college.

Upon graduating from high school, Charlotte enrolled in a local secretarial school. For the first time, Charlotte excelled academically. Her organizational skills made her the most efficient student in the school. Added to that, her perfectionist tendencies made her shorthand and her typing perfect. She practiced until she never had a need for correction tape. When she finished at the school, with glowing recommendations, she immediately began looking for a job.

The advertisement in the paper said the job was for a new dental practice in the next county. She was warned by her mother not to expect to get the first job she interviewed for, not to expect a job too quickly. So she was surprised when they offered her the position.

She signed the contract, found herself a small, neat apartment nearby, and moved into it within two weeks. It felt great to be away from her mother's constant picking and insults. She even went out, after her first paycheck, and began to buy professional clothes for her new career, something her mother would never have approved of. Victoria believed, and thought she had raised her daughter to believe, that dressing well only led to bad endings. That the need to be fashionable, to be attractive to men, was a regrettable sin, a lack of judgment and decorum. But Charlotte was not Victoria and she wanted to look nice for work, to have a man look at her with enough interest to consider her as a potential wife and, if she was truly lucky, a mother for his children.

As Charlotte grew to know the doctors and learn about the practice, she developed a system for appointments and filings. It worked well, and the practice flourished. It was rare when there was an opening in one of the doctors' schedules. So, when Nathan walked in unexpectedly, Charlotte did her best to find him space. She could see the pain in his face, and she felt the need—almost maternally, although she was only about six years his senior—to help him. She gave him the obligatory forms to fill out and quickly went to the back to let Susan know her plan.

Charlotte had set up an appointment for herself that afternoon, to have her teeth checked. She had begun to feel a dull pain in her front teeth even though she flossed and brushed three times a day.

All three of the dentists had commented at one time or another about her habit; about the damage she might end up doing to her teeth. At first, she had ignored their concerns, but lately over the past few months her teeth and gums had begun to feel sore. She had decided to take them up on the offer and penciled her name into the schedule.

She chose Susan for the exam because she was nervous about the prospect of having one of the men touch her teeth. She felt, and always had felt, more comfortable with women doctors. For although she was not her mother and felt no repulsion toward men, she had been raised to believe that women should go to women doctors and had been unable to shake the uncomfortable feeling of a male doctor.

However, when she had witnessed the grimacing pain on Nathan's face, she had decided to sacrifice her appointment. She could live with a small amount of pain for a while longer, if it helped to relieve Nathan's obvious suffering.

She decided to bring Nathan to the end room, a room that was rarely used and was empty at that moment. In fact, as far as Charlotte knew, only Dr. Susan had ever used the room, and even that was a rarity. Charlotte was unable to think of a time when either David or Keith had visited a patient in that room.

As she led Nathan into the room, she saw a film of dust covering everything in the space. *Disgusting*, she thought. *How have I never noticed this filth before?* She truly could not understand how she had missed this, how it had gone by her unnoticed. The more she thought about it, the more she realized that she could not remember the last time she had entered the room. Could not recall the last patient to use the room.

She left Nathan in the room and headed off to tell Susan that she had a patient in room 5. She stood in the doorway of one of the examination rooms, waiting to get Susan's attention. As Susan turned to look at her, Charlotte smiled nervously and signalled that she needed to talk to Susan immediately. "Dr. Andres, I have put your new patient in room 5. All the other rooms were … "

Before Charlotte could complete her sentence, Susan quickly ran from the room. Charlotte followed Susan down the hall and into the room just in time to see Susan coaxing Nathan out of the examination chair and trying to convince him to change rooms. Susan desperately looked at Charlotte, her eyes pleading for help. Charlotte came to help move Nathan to another room.

As Nathan settled into another room down the hall, Charlotte apologized to Susan and promised to not use the room without Susan's prior knowledge again. She could see anger in Susan's eyes and needed to placate her, needed to make everything perfect again.

At first, she didn't understand why the doctor had reacted the way she had. But as she lay in bed that night, images of the room flooded through her mind. She realized Susan had not wanted a patient to see the dust in the room; she had not only been embarrassed by the dust, but it had made a bad impression. Who would want to go to a doctor whose office was so filthy? Charlotte's lack of judgment could have lost them patients, could have cost her job. She would have to fix the problem.

She decided to go into the office early and clean the offending room, so she set her alarm to wake her two hours earlier than usual. She awoke with the alarm, forcing herself to leave her warm bed and to begin her morning ablutions.

She drove to work in the darkness of early morning. Charlotte parked her car in her designated parking space, surprised to see Susan's car already there.

*Perhaps, she had the same idea. Well, two of us cleaning will get the job done more quickly, and then afterwards maybe Susan will have time to check my teeth,* thought Charlotte as she briskly walked through the early-morning coolness.

Charlotte unlocked the front door, locking it again once she was inside. She dropped her purse on her desk, walked into a back room, and grabbed some cleaning supplies. On her way to room 5, Charlotte noticed Susan's office light was on. She tiptoed past her door, hoping to not disturb Susan, hoping she could still surprise her with the clean room.

Charlotte tried to open the door to the room and found it was once again locked. As her hand rested on the doorknob, she felt a strange sensation, a tingling feeling, as if a thousand butterflies were fluttering their wings against her brain. It wasn't an unpleasant feeling—in fact, it tickled, and Charlotte found herself giggling with the sensation. As she stood there, enjoying this new sensation, she felt a small part of her mind reel. The rebellious section grew larger and soon a majority of her mind did not want to stay attached to the door. She released her hold on the door and took a step back from it. With the link broken she no longer felt the tickling sensation. Although part of her wanted to reconnect, most of her mind felt relief.

She glanced at her watch and saw that it had been over an hour since she had entered the building. She had somehow lost an hour of time standing there holding a doorknob. Could she have been standing there that long? Was it possible? Charlotte shook her head and slowly walked away from the room, glancing over her shoulder at the door every few steps, wondering.

# SUSAN

SUSAN SAT NEXT to her patient, rolling on her stool, looking back and forth between the x-rays and the patient's open mouth. She glanced at the x-rays one more time, deciding on the action she would have to take. She pushed the intercom, calling for the dental assistant to come in with the Novocain so she could begin the procedure. She swabbed the patient's gums with a numbing gel so the shot would not be painful, merely uncomfortable. The root canal itself was straightforward. Susan did not anticipate any problems today.

As she turned to give the nurse directions, she saw Charlotte standing in the doorway. She assumed Charlotte was here about her appointment later in the day; she was probably nervous about what they would find wrong with her teeth. Susan understood this anxiety; she just didn't have time to hold Charlotte's hand right now.

"Can I speak to you for a second?" Charlotte asked tentatively, noticing the slight exasperated look on Susan's face.

"Um, of course. But only for a second. Give me one minute and I'll be right there," Susan replied as the dental assistant came in with the syringes. Susan carefully lifted a syringe and slid it gently into the patient's mouth. She pushed on the plunger and watched as the anesthesia oozed out of the clear tube and into the woman's gum. She repeated this procedure three times and then left to find out what Charlotte needed, knowing that the Novocain would take a few minutes to begin working. She hoped that would be enough time to calm Charlotte down.

Susan followed Charlotte down the hall, once again noticing the slight hum of the brightly lit fluorescent bulbs. Thinking back over her life, she had never noticed this sound before. But since discovering the machine her sense of hearing had improved exponentially.

"So, you know how I was supposed to be your next appointment?" asked Charlotte.

"Of course," Susan replied. She was about to reassure Charlotte when she realized that Charlotte was canceling the examination altogether.

"Charlotte, you need to be examined. Your teeth have been bothering you for a while. Let me see what's wrong before you start to get nervous. It could be nothing more than sensitive teeth. Maybe you'll need to buy special toothpaste. But please let me check. I—no, we—want to make sure."

"It isn't that," Charlotte replied. "A new patient just walked in off the street. He is in a lot of pain, so I gave him my timeslot. I can reschedule for another day; this young man is really suffering. I had to help him."

"Oh, okay," Susan stammered, surprised and a little disappointed. She, as well as David and Keith, had been trying to get Charlotte in a chair for months, ever since they'd seen her adding cold water to her coffee because the heat of the coffee made her wince.

"I put him in room 5 … " Charlotte started to explain,

wanting to add that she didn't want other patients, especially children, to see the poor man's suffering. However, she didn't get the chance Susan was already running down the hall toward room 5.

*No, no, no, no* ran through Susan's mind. *Please let me get there in time. Please don't let this happen.* Susan slammed into the door, sending it flying open.

She ran into the room, thankful to see the young man sitting there, breathing; thankful to see that the suction straw still sat perched in its holder.. With Charlotte's help, Susan relocated Nathan to room 3 and promised to be back as soon as she could be. She sent Charlotte down to check on the status of her root canal patient, so she could slip into her office, grab the key, and lock room 5 so no one else could enter. She knew that she had to be more careful from now on; she had to double, even triple, check the door each morning. It had to stay locked.

Susan finished the scheduled surgery and went to examine Nathan, curious to see if there was any effect from the machine. She wasn't sure what to expect but maybe she would see something in his behavior, something in his eyes that would tell her It had called to him but that he had resisted.

She sat next to Nathan and checked the x-rays the dental technician had taken. She saw that he had a severely impacted left molar and told him that it had to come out as soon as possible. She stressed that they didn't want the infection to spread to other teeth. When she saw the hesitation in his eyes, she wondered if it was from the idea of surgery or from the idea of being so close to the machine.

She had to find out if there had been an effect, so she again stressed the dangers of an infection like his, the jeopardy he would be putting his other teeth and jaw in if he didn't get the tooth pulled. Nathan reluctantly agreed and made an appointment for the next day.

Susan knew she would have to rearrange her schedule for this, but she had to prioritize. He had been exposed to It, the machine; she had to know if any influence was developing. She was interested in seeing if there would be a reaction tomorrow; did the machine call him? Did he sense Its power? And if so, how did he resist Its pull?

She decided to find out while he was under anesthesia. She would spend tonight thinking of ways to get the assistant to leave during the procedure so she could question Nathan. She had to have a plan. She had to know what he knew.

That night Susan decided she had to get out of the building; she needed to try to clear her head of the cacophony of the machine. She went to a local restaurant and ordered a Caesar salad and burger for dinner. She then opened her notebook and began to brainstorm ideas.

Susan knew that she did her best thinking while occupied with other things, so she let her mind wander while her subconscious worked on her dilemma.

As Susan ate her salad, she saw Charlotte walk into the restaurant on the arm of a man. They sat together in a dark corner, whispering and holding hands across the tabletop. Susan tried not to look, she tried not to pry into her employee's life, but she found that impossible.

The man was an older gentleman, perhaps twenty or even twenty-five years Charlotte's senior. His black hair was peppering with grey, while small lines were etched around his eyes. He was a handsome man, and Susan could see why Charlotte would find him endearing. Susan knew that Charlotte had never known her birth father, or any father figure for that matter. *Maybe Charlotte has a daddy complex,* thought Susan.

She knew it wasn't her concern and that she shouldn't pay attention to her employee's personal life, and Charlotte was an exceptionally good employee. It didn't affect Charlotte's work if she had a "daddy complex," so Susan shouldn't care. But Susan continued to think about it while watching Charlotte and her gentleman. She recalled how Charlotte would sometimes look at Keith, laughing at his corny jokes. Again, Susan tried to shrug off the thoughts; she tried to bring her mind back to her problems. But she couldn't. Charlotte was seeing one man while flirting shamelessly with Keith, her boss. Susan knew that Keith was no longer hers to worry about, but something inside her didn't like watching someone—anyone—flirting with him. She knew it wasn't her problem, that she had allowed Keith to be free. And it wasn't only Charlotte who flirted with Keith; Susan saw many women flirt with him, but she continued to ponder Charlotte. It was different with Charlotte. She worked with them.

She had bigger problems of her own to deal with. She refocused her mind. She had to figure out what had happened today; how did Nathan resist the pull? Until now, she knew about no one who was able to withstand the call of the machine. No one except herself, but she didn't know how long that would last. She believed—no, she knew—her fate was to one day place the suction straw in her own mouth and feel the liquid slowly slip out of her body. She shuddered as she thought about it.

But what to do about Nathan? Maybe sleep would help her decide; if, of course, the machine would let her sleep tonight. If …

# NATHAN

Nathan lay on his bed, drugged on painkillers and experiencing some of the wildest dreams he'd ever had. His mind raced with images; horrifying, terrifying nightmares crashed from his subconscious. He had spent the nights since his time in room 5 in fitful, evil-fueled dreams. No matter how or where the dream started, it always ended in room 5, with Nathan's hand reaching for the suction straw. The room was dark, ominous, as Nathan entered, but the machine glowed with an eerie light—an unrecognizable hue; an almost-painful-to-the-eyes white. Nathan walked across the room slowly, trembling. Although the room was cold, icy, Nathan felt sweat covering his body. The room seemed to grow as he stepped forward, a foot for each footfall. He began to run but the room just grew faster. He had to reach the machine; he had to destroy it; destroy it now, before it was too late.

    His dream-self felt the compulsion to hold the straw, what his dentist back home called "Mr. Thirsty," and to slowly, methodically break the machine. He wanted to snap it into pieces and then further destroy each piece until nothing was left but a pile of rubber and metal, unrecognizable even to a trained eye.

When Nathan awoke from the dreams, he found himself drenched in sweat, trembling. He wasn't sure if it was from being cold or from being filled with adrenaline or fear. But it was from the dreams, the medication fueling their brightness.

"Are you okay? Here, let me get you more blankets," Annie said as she laid another afghan over Nathan. He looked at her and smiled, thinking about how lucky he was to have her in his life. She wiped his brow as his eyes closed and he drifted back into terror-filled sleep.

The next time he awoke, the painkillers had worn off, and Annie was standing there with a tumbler of water and his next dose. He shook his head slowly and mumbled, "No more. I want Tylenol instead."

"But the doctor said … " she began. Nathan again shook his head.

"No more of those. The dreams. No more of those."

Annie brought Nathan the water and two Tylenol and sat watch over him as he drifted into another tumultuous sleep.

Even with the painkillers leaving his system, the dreams persisted. They became more vivid and slowly began to seep into his reality, his wakefulness.

As he sat in the lecture hall, trying to follow the professor's ramblings, he would suddenly see room 5. It felt as if he was transported back into the scape of his nightmares. He could feel his pulse quicken with each passing minute. Most of the time, he would just close his eyes, and when he opened them again he would be back, sitting in the molded plastic chair, surrounded not by darkness but by his classmates.

But sometimes he wouldn't be. He would have to relive the dream; he would have to try to destroy the machine, to dismantle Mr. Thirsty. The question was how. Each time he entered into that world, he would try a different approach. He always failed.

He decided to go back to the office, to see if the pull was still there. He hoped it had all been a wakeful dream, that the infection had caused him to believe something sinister was happening in the dental practice. He had to find out the truth; he knew he would be haunted until he did.

He stood on the sidewalk outside of the practice. He stared at the blue wooden building, the yellow door bookended by two triangular pine trees. So far, he felt nothing, no pull to enter the building. Maybe it had been a hallucination, but he had to be sure even as relief flowed over him. Taking a deep breath, Nathan walked toward the building, stepping carefully over the fallen pinecones that were scattered on the front lawn. He entered the building, inhaling the stale air of the dental practice, and smiled at Charlotte.

"Well, hi there. Are you having a problem with that tooth—or, the spot where the tooth was—again?"

"Um, no. I, lost, um, a pen last time I was here. It was silver and kinda old. Did you find anything?"

"No. Where do you think you lost it?"

"I was hoping if fell out of my pocket when I was in the examination chair. Do you mind if I look for it?"

"No. Do you remember which room you were in? I can see if it's empty right now."

"I think it was the second door on the left."

"Okay, that's room 3," she responded, checking the dental schedule, "It isn't being used right now. Let's go look."

Charlotte led Nathan down the hall and into room 3. As they glanced around the floor of the room, Nathan rapidly tried to think of ways to get into room 5, alone. How was he going to get Charlotte back to her desk? And what was he going to do once he was in room 5? Was he going to dismantle the machine or just look at it, trying to figure out how it worked? What if it pulled him in again? What if he couldn't get away this time? He wondered what that meant. What would happen to him?

But what if it had all been a dream, a painkiller-induced hallucination? Maybe too many horror movies had somehow warped him like his grandmother had always warned.

Nathan knew he had to find out, and he needed to know now. This simple task had infected him, taken over his life. He had to know the truth.

"I don't see it anywhere," Charlotte said, turning to see Nathan standing near the door.

"Huh? What?" Nathan stammered.

"Your pen?" Charlotte said, "I don't see it here. Are you sure you lost it while you were here? Maybe you lost it somewhere else."

"Oh, right," he whispered, then speaking louder, "It has to be here. Maybe one of your dentists picked it up. Can you ask them for me, please? It really is important to me."

"Fine," Charlotte sighed. "But you'll have to wait in the reception area."

"Okay," Nathan followed Charlotte into the reception area and sat down. As soon as Charlotte left the room, Nathan walked to the doorway, glanced down the hallway, stepped through the opening, turned right, and headed to room 5.

The closer he got, the more he felt the strange pull. It hadn't been a dream or a hallucination. This was very real.

Nathan reached the room, gently placed his hand on the doorknob, and slowly began to turn the handle. The door was locked. He pushed on it, suddenly becoming desperate to get into the room. He didn't understand why, but he had to get inside the room; he had to touch the machine. He saw an image of himself inside room 5, holding the suction straw in his hand, slowly, deliberately placing It into his mouth.

"What are you doing?" Charlotte hissed, walking briskly toward Nathan. He realized that he had been hitting his shoulder against the door, attempting to break it down.

"I was in this room that day. I thought my pen might be in here," Nathan said as he glanced down the hall and saw patients and doctors standing in the doorways of the other examination rooms with their mouths agape.

"That door is locked for a reason. Please leave now!" Charlotte stated, pointing toward the exit door in the back.

"But maybe my pen is in there," Nathan argued. He could see the three partners moving toward him.

"You heard her," Dr. Caine said. "Leave or we call the police."

"Nathan, right?" Dr. Andres interrupted.

"Yes."

"That room is being renovated, updated. I'm sure you understand why. It's not safe for you to be in there right now. Insurance liability and all. We wouldn't want you to get hurt. The room had been gutted. I'm sure if there was a … "

"Pen," Charlotte filled in.

"Right. A pen, we would have found it."

"Oh," Nathan replied. "Thanks." He slowly left the building. As he walked down the steps, he knew that there were no renovations. Whatever was in that room, Dr. Andres knew about it and wanted to keep it a secret. Now Nathan was sure that something was happening in room 5—something sinister.

# KEITH

An hour after Nathan left, David and Keith came knocking on Susan's office door. "Come in," Susan called. She was sitting on a Queen Elizabeth chair, gently sipping a cup of warm tea, while reading a patient's chart. *Nocturnes* by Chopin wafted across the room.

"Hey, Suzy," Keith said, smiling his perfect white smile at her. "That was some quick thinking you did back there. What was with that guy, anyway? Trying to break down a door for a pen?"

"Who was he? You seemed to know him," David commented.

"Nathan? A former patient. He was a walk-in with an infected tooth. I can promise you, he is a *former* patient. I do not intend to see him again. He seems to be unstable."

"Good. People like that are bad for business. My patient was really shook up after all that commotion. People are nervous enough at the dentist; they don't need that kind of craziness."

As David and Keith left Susan's office, Susan quickly yelled after them, "Oh, and Keith—I hate 'SUZY!'"

"Right, sorry ... Suzy." Keith smiled back as Susan shook her head, sipping her Oolong tea.

*I might have a "friend" for Keith to meet one day*, she thought, smiling to herself.

. . .

Hours later, after everyone had left for the night, going to their homes or out with friends, Susan once again reached into her desk and removed the ancient key. She walked down to room 5, put the key in the lock, and slowly turned the handle. She knew what she would find, and what the police would have seen if David had called them earlier after Nathan's stunt. She dreaded this part of the deal, the arrangement she had accidentally, unknowingly, made with the machine.

She had never planned for this to happen, but she too had felt the allure of the machine. But instead of wanting to place the straw in her mouth, dehydrating herself with Mr. Thirsty, Susan felt compelled to help the machine feed.

Since the day she found it, her consciousness had been taken over. It didn't happen slowly; it wasn't a progression. It was instantaneously. She had put one hand on the relic and she was Its unwilling cohort, Its slave. She couldn't remember a time when she wasn't under Its hold. Sometimes images would enter her mind—she could see herself laughing with friends or curled up at home reading a book. But these were distant memories, and they were fading from her fast. All that mattered now was feeding the machine. That was how she now thought of it—feeding. She had begun to rationalize her actions, her crimes, this way. She saw it as being no different than someone buying live mice for a pet snake. All living things must feed. The machine needed the liquid, so It, too, could survive. All she did was bring It Its meals.

Susan walked into room 5, exhaling as she approached Mrs. Sheila Danvers. Susan began to examine the elderly body for any signs of liquid retention. As she bent over the mummified Mrs. Danvers, Keith appeared in the doorway.

"Who do we have here? An emergency? Can I help in any way?" Keith said standing in the doorway. "No, Keith, um, I have it. Go home or out or wherever it is you go nowadays. I have this," Susan quickly said, moving toward him; she hoped to block his entrance into the room, but he made his way in, skirting around her. He moved to the foot of the examination chair. His charm-filled smile quickly faded as he looked on the remains of Mrs. Danvers.

"What the hell happened? Susan? What is this?"

Susan panicked, her mind racing for an explanation, anything reasonable. But then she realized that she didn't need one, not really. The machine would tell her what to do; as always, she would follow Its instructions perfectly, no matter what It wanted her to do.

"I don't know, Keith. Something went wrong. Help me, please!" A piece of Susan, the old Susan, crept into her voice. She felt the machine's pull grow stronger, barricading the old Susan back into her subconscious mind.

"What can I do?" Keith asked, horrified. He knew they should call someone, but what would that do to their practice? He had no explanation for the condition of the body that sat before him. He wavered for a moment and then said, "Susan, we need to call the police. We have to report this."

"Why?" she said desperately, "We could just get rid of the body. Destroy all the evidence. No one uses this room anyway." She knew what the machine wanted, but the old Susan, the Susan who'd once made love to Keith, could not accept the plan. She wanted to tell Keith to run. She started to form the words in her mind. The machine hummed louder, drowning out the objections in Susan's subconscious.

Keith looked at his friend, wondering if he had ever really known her. For the first time in a while, he truly looked at her and saw her for who she was now. He saw the tired eyes and disheveled hair. How had he not noticed all these changes? He couldn't remember the last time they had talked. He had been so angry at her for pulling away.

"Suzy, Susan, we have to call the police." He reached out, placing his hand on her shoulder. "What if she had family? Someone will know she is missing; someone will know she came here and was never seen again. I am not going to prison for this." Keith turned around to leave the room.

"You're right, of course. Just help me put things back the way they were. We shouldn't disturb any of the evidence. Can you put the suction straw back into her mouth? I removed it when I came into the room and first saw her." Susan held the device out to Keith as she straightened the fallen tray.

Keith reached for the straw and felt the overwhelming compulsion. He turned to Susan and saw a playful smile on her lips.

"What's wrong, Keith? Having second thoughts?" the old Susan had once again been subdued by the persistent machine.

"I ... I ... don't know," he stammered as his hand involuntarily moved the suction straw toward his own mouth. "Susan, something is wrong." As he moved the straw closer to his mouth, he began to realize what had happened to Mrs. Danvers and that it was not an accident. "Susan ... Suzy ... help me!"

Susan looked at Keith. "I'm sorry," she said as Keith put the suction straw into his mouth. "Why don't you sit down, here on the floor. It will be easier, more comfortable that way. Don't fight It, Keith. It won't take too long." Susan helped Keith slide onto the floor, his back resting against the wall, his legs splayed out in front of him.

Susan lifted Mrs. Danvers out of the dental chair and carried her out of room 5. Before shutting the door, she glanced at Keith. His eyes stared back at her, pleading for help. She closed the door, saying quietly, "I am sorry, Keith. I'll be back for you later."

As she carried Mrs. Danvers to the basement, she thought she heard Keith cry out for help. She laid Mrs. Danvers down and walked back to room 5. She placed her hand on the doorknob and silently locked the door, resting her right hand on the door and sighing. The machine would take care of any problems Keith may be having.

After Mrs. Danvers' burial, Susan went back upstairs, put on gloves, and entered Keith's private office. She found his computer was still turned on, his email open. Realizing her good fortune, Susan composed a quick email to Charlotte from Keith.

> Met a real beauty tonight. Have flown to a secret location with her. Cancel all my appointments for this week.
>
> —Keith

Susan clicked send and walked out of his office, thankful for Keith's past behavior and indiscretions. In a week, Susan would have Keith send a farewell email to Charlotte, David, and herself saying that he had fallen in love, that he was giving them his share of the practice and would not be back.

With her plans about Keith solidified, Susan went to the file room, where she removed Nathan's file from the cabinet and carried it to her office. And as she waited for the machine to finish with Keith, she brainstormed ideas for Nathan. He also had to disappear, but he had parents—involved parents, she assumed, since he had listed them as his emergency contact. This one would be tricky.

Susan drifted off to sleep, her original memories flooding back. Images of Keith, David, and herself laughing together in hotel bars, laying out the plans for their practice. Late-night phone calls with Keith, ones that started out professionally but always ended up personal.

Flashes of the times she and Keith would secretly meet. It always started with talking. They would discuss the practice, their dreams for its success. And as they talked, Susan would rest her hand of the tabletop, Keith's hand covering it. They would walk along the lakefront, holding hands. Susan knew she was falling in love with Keith, as he was with her.

Susan awoke just as her dreams began to reawaken her love and desire for Keith. She jolted up and ran to room 5, hoping she wasn't too late, knowing that she was. Quickly unlocking the door, she entered the room and went to Keith's side. He was gone. Nothing in the husk that was now Keith resembled the man she had once loved, the man whose heart she had broken when the machine took over her life.

She had sent Keith into other women's arms and into their beds. She hated him for it, for not fighting harder to keep his Suzy. And now she had killed him, or at least helped to facilitate his death.

Susan knew she couldn't bury Keith with the others. He was not just some anonymous person; he was her friend, more than her friend. She gathered his body into her arms and carried him to her car. Under the darkness of night, she gently, lovingly placed him in her trunk and drove off toward the woods. She would bury him near his cabin, the one she and Keith had made love in so many times. She would bury him there and then sleep in the cabin that night, to hold him close one more time.

As Susan pulled out of the driveway, another car, which had been parked on the road, started up and headed in the same direction.

Nathan sat behind the wheel of his roommate's car, a ten-year old Toyota Corolla, wondering what Dr. Andres had just placed in her trunk. He knew he had to follow her to find out.

Susan's mind raced as she drove out of the town limits and headed into the mountains. She began to remember more and more of her life from before. She discovered that the farther she drove from the machine, the weaker its pull felt. She was still tied to its pulsing call, but her memories were becoming free. The farther she drove, the more Keith entered her consciousness. Guilt, real guilt, began to fill her as tears, actual tears, started streaming down her cheeks. The realization of all she had done weighed on her as she parked her car outside the cabin.

She hoped Keith still kept the key in the same place. Susan walked to the front door, bent down, and picked up a small purple frog that was perched on a gray rock. She turned it over and reached inside. Her fingers found the key. She placed the key in the door and went inside. More memories invaded her, her breathing became erratic until she dropped to her knees sobbing. As she regained her composure and her breath evened out, she looked around the room. It was exactly as it had been when Keith had taken her here; what felt like years ago. The stone-faced fireplace dominated the back wall; the small kitchenette was on the adjoining wall. A Navajo rug lay on the wood floor. A couch, coffee table, and armchair were the only furniture in the room. Susan could sense Keith in the room as memories of their many weekends together bombarded her mind.

She could see him lounging on the couch, his flannel shirt finishing the picture of rustic life. She sat on the rug in front of him, leaning against the couch, his fingers entangled in her hair. They had spent the day hiking in the woods, picnicking near a riverbed. Now they rested, a fire blazing. The smell of dinner enveloped the room. Susan smiled up at Keith; she knew that she was falling for him. She didn't want to leave this room, this ideal place. But she knew that she had to; she had to show Keith and David her plans for the building she had found for their practice. For now, she was going to stay in the present, in Keith's embrace. She was going to relish the warmth of his skin next to hers. Work would be there tomorrow; today and tonight were just about Keith and herself—and she was going to enjoy each minute of it.

Susan could once again feel tears rolling down her cheeks.

But then, she felt It. The machine was pushing harder, trying to reestablish the connection. She fought against It, trying to break its grip. It screamed at her to bury the body and come home. Over and over she heard It, felt its desperation for her. She could feel It winning. She slowly rose and walked out of the cabin to a small shed. She found a shovel, walked into a line of trees, and began digging a grave.

When the grave was deep enough for her purpose, she walked to the car and retrieved Keith's body from the trunk. She carried him to the gravesite, lowered him into the ground, said a final farewell, and slowly placed the dirt on top of him. She then returned the shovel to the shed and reentered the cabin to sleep.

. . .

NATHAN HAD LEFT HIS CAR ON THE ROAD A QUARTER mile back. He sat in the shadow of some trees and watched Susan bury her cargo in the woods. After she stood quietly over the fresh mound of dirt, Susan slowly walked back to the shed, returned the shovel, and made her way back to the cabin. Nathan waited to see if Susan would reappear, but she didn't. He stayed hidden in the trees until the cabin's light went out. Then he quietly entered the shed, grabbed the shovel, and began to dig up the loose dirt.

After a few minutes, he unearthed what Susan had just buried. He shone a light onto it and recoiled at what he saw. He recognized the face as one of the doctors from Susan's practice, but he could not understand what had happened to him. His face had darkened and had a leathery appearance. His body was shriveled to half its normal size. His fingers and toes were curled as if grasping something invisible in the air. His lips were frozen in a grimace, revealing the pain of his death.

Nathan realized that this was what the machine did, and that Dr. Susan Andres was somehow involved and responsible for this death. What he didn't know was whether Susan controlled the machine or if the machine was in control of Susan. He hoped it was the former but feared the latter. He had felt the machine's powerful pull; he feared that he knew who was in control.

After Nathan re-covered the body with the dirt and placed the shovel back in the shed, he hiked back down the dirt path to his car and drove slowly back toward campus. He arrived at his apartment and was happy to see that his roommate was not around. He went upstairs and lay in his bedroom, the image of Keith plaguing him.

The police would never believe his wild story, and if he brought them to the body, they would demand to know how he knew its location. He couldn't think of how he would explain this to anybody. He only knew that he had to—needed to—do something. He couldn't allow more people to die. He just didn't know how he was going to stop it.

. . .

WHEN SUSAN AWOKE, SHE REALIZED THAT SHE HADN'T FELT this rested in a long time. Last night was the first night she had slept straight through, no interruptions to awaken her.

She slowly stretched before exiting the bed and then took a long, hot shower. As the water cascaded around her, she became more aware of the quiet. Not just the lack of cars and people, but the quiet in her mind. The machine, which usually screamed Its way into her, was now just a whisper.

She soon noticed her hunger—not the machine's, but hers. Susan remembered a small diner where she and Keith had eaten. She walked to her car to head into town. As she left the woods, heading back to the highway, the whisper grew louder. Susan stopped the car and sat. Her mind was split between her thoughts and the machine's growing demands. She opened her phone and wrote an email to Charlotte. She told her to cancel all her appointments until further notice. She knew that David would be furious—first

Keith and then Susan—but she knew she had to do it. She had to disconnect from the machine. Or at least she had to try.

Exhaling, Susan restarted the car, made a U-turn on the road, and headed away—as far away as possible. She needed time to think, to regroup. She needed to decide what to do next.

# CHARLOTTE

CHARLOTTE HAD NEVER known her father. Victoria, full of the shame of a fallen woman, had filled Charlotte with lies about him. Shortly after discovering she was pregnant, Victoria resigned from her job, packed her few possessions, and moved away from her parents' house. She had to start over, had to find a place where her shame would not be known.

Victoria found a job as a receptionist in a small town, a place she had never heard about before. Once there, she began her new life based on a simple lie—she was a widow. Her beloved husband had died tragically in a car accident, before his first and only child was born. He, sadly, would never lay eyes on her; there would never be pictures of him with her.

As Charlotte grew older, she began to question the story. Why were there no picture of her father? Not even a wedding photo. Victoria explained that she had destroyed them in her grief; it pained her so much to see them. Charlotte wondered why she didn't know his family, no grandparents or cousins. Victoria said that they, too, had died. Charlotte began to fixate on a family curse. How could every member of one family be dead? Did this mean that she was also destined to die young?

She would dream about the horrible way she would die. Would it be in a fire? Drowning? Maybe she would be buried alive or devoured by an animal. She even allowed her mind to play with the idea of a supernatural death—werewolves, vampires, or maybe a vengeful ghost or demon. She knew that however she was going to die, it was not going to be ordinary.

Victoria had no answer. She had begun to run out of lies. She decided that it was time to tell Charlotte the "truth." After school one day, when Charlotte was fourteen years old, Victoria sat her down to tell her the real story of her father, the secret she didn't want to be found out.

"Charlotte, my daughter," Victoria began. "It's time you knew the truth. Your father is not dead. To be truthful, I don't know that. He might be dead; I really don't know, nor do I care. Your father is, or was, a very bad man. He took advantage of innocent young women after plying them with alcohol."

"What does that mean?" Charlotte asked.

"You know how I never drink alcohol?"

Charlotte nodded.

"Charlotte, darling," her mother said in her exasperated way, "answer with words. Anyway, there is a reason why I never drink. I want to tell you why. One night, when I lived in another city, I went out with some of the other young single girls from work. It was the one and only time that I ever did. They tricked me into drinking and then left me in a compromised condition." Anger burned in Victoria's eyes.

"How?" Charlotte interrupted.

"Don't interrupt," Victoria chided. Charlotte meekly whispered an apology as Victoria continued to weave her story.

"Well they, these girls, told me my drinks were virgin, but they weren't."

Charlotte began to open her mouth to ask what "virgin" meant, but quickly closed it when she saw her mother's tight-lipped expression.

Victoria again continued her story. "There happened to be a handsome man—you get your black hair from him—at the bar that night. He came over to talk to me. Well, I was so drunk that I couldn't think straight. I accepted his offer for a ride home. I thought I had come down with a flu and was afraid to drive, you see." Victoria sighed, shaking her head.

Charlotte looked at her mother, trying to picture her always-in-control mother unable to drive. She couldn't quite see her mom out drinking with friends; she had never known her mom to be even friendly with another person. She was polite, even cordial; but friendly, never.

"That was my second mistake of the evening. The first being trusting those women. I should have called for a taxi, but hindsight and all. Charlotte, my child, your father was not—probably still isn't—a good man. That's why I am so strict with you—genetics, you never know whose genes you got. Well, now, I'm sure you can figure out the rest of this … sordid tale. I won't go into any more of its gruesome details." Victoria then rose from her chair, absentmindedly brushing imaginary wrinkles from her skirt, and briskly walked out of the room.

Fourteen-year old Charlotte didn't understand the story, didn't grasp the underlying meaning. But as she grew older and thought more about her mother's story, she began to piece together what happened that night.

By the time Charlotte was eighteen years old, she had realized what her mother had been trying to tell her: that she, Charlotte, was the product of rape. Her father was a rapist. She understood why her mother had lied all those years. How horrible it must be for her to have to look at her rapist's child every day. So much of Charlotte's childhood made sense to her now. She now understood why her mother never hugged or kissed her, why she never said "I love you" to her daughter. Why she never even tucked her into bed at night.

It was around this time that Charlotte began to think of ways to punish her father. She fantasized about confronting him. When Charlotte was hired at the dental practice, she found a private detective and told him all she knew about her father. She had already discovered the name of the town where her mother used to live—it just took a little snooping when her mother was out shopping; she had found an old tax return in her mother's files. Her old address, her place of employment. The detective set out to find this unknown man. Within a few months, he called Charlotte to tell her that he had found her father. His name was Kenneth Donovan and he was a high-profile attorney living about two hours from Charlotte. The detective brought her his dossier, which included multiple photographs plus an address and number with which to contact him, if she wanted to.

She held the folder for a few days before deciding to call him, posing as a potential client. She would feel him out and then choose the right time to tell him who she really was.

But when Charlotte finally did introduce herself to her father, she was surprised to find that she found him to be not only handsome (as her mother had told her) but charming as well. She found herself falling for his endearing ways, his fatherly attention. She found that she had to repeatedly remind herself that this man was not as he seemed. He was conning her; he was a rapist—her mother's rapist. And he had to pay for his crime.

She knew that she needed to make him trust her; she needed to catch him off guard if she was going to punish him. Keeping this in mind, she started spending time with him. They grew close, so close that she would be able to find a way to wound him as he had her mother.

. . .

CHARLOTTE CAME INTO WORK THAT MORNING TRYING TO decide what to do about her father. She enjoyed the time she spent with him and was having trouble picturing him as the man her mother had described. She wasn't sure if she could continue with her plan; she didn't think she would be capable of killing him.

Whenever Charlotte found herself in a quandary, she found it best to stay busy, to give her mind a break from the questions at hand. She felt a wave of disappointment as she checked the day's schedule and saw it was so light. With Susan and Keith both on vacation, David was the only specialist available. The hygienists had patients coming in, but it was not enough to keep her occupied, plus they were all regulars and had no paperwork for Charlotte to fill out or file. Charlotte sighed as she looked at her desk—it was spotless. She had stayed late to finish her paperwork last night and had already put the week's insurance claims in the mail.

Then she remembered room 5. Susan had said that it was under construction, but Charlotte knew this wasn't true. But what if Charlotte were to thoroughly clean the room, give it a fresh coat of paint, hang some new posters. Maybe even order some new equipment. David would have to sign off on the equipment, but if she made the room inviting, then maybe it was doable. Room 5 would be useable.

She smiled, rechecked the schedule, and saw that she had two hours before a patient was due. She left the front room and headed down the hall to room 5. She removed her keys from her front pocket and placed her hand on the doorknob. The door slowly swung forward, slightly ajar.

She put her keys back in her pocket, wondering who had opened the door earlier, and entered the room. She surveyed what work needed to be done and decided on what supplies she would need. She turned to leave and headed toward the supply closet When she returned to room 5, her arms were laden with rags, brushes, cleaning supplies, and a can of leftover paint. She walked to the counter, put her supplies down, slowly exhaled, and began to clean the room.

After an hour and a half, she began to see some progress; she also heard David enter the building. She quickly brushed dust off her clothes and ran her fingers through her disheveled hair. She walked briskly to the front and greeted David with her best smile.

"Morning, Charlotte. What's our schedule like for today?" David asked, placing a cup of coffee on Charlotte's desk.

"Light. You have a ten o'clock and then two more patients this afternoon."

"Okay," David sighed irritably. "Have you heard from Keith or Susan?"

"No."

As David walked to his office, Charlotte could hear him mumbling, "When are they coming back? Maybe I should start to look for new partners." As he walked down the hall, he saw room 3 was already in use and thought that at least they still had those patients. He entered his office and began to review the day's cases.

Charlotte took a sip of the coffee David had brought her. She sat down and waited for the ten o'clock patient to come in. As soon as she had the patient settled in the exam room and had filled out the required insurance forms, she headed back to room 5.

# SUSAN

Susan drove west. She had no destination in mind; she just needed to get beyond the machine's reach. She drove until she ran out of road. She parked, left the car, and sat on the white sands of the Pacific Ocean. She had no idea as to where she was, only that she no longer felt the pull of the machine. She was finally free.

As she sat, watching the waves roll onto the beach, the memories of what she had done filled her mind. Tears rolled down her cheeks as she tried to figure out how she had become a murderer. Not just a murderer, but a mass murderer—or was it a serial killer? She wasn't sure which one she was, but it didn't matter. She was going to spend her life in prison, where she herself would agree she belonged.

In the distance she heard music accompanied by laughter. She slowly looked around and saw what appeared to be a bar in the distance. She stood up, removed her sand-filled shoes, and plodded her way down the beach toward the alcohol-infused oasis.

When she arrived at her destination, she went inside and ordered a glass of whiskey, the first of many drinks that afternoon. She spent the afternoon sitting on a barstool, drinking glassfuls of whiskey, while watching patrons come and go throughout the day. By closing time, she could barely stand as she stumbled her way back down the beach. In her drunken stupor, she fell onto the sand and passed out. The next thing she was aware of, it was morning. The sun shone blindingly down on her. Her eyes burned from its intensity; a hangover headache pounded in her temples. She rolled over, threw up the alcohol left in her stomach, covered the spot with sand, and then crawled five feet over.

Closing her eyes once again, Susan laid back down and replayed the past years in her mind, trying desperately to understand how she could do something so evil. It was so difficult for her to see herself for who she now was—a murderer. Plain and simple, she had killed—or to rationalize it, allowed a machine to kill. She had *helped* a machine kill more people than she could now recall. People she didn't know; people she held no grudge against—except for Keith, whom she had loved. Yet she had led him to this death, knowingly. If she were to be truly honest with herself, maybe even willingly.

She could taste the salt from her sweat and tears on her lips, but she didn't move. She lay there and thought. Why had she been so vulnerable to the machine's manipulations? She never felt the need to put the straw in her mouth; she just needed to bring others over, allowing the machine to go into their minds, convince them that they wanted to place the straw in their mouths, that they didn't want to ever remove it. That they wanted to die for the machine. She had never felt the desire to die for the machine, just to feed it—to kill for it.

Susan breathed in the salt air, slowly exhaled, and let her mind play over her memories. She allowed it to travel back to her childhood, desperately trying to find the incident that had allowed her to become who she now was.

She remembered an average childhood. She had been an only child for the first twelve years and then her brother, her perfect brother, had been born. She remembered the way her parents looked at him with such love and acceptance; everything he did was a marvel. Susan faded into the background as Erik emerged. Susan could not remember a time when her parents looked at her the way they looked at Erik.

Susan sat stone-faced, thinking about what had become of this perfect child. Erik had not lived past age four. He had fallen ill after a night of burgers and fries and died within a few hours. The doctors said it was *E. coli*. Susan pictured his casket; it had surprised her at the time—it was so small. She had not known that caskets were made so small. She had stood next to it throughout his funeral. Her mother spent most of the funeral standing next to her, sobbing, gripping Susan's arm with such strength, such desperation to cling to any hope, that she left a bruise. Susan had been afraid that her mother would throw herself onto the coffin in her grief, and she stood ready to catch her if she did.

Susan could feel the cold of that day as she lay on the hot beach. It had been a chilly fall day, made colder by a mist coming down. Her family stood in the rain, looking at the small casket as it was lowered into the ground. As the priest spoke words of comfort at the gravesite, Susan tried to hold her mother's hand, but her mother pushed her hand away, rebuffing her daughter's need for comfort. She was the one who had lost the most. The loss of a child, the unexplainable grief. She was the one truly suffering. There was nothing left in her to give to Susan.

Then a memory, one she hadn't recalled before, came back to her. As she, at sixteen years old, stood above her baby brother's grave, a fist of dirt at her side, her mother hoarsely whispered to her. Susan had never remembered what her mother had said that day until now. She had hidden it deeply inside her, not wanting to accept the truth of the harsh words, but today she heard her mother's voice clearly say to her, "It should have been you and not my Erik. Why wasn't it you instead? Why didn't you get the tainted burger? Why?"

A seagull's cry intruded into Susan's memory, and she opened her eyes. Her mother's words echoed in her mind as she lifted herself up and headed back to her car. As she started the engine, she wondered if her mother had been right. Maybe it should have been her; maybe Erik would have been a better person than Susan. But Susan could still change that. She could never undo what she had done, or had allowed to happen, but maybe she could stop it from happening to anyone else.

Susan knew what she had to do. She headed back east. She had to stop the machine from killing. She didn't know how to stop It or if she would be able to resist Its pull, but she knew she had to try. Erik would have stopped It, probably before Its first kill. Now, Susan had to try; and she had the long drive to figure out how.

# CHARLOTTE

IT WAS SUNDAY; the office was closed. Charlotte pulled into the parking lot. She planned to paint the room today so it would be dry by Monday. She entered the building, playing David's reaction to her efforts in her head. She hoped he would be pleased; maybe he would be so excited that he would take her to lunch—or, even better, dinner. Charlotte smiled to herself as she pictured David, looking handsome in a suit, picking her up for a fancy dinner. And maybe a second date would follow, and then ... Charlotte shook her head. "Stop daydreaming and get to work. If you don't get the room done, none of it will come true." She picked up her painting supplies and started the work.

She had finished the first coat of paint and was washing her hands when she heard the front door open.

"Hello, Charlotte, honey? Are you here?"

Charlotte looked at the clock and realized that she had lost time again. It had taken her much longer to paint than she had thought it would. She had made plans to have lunch with her father that day and had assumed that she would be able to clean herself up and still meet him on time.

"I'm back here," she yelled. Her father walked toward the back rooms. She emerged from room 5, still covered in paint.

. . .

"I guess I'll have to wait for you to get cleaned up," Kenneth laughed, smiling at Charlotte.

"Just give me a few minutes." Charlotte moved to her desk, grabbing a bag of clothes she had brought with her. She went into the bathroom and began to wash the light-green paint off her hands, arms, and face.

While Charlotte was getting ready for lunch, her father walked to room 5 and peeked in so he could see what she had been doing. Charlotte had told him her plan, how she wanted to help the practice by sprucing up the room. He smiled at his daughter's work and gingerly stepped into the room.

At first, Kenneth was unable to detect the low hum, but as he walked farther into the room, his ears began to pick up the vibration. The farther into the room he went, the more the vibration grew to an audible hum. He looked around the room, trying to detect where the sound was coming from, as he slowly made his way to the suction straw. He felt his hand involuntarily reach out and stroke the straw, feeling the vibration throughout his body. He picked up the straw and brought It to his mouth. He didn't understand why he was doing this; his brain was trying to command his hand to stop, to reverse its course. As he placed the straw into his mouth, he felt a sharp, yet pleasant, pain. The straw anchored Itself into his mouth. Slowly, methodically, the straw began to remove all the liquid from his body. His mind screamed out, and then faded to nothing more than a single vibration as he lowered himself to the floor and waited for death.

"I'm ready, Dad," Charlotte choked out, feeling the nausea she always fought using the word "dad." When he didn't respond, Charlotte went to look for him. She saw his car still in the parking lot and began to search the building.

She walked around looking in the various rooms, calling for him, until she got to room 5. She went into the room and saw what was left of him. Stifling a scream, Charlotte approached the body. Looking down on the mummified body, she puzzled about what she should do. Suddenly an image came into her mind—a key. She could see it perfectly in her mind, an antique key with a fleur-de-lis on it. She instinctively knew she could find it in Susan's desk. After retrieving the key, she carried what was left of her father down the cellar stairs, placed the key into the hidden lock, and buried him alongside the other victims.

Charlotte relocked the door, returned the key, and went home. She didn't understand how she'd known about the key or the secret room. She wasn't even sure what had actually happened in that room, what she had seen and done that day.

That night, Charlotte felt the pulse for the first time. The machine was calling for her to kill again—soon.

When Charlotte woke the next morning, her memories from the day before slowly slithered into her consciousness. She shuddered when she realized that she felt no remorse about her father's death. It was what she had wanted—to make him pay for his crimes against her mother. She had fulfilled her goal. She found herself smiling—a gold star for Charlotte.

As she poured hot water into her teacup, she noticed a slight humming noise. She looked around her kitchen for the sound's origin but couldn't find it. After searching her apartment, she left for work, hoping that the hum wasn't anything important or dangerous. She made a mental note to let her landlord know about the strange sound.

As she drove to work, she realized that the humming wasn't something dangerous going on in her house. It was in her head and was getting louder the closer she got to work. By the time she pulled into the parking lot, it wasn't a hum; it was words, commands for her to find another food source. She didn't understand what was happening but quickly realized what she was being told to do.

Charlotte shook her head, hoping to clear the thoughts from her mind. They just got louder and more plaintive. She walked to her desk, resisting the urge to enter room 5, turned on her computer, and printed the schedule. As she pulled the day's charts from the files, she became grateful that the day appeared full and busy. She would be too swamped to worry about a voice in her head; for that's all it was, a voice in her head. It couldn't be anything else. She carried the files to her desk and organized them into piles by appointment time, the earlier appointments on top. She placed each pile into the box of a different employee, so everyone had the charts they would need for that day. She then went through Friday's charts and invoices.

As she shuffled through invoices, her mind began to wander. She dwelled on the way her father looked after the machine. What had happened to him? She had never seen anything like it before. She knew that she should be scared, should at the very least be freaked out by what she had seen, but she strangely was not. If anything, she was somehow comforted by it. She felt waves of guilt wash away from her. For the first time, Charlotte did not feel responsible for anyone else's suffering or pain. She just felt relief.

The voice grew even louder; It went from a childlike whine to a scream of suffering. It ordered her to find someone. She tried to shut It out.

How had her father died? Could that have something to do with this voice?

Charlotte wondered what she had unleashed.

# EMMA ROSE

Emma Rose had been a promising attorney. She graduated from law school at the age of twenty-four and began working at a prestigious law firm. Passing the bar on the first try only made her more impressive to the firm's partners. She was quickly put on some of the firm's most important clients' law teams. But as the stress began to build, Emma Rose found herself unraveling.

Emma had successfully been keeping a secret from everyone. She had begun to hear voices at the age of twenty. Emma's type A drive had aided her in relegating the voices to background static, but as the pressure at the firm grew and sleep became more and more elusive, the voices started to press forward.

It came crashing down around her one afternoon. She was taking a deposition from a very important client when the voices finally broke free. She had been preparing for this deposition for the past week, pulling twenty-hour days. The lack of sleep and the poor eating habits she had developed weakened her restraint.

She was in the middle of asking the witness a pivotal question when she turned to the empty chair on her right and loudly said, "Shut your fucking mouth already." She then stood up and began smacking the sides of her head with her hands, whispering, "Shut up, shut up, shut up. Stop asking me that. I won't do it. Shut up, please." It took two attorneys to calm her down and escort her out of the conference room. She continued to behave erratically, until her colleagues began to fear for her well-being and safety. One of the receptionists called for an ambulance after Emma Rose grabbed a hot coffee pot while screaming, "Shut your cock-sucking mouth, you motherfucking bitch." The EMTs took her to the hospital. She underwent a three-day observation, after which the doctors admitted her to a local psychiatric hospital and began to create a medication system for her treatment. She was hospitalized for six months. Emma Rose never worked as an attorney again.

When she was released from the psychiatric hospital, she had nowhere to go. She had dedicated her life to the study of the law, so she hadn't cultivated friendships and had become estranged from her family. She couldn't tell them what had happened; she knew they would be ashamed of her. They would think that she had brought this on herself. Her mother would probably insist on bringing her to the family's priest for an exorcism.

So, Emma left the hospital and disappeared into the world of the homeless and sick. Once she was out of the hospital, she stopped taking her medications. She had no way of procuring them without money or proper identification. She tried staying in shelters, but the voices would cause her to rant and yell throughout the night and she would be asked not to return. Emma Rose, a Harvard Law School Graduate, was now one of the faceless street people. She became the one you would cross the street to avoid, as she yelled and gestured obscenities at all who came her way. Soon she started to wear aluminum, trying to cover herself with it, yelling about conspiracies and the monster who took the other street people away.

As she walked the streets one day, she passed the dental practice of Andres, Brenner, and Caine. She suddenly heard a new voice in her head. It was an inviting voice, one that told her to go into the dental practice. That all her problems would be solved if she had the metals in her teeth removed. The voice was so appealing, so pleasant, that she decided that it made sense. If she had her fillings removed and replaced with non-metal ones, she would no longer hear the voices. Then she could practice law again. She walked into the practice and approached Charlotte at her desk.

"I need help, fast," Emma said, her eyes darting around the room, looking for anyone dangerous or suspicious. She knew she had to be careful if she didn't want to disappear like the others had.

"Do you have an appointment?" Charlotte inquired, wrinkling her nose against the odor of this woman.

"No. But it is urgent." Leaning closer to Charlotte, Emma whispered, "They wiretapped my teeth, so They can talk to me, inside my head. They tell me what to do. If I have them removed, the talking will stop. Please."

Charlotte heard a humming growing louder in the back of her brain—her subconscious mind was summoning her again. "Um, okay. Do you have any insurance?"

"No. You know that They can track you that way."

"Okay. Do you have any family or friends in the area? Someone who can pick you up if necessary?"

"No."

Charlotte smiled. The humming was now reverberating through her skull. "Follow me, please. I am going to put you in exam room 5. Then I'll see which dentist can help you."

Charlotte led Emma down the hallway and opened the door to room 5. She helped Emma into the examination chair as she said, "Just sit back. Someone will help you soon."

Charlotte closed the door and walked back to the reception area. She wasn't sure how long it would take, but she had nowhere else to be; she could wait.

Emma sat in the dental chair, quietly waiting for help, when she sensed a presence in her mind. The new voice emerging. At first It was quiet, barely audible in the chaos of her brain. But the voice grew until It was all she could hear.

She didn't like this new voice; It sounded metallic, almost robotic, and she didn't quite understand what It wanted her to do. Emma tried to force the voice down, to restrict It to the background. But each time she did, It struck back forcefully, pushing Its way back to the forefront.

Finally, Emma could fight It no longer. She reached over and picked up the suction straw. She didn't understand why the voice wanted her to do this, but she followed Its instructions anyway.

She placed the straw behind her bottom teeth and then sat back. Emma Rose slowly felt her life drain out of her, a drop at a time.

# NATHAN

NATHAN HAD NEVER had trouble sleeping before. He was one of those people who could put their head down and be asleep instantly. But ever since he had had that tooth fixed, he found sleeping difficult. He tossed and turned all night plagued by nightmares that he couldn't clearly remember the next morning. He just had a feeling of foreboding when he awoke.

His eyes felt heavy all the time, the circles under them growing larger each day. He drank copious amounts of coffee, sometimes up to fifteen cups a day, just so he could stay awake enough for his classes. Even so, his grades fell until he was failing every course.

His professors assumed he was out partying, the way some less-serious students do. And therefore, they lacked the sympathy Nathan needed. He needed to find someone to talk to; someone who wouldn't think he was either playing a prank or crazy.

He hadn't gone to the police after finding Keith's body, for fear that they wouldn't believe him. They'd accuse him of trying to pull a college prank on them or even of being the murderer himself. He couldn't figure out who to tell, afraid of what they would think. How could he explain to someone, anyone, that there was something evil, sinister, in a local dental practice—that a well-respected local dentist was somehow draining patients of all their bodily fluids and then burying the mummified bodies in the woods outside of town?

Even to Nathan it sounded crazy, like the plot of a bad science-fiction movie. He had to find evidence of what was happening. Something tangible that he could bring to them.

Nathan, his sixth cup of coffee in his hand, headed to the local library to do some research on missing people. He had to assume that the mummified dentist wasn't the only victim.

After spending what seemed like hours in the library, he found only a few references to some missing homeless or elderly people. Nathan needed to stretch, so he decided to go for a walk to clear his mind. As he walked down the streets of the town, something pulled at his mind. He knew something was not right.

He soon found himself standing on the sidewalk in front of the dental practice. He stood there, looking at the old Victorian house. He had to know what was happening inside there. He realized that he would have to come back at night, when the practice was closed. He walked away, already planning his next visit to the dentist.

# OLLIC

Oliver Sebastion's parents never thought that they wanted to have children. They liked to spend their free time travelling to exotic locations, climbing mountains, hiking, or pushing themselves for the adrenaline rush. A child didn't fit into their model life. But when they found themselves expecting, they were overjoyed. They began to research how to travel with a young child, what locations were more child-friendly yet still exciting. They bought hiking gear for hiking with babies, bike attachments for children. They not only adapted to the idea of having a child but began to see how a child could push them in a new direction.

When their son was born, they dissolved into him. They quickly discovered that Oliver didn't like the feel of the sun on his face or the way wind blew on him. He was not an outside person. All their plans disappeared as they adjusted to life with their son. They pampered their only child with attention and material objects; they heaped him with praise and reassured him of his brilliance. Oliver drank it all in; he was the center around which their world revolved, and he knew it.

He never played sports or learned to enjoy the outdoors, instead preferring to interact with other children at school or to stay at home playing video games. When Oliver started high school, his parents bought him all the latest computer equipment. As he played the newest games, he couldn't help but think about how great it would be if the graphics were better, if the games were more involved and intricate.

He dreamed up games where the images were realistic, where there were actual storylines and in-depth characters. He decided to go to the library one day and borrow books on computer gaming and coding.

He began to practice writing code after school one day and discovered his true passion in life. His academic focus deepened, and upon graduating he went to college to study computer engineering. During his first two years of college, he could be found on his computer when not in class or in the cafeteria.

During his junior year of college, he met Lynne. She was using a computer terminal in the lab where he was working as an assistant. Lynne was writing a research paper and was having difficulty using the new programs. As Oliver and Lynne talked, they found an instant rapport.

Lynne and Oliver began hanging out together more and more often. He introduced her to the world of virtual reality. When Lynne first played Oliver's latest game, she began to laugh at the unnatural way in which the avatars behaved. Confused, Oliver asked her how he should make the characters act. Smiling, Lynne told him, "Have them act like real people. You know, how you and your friends act. Your characters—"

"Avatars," Oliver interjected.

"Right, avatars," she continued, "are stiff and seem uncomfortable."

Oliver nodded, "But, like how?"

Lynne looked at him, asking, "Do you have friends? You know, like normal, non-computer friends? Not on Facebook or Twitter, but real, in-person friends?"

Oliver mouth dropped as his face reddened. Lynne jumped up, saying, "Come on."

"Where?"

"Just come with me." Lynne led him out of the dorm. He followed her across campus, his stomach cramping as he heard the music pulsating in the distance.

She introduced Oliver to the real world. She brought him to parties and events on and off campus, and as he met more people, his life became more social. His avatars also became more real.

Oliver began to go to underground raves, enjoying the adventure and the unknown. At first, he would just sit in a corner, watching the interactions between people. He made mental notes of behaviors so he could adapt them into his games. Within a few weeks, he began to participate in the events. Oliver took his first hit of ecstasy four months after meeting Lynne. But even so, he never missed a class or let his grades drop.

But then one night, as Oliver sat at his computer, he heard a knock on his door. One of Lynne's good friends, Carole, was standing there, tears streaking her face. Choking back sobs, she told Oliver that Lynne had died the night before from an overdose.

Oliver sat down hard on his bed, not comprehending what she was saying. Carole sat next to Oliver, placing her hand on his. They cried together.

Carole and Oliver began to spend time together, feeling Lynne's presence in each other's company. The more time they spent together, the more Lynne felt alive to them.

Oliver and Carole married right after graduating. Children followed a few years later. After their twins were born, Carole left her job to stay home with the children.

Oliver found a job in computer programming and thrived. He spent his nights creating his games. In the beginning, he helped Carole with the twins—feeding, bathing, and getting them to bed. But as time went by, Oliver spent more time locked in his office. His games began selling and were becoming more popular. He quit his job and began to work from home.

Carole had supported Oliver when he decided to venture out and focus on his true passion—games. She understood that he would be keeping strange hours; she adjusted the family's schedule accordingly. What she hadn't realized was how much time Oliver would spend on it; how little time he would give to his family.

Oliver Sebastion was better known as Ollic to video game enthusiasts. His games were considered the best, and he knew that the one he was currently working on was his masterpiece. He had spent months working on the game, holed up in his man cave, the office space in his basement. His wife kept his mini-fridge stocked with Stewart's root beer and cream soda plus an ample supply of snacks. For meals she left trays of food outside his office door.

Ollic sat at his computer screen, admiring the code he had recently entered, when he realized that he had not eaten in a while; his stomach was gurgling uncomfortably. Ollic rose and walked over to the door, noting that both his feet were numb from lack of circulation. He opened the door, looking for the tray of food that must be there waiting for him. But the table was empty. Curious, he walked up the stairs, calling for his wife. There was no answer.

He went into the kitchen and opened the fridge. All inside was covered in green and grey mold. Where was his wife, he wondered as he walked through the house. He entered their bedroom and went into their closet. Again, it was empty. All signs that anyone else had ever existed in this house were gone. He peered into his children's room, only to discover that it, too, was empty. Ollic returned downstairs and spotted an envelope on the mantle. A note from his wife.

She was gone. She had packed up the kids and left him three days earlier and he hadn't noticed. He picked up the phone and ordered a pizza. He spent the rest of that day setting up a food delivery system and a way to pay all his bills on a schedule. Now, at last, he could write code undisturbed.

He slept in his bed that night and made sure to shower in the morning. He checked his front porch. On it sat four grocery bags. His system working already. He brought the groceries to his man-cave and began to work on the game again. He moved the microwave downstairs, so he could heat up food when necessary. It would be fine.

Then the toothache began. He tried to ignore it, but it interrupted his concentration. Not remembering his dentist's name, he looked one up and called the office of Andres, Brenner, and Caine. His appointment was set.

When he arrived, he dutifully filled out the paperwork. Where it asked for an emergency contact, he wrote "none." For the first time, he felt a pang of loneliness; he missed having a wife, an emergency contact person.

Charlotte took note. She brought him to room 5 and prepared him for his visit.

Oliver "Ollic" Sebastion's masterpiece was never finished. But that was okay, because no one ever knew.

# ANNIE

Annie sat in her psychology class, trying desperately to pay attention to the professor's lecture. All she could think about was Nathan. She couldn't understand what was happening to him; he had become so distant. She knew something was weighing on him; something beyond schools, tests, and GPAs. Something bad had happened.

His screams at night, the look in his eyes after he woke from night terrors, frightened her. She lay in bed at night, listening as he struggled in his sleep as if some unseen force was holding him, perhaps even hurting him. And when he awoke, he would tell her that he didn't remember the dreams. But she wasn't sure it was true.

Her friends begged her to just leave him; they had only been together for a few months. They speculated about the possibility of a drug addiction, or maybe he had committed a violent crime. Maybe the guilt of it was plaguing him.

But Annie couldn't leave him; she had to help him. She had to be a good girlfriend. She skipped her afternoon classes and sat in the library, reading psychology journals, desperately looking for an answer, a way to get him to open up to her, to share his pain. She had to find a way to help him, to take care of him.

. . .

Annie had grown up on a working farm, miles from any neighbors, let alone a town. She rode the bus for an hour to school every morning and then again in the afternoon. Annie woke up in the morning around four so she could collect eggs, milk the cows, and make her father breakfast before getting ready to catch the six o'clock bus to school. When she came home, she would make dinner and the next day's lunch, and clean up the kitchen before beginning her homework. On a good night, she was able to go to bed around one or two.

Annie was a caretaker by nature and necessity. Her mother had passed away when Annie was six years old. He mother had been her world. She was Annie's caretaker, her nurturer, her place of repose in a house of men. Her father had never been loving toward his only child—his disappointment in having a daughter instead of a son was obvious even to a six-year-old child. So, when her beloved mother died, Annie became the only woman in a house of farmers. She was expected to "help out" whenever possible. Annie spent her days either studying or running the farmhouse. She fed all the farmhands for three meals a day. She couldn't recall the last time she was thanked or told that she was loved. She vaguely remembered her mother whispering it to her as she tucked Annie into bed each night. But that was long ago and only a passing memory.

This was now her life, work and school. If she was lucky, she could get a few hours of sleep each night, but that was all her life would be—there would be no parties or dates, let alone prom. But Annie would never complain. She had detached herself from the dreams of young girls when her mother left her.

Then one afternoon, when Annie was seventeen years old, she came home from school to a bevy of police cars and emergency personnel at her house. Annie stood at the gate to her home, just watching the scene play out in front of her, when a black body bag, bulging with its cargo, was wheeled out of the barn.

Annie dropped her books and started to run, pushing through the farmhands. She could feel the hands and arms of the men as they attempted to grab her, to stop her from reaching the barn. She was no longer thinking; she was reacting. Her father was dead. He'd had a heart attack while working in the barn. Annie was alone. She was unable to run the farm on her own, so she reluctantly sold it and moved herself into a small studio apartment in town. Her social worker, Jean, had helped her become emancipated, so she wouldn't be put in foster care for the sixth months before her eighteenth birthday.

Annie continued in school while running her small household. She found that she now had more time to dedicate to her studies and herself. Jean checked on her with weekly phone calls and monthly visits. But Annie had no one to take care of, and she needed to take care of someone. She had to be necessary to another.

She started college the following fall, moving into her dorm with minimal property. Her studio apartment had come furnished, so all she had was her clothes and a few mementos from her parents and the farm. The small amount of money that she had received from her parents had either been used for her rent or was now paying her tuition. When she met her roommate, Lyra, she was thrilled. Lyra brought with her a minifridge and a TV with a Blu-ray player. They stayed roommates through freshman and sophomore year and into their junior year. Even though Lyra was too independent to fulfill Annie's need to mother someone, their friendship stayed solid through bad grades, boyfriends, and dorm fights.

When Annie met Nathan, she saw in him what she needed—someone in need of nurturing. Nathan still carried the scars from his early childhood—the dismissive attitude of his parents, the numerous nannies hired to raise him. Their relationship started at the beginning of their junior year when they met in the school's quad. Nathan was playing Frisbee with some friends when the Frisbee hit Annie in the back of her head. Nathan went over to apologize. They started talking, and Nathan invited her out for "I'm so sorry I hit you with a Frisbee" pizza. It didn't take for long for them to start dating.

From that point on they were inseparable: they studied together, ate meals together, and quickly started spending nights together. Lyra liked Nathan for Annie; they seemed so happy together. The three of them became friends. And on the nights when Nathan stayed at Annie's, Lyra would crash at a different friend's room for the night. She was genuinely happy for her friend.

But then, Nathan changed. He became almost erratic, different from the calming person he had been.

. . .

Annie knew that Nathan's problem started after his appointment at the dentist's. So that was where she would start. All she knew was that he saw a woman dentist and that the office was in an old Victorian house in town. She decided to walk around the town, taking note of any offices that fit the description, hoping there wouldn't be a lot of practices.

As she exited the library, she was shocked to see that the sun had set. It had grown dark—too dark for her planned walk. She would have to wait for the next day.

Annie walked to the cafeteria, hoping she would see Nathan there. She tightly grasped her tray of food, glancing around the room, looking for him. He wasn't there, again. Annie sat down at an empty table and ate her dinner. After sneaking some rolls into her bag, she left the cafeteria and headed to Nathan's off-campus apartment. She would drop the rolls off for him and then head back to her room so she could study. She gave the rolls to Nathan's roommate, Kevin, and then headed back to her room.

That night she told her roommate, Lyra, her plan for the next day. She would attend her morning classes and then go for her walk. Lyra offered to go with her, but Annie, the constant caretaker, wouldn't let Lyra miss any of her classes. Lyra was a type A stresser; if she missed a class, one class, she would panic, convinced that she was going to fail, flunk out of school, and have no future. Annie could not let that happen. She couldn't put Lyra through that. As she fell asleep, she promised to tell Lyra everything that happened.

The next day, as her morning classes wound to an end, Annie picked up her books and walked back to her dorm room. She dropped off her books and notes, grabbed a heavier jacket, and set off to find the dentist's office.

Nathan had described the Victorian house to Annie and had given her a vague idea as to its actual location, so she recognized the building when she came to it. The large wraparound porch with a double door in the center. The lilac paint with violet shutters. The house was distinct.

But now that she had found it, she didn't know what to do. So she sat on a bench down the street from the office and watched as patients went in and out.

For hours, Annie sat and watched. She began to think that this was a dead end, that this was not going to explain Nathan's strange metamorphosis. She saw so many patients come and go that she had to assume that the practice couldn't be the problem.

It was getting dark out. She had just decided to go home when she realized that she hadn't seen the last patient leave the building. She sat back down. She figured that she might as well wait for the last patient to leave.

Within a few minutes, she saw the doctor and three hygienists leave the building and lock the main entrance. She waited for another hour. The back door of the practice opened, and a young woman appeared. She glanced around furtively and then walked to her car. She opened the trunk of her car, looked in it, shook her head, then closed it and reentered the building.

Annie sat. She searched her memory, trying to remember seeing the last patient leave, but she knew he hadn't. So, she sat. The streetlights came on. Just as she rose to leave, wondering how she could have missed him, a slice of light shone on the pavement behind the building.

She walked toward the light, getting close enough to see the door. A woman, moving covertly, exited the building. She was breathing heavily, as if she had just completed some intense physical labor. The woman took a few deep breaths, looked up at the sky and then reentered the building.

Annie stood in the shadow of the building, confused. The light had revealed streaks of dirt on the woman's clothing and face. Annie's curiosity grew, as did her determination to find out what was happening in this building.

. . .

Annie lay on her dorm bed, retelling her adventure to Lyra. When she had finished describing the woman, she stopped and looked at her roommate.

"Don't go back," Lyra said. "This is too creepy. Any horror movie aficionado would tell you not to go back."

"I have to find out what is happening; this could explain what happened to Nathan, why he has changed so much."

"Who cares about how Nathan has changed? Don't go back. Please. What if something happens to you? Please."

Annie yawned and sleepily said, "I have to."

# EMMETT

BY THE TIME Emmett was two years old, he was dribbling a basketball and could throw a baseball with basic accuracy. His father, Charlie, was thrilled. Charlie had been a star athlete in high school and continued to play in college, but he did not have the skills nor the natural abilities needed to become a professional athlete.

But when his son was born, Charlie saw in him great potential, the possibility of becoming not only a professional athlete but a Hall of Famer. Charlie bought him every conceivable sporting item and piece of equipment, hoping he would choose a sport early so he could focus and hone his skills.

And Emmett did—baseball, pitching to be precise, became his passion. Emmett spent hours practicing every day. And when he couldn't go outside to actually throw a baseball, he was building the muscles in his arm and wrist. He would sit at his desk in school, squeezing a tennis ball, while imaging the form of a perfect pitch. Emmett became obsessed with being the best pitcher baseball had ever seen.

And all his hard work and practice paid off. By the time Emmett was twelve years old, he was being recruited to private school. Emmett and Charlie chose the school with the best baseball program.

Emmett Elijah was named one of the best high school pitchers his freshman year. He knew that baseball was his future. That was all he cared about; academics lost all importance. He would attend classes only because he had to if he wanted to maintain a 2.0 average and continue to play ball for the school. But he remembered nothing that he learned. He only focused on baseball.

. . .

EMMETT ELIJAH HADN'T ALWAYS LIVED ON THE STREETS, addicted to painkillers or whatever drug he could get. He hadn't been choosy for a while now; whichever drug would numb the memories, he took. He didn't want to remember his life before.

But every once in a while, it came back. The memories of him standing on the pitcher's mound, crowds chanting "Em—mett, Em—mett" as he wound up his pitch. He could hear the ump yell, "Strike Three. You're Out!"; he could see all the Yankees rushing onto the field. Emmett Elijah had pitched the winning strikeout of the final game of the World Series.

Soon after, he had gone to his summer house and made what would later be described as the tragic decision of his young life: to jump off a nearby bridge. He had done this for many years, since he was a child. But this time, something went wrong. He hit the bottom of the pond, fracturing both his ankles. Three surgeries later, he still walked with a limp and found himself addicted to painkillers. When his prescription ran out, he found other sources for the drugs. Emmett Elijah's career was over, as was the life he had known so far. He soon had to auction off his cars and his mansion. Within a year, he had sold off all his property and had lost all his money.

Emmett wandered the streets now, wearing his old Yankees cap, unrecognizable to all but the most ardent of fans. Sometimes, someone would see a glimpse of him, of who he once was, under the dirt and sallow pallor. He even had a few people ask him for an autograph. He would oblige for a fee. He needed the money for drugs.

Emmett Elijah, a man who was once surrounded by people chanting his name, was now alone. Then he met Charlotte.

Charlotte spotted Emmett months before. He was frequently outside of her building, trying to stay warm in the frigid winter temperatures. She frequently brought him warm soup to eat or bottles of water. She even gave him a blanket one particularly cold winter night. He liked Charlotte; he trusted her. She was one of the few people who was kind to him, who didn't care who he used to be.

So, when Charlotte came to him and offered him a free dental cleaning, he agreed to go with her. He walked with her to the old Victorian house and watched as she unlocked the door. He immediately felt an urge to run, to get away from there as soon as possible. But then he remembered why he had come. Drugs. A dentist's office should have drugs; maybe he could even get hold of a prescription pad. His need for painkillers overrode the ominous feeling. He entered the building and followed Charlotte to room 5.

Charlotte unlocked the door, turned on the lights, and showed him into the room. He scanned the room for possible medication locations as he sat in the reclining chair. He eased into the chair, thinking about how comfortable it was after all that time on the streets.

Charlotte left the room. Within seconds, Emmett's drug-addled brain was taken over by the machine. He had no ability to resist, to withstand the machine's command. He placed the suction straw into his mouth. Even as the machine drained him, he decided that some of the cabinets looked promising. As he slipped into unconsciousness, he planned on searching them.

The last though of Emmett Elijah, hero of the World Series, wasn't about baseball.

# CHARLOTTE

CHARLOTTE SAT AT her desk, trying to concentrate on the insurance forms in front of her. The machine's pulse in the back of her mind had turned into a rhythm. It pounded at first but quickly turned into a screaming insistence. She was finding it difficult to ignore the machine's pleas for food.

*Later,* she thought. *I will feed you later.*

The phone's ring snapped her out of her trance. She picked up the receiver and by rote said, "Hello, Andres, Brenner, and Caine, dentists. How can I help you today?"

"I was hoping to get an appointment. Are you accepting new patients?"

"We absolutely are. Is this an emergency?"

"No, I just need a cleaning. Haven't had one since the beginning of the summer.."

"Okay. Let me see what we can set up." Charlotte checked the appointment book. "I have an opening today at 3:15?"

"Great. Thanks."

"Your name?"

"Annie Coller."

"We will see you then."

. . .

Annie left a note for Lyra, telling her where she had gone, and then walked back to the dental practice. This time, she went inside. She noticed the juxtaposition of the Victorian architecture with the more modern office furniture. She glanced at the pile of random magazines spread across the glass-top coffee table. Just as she picked up a recent tabloid, Charlotte came into the office. She handed Annie a clipboard with all the forms that needed to be filled out.

Annie sat, filling in paperwork, when she began to hear a low thumping noise. She looked up, glancing around the room, trying to find its source. As she looked around, she realized that no one else seem to be reacting to the sound, even as it got louder.

When Charlotte called to another patient and led that patient down the hall, Annie stood up and walked toward the sound. She didn't understand why she needed to find its source, but she did. She left the waiting room and headed down the hall, in the opposite direction from Charlotte. She followed the sound as it grew louder and more demanding. It seemed to be calling her, and she had no choice but to obey.

Just as Annie's hand began to turn the doorknob on room 5, Charlotte came running around the corner.

"What are you doing?" Charlotte demanded.

Annie, still pulling on the doorknob, looked at Charlotte. "What is making that sound? It sounds … sounds … scared? No, It sounds hurt, or maybe hungry. Yes, It sounds hungry. What is It? We have to help It."

Charlotte stood frozen, staring at Annie. Her brain raced. *How could she hear It? Who is she? I can't let her know. No. I can't let her meet the machine.*

'You need to leave," Charlotte said.

"I must help It. It needs me. What is It? Please, let me help It. I grew up on a farm; I know how to take care of injured or sick animals. Please, let me help," Annie whispered desperately.

Charlotte placed her hands on Annie's. She pulled her away from the door and escorted her out of the practice. "You need to leave," Charlotte said, emphasizing the word "Need." "Don't come back here, ever. Run far away if you must. Just leave."

Annie looked at Charlotte, nodded slowly, and walked away from the building, down the street, away from the pleas for help. As she got farther away from the building, she felt the desperation loosen. By the time she was back at her dorm, she was confused. She didn't understand what had happened there, but maybe Nathan did. Should she ask him? Should she share her experience with him? She wasn't sure. What if this wasn't his problem? Would he think she was crazy? Would he leave her?

All she knew was that she had to return to the office. She needed to know what that sound was; what had happened to her. She needed to have a plan; a way to get into that room without the receptionist knowing. Annie fell asleep, her mind continuing to solve the new problem.

. . .

CHARLOTTE SAT AT HER DESK, WONDERING WHO THE GIRL was. How did she connect to the machine so quickly? How did she understand what the noise was and what It needed? Charlotte felt an overwhelming need to protect this girl and to keep the machine to herself. Charlotte knew it was time to move out of her apartment and into the practice; Susan's empty office would make the perfect hideaway.

. . .

Annie woke up the next morning with a plan. She would spend the next few days watching the practice, learning the various employees' schedules. Then, once she knew when the practice was empty, she would …

She didn't know what she would do then. Annie had never broken the law before, at least not a felony law. She wasn't sure how to get into the locked office or what she would do once she did.

# SUSAN

Susan was on her way home. She drove slowly, not because she was a cautious driver but because she was nervous to return. She hadn't felt the pull of the machine in weeks and had a feeling of clarity for the first time since she had found that office space and had touched evil.

She was fearful as she headed back to the university town. What if the pull came back? What if she began to kill again? How will she explain Keith's disappearance?

An avalanche of guilt covered her as the realization of Keith's death came to her again. She had killed him, as well as countless others. She had no idea as to how many had died, nor could she recall names or even faces. But they were dead, horrifically murdered and hidden in the basement.

She knew that the machine would never allow the bodies to be found; she could just leave town, open a practice elsewhere. She could tell David and Charlotte that Keith had left her and had run off with some younger woman. That she was too devastated to come back. It would be too difficult to work there without him. It was believable; only she knew the truth. She knew where Keith was, or at least where his body was.

But what of the machine? Had it found someone else to help it feed? She felt a need to stop the machine. She had to stop it from corrupting another person; she must not allow another person to die.

She continued down the highway.

As Susan neared home, she realized that she no longer felt the machine's pull. She was still free of the constant drone and thrumming. She realized that the machine had found another helper. She pulled the car over, turned off the engine, and sat, staring out the car windshield.

Her mind raced with ideas on how to not only stop the machine but destroy it so it could never inspire someone to kill for it again.

# ANNIE

Annie left her dorm room that morning carrying her backpack. But instead of her books and laptop, she had her iPad plus snacks and bottles of water.

She knew she was going to have a long day watching the dentist's office, looking for a pattern to their day. She had to find a time when she could slip in unnoticed; she had to find the plaintive call that had been haunting her. She had to help whatever it was that she heard ceaselessly crying out.

Its call had become stronger and louder over the past few days, and Annie found herself unable to resist much longer. She had to find It, had to nurture It so It would stop crying. She had finally found something that needed her, something that she could take care of.

Annie quietly left her room and headed down the well-lit hallway. The dorm was just beginning to wake up for the day. Students were crawling out of their warm beds and getting ready for class or attempting to cram one more fact in before an exam. Computers were being turned on, social media sites checked for any news, and papers were being edited one more time before they were due.

Annie headed out the front door, double-checking that it locked behind her. Ever since moving into the dorm, Annie had felt an overwhelming need to be sure that her dorm mates were safe from a madman. The thought that her carelessness could allow someone evil, a Ted Bundy type, into their quiet collegiate life haunted her. So she took precautions—she double-checked the doors compulsively, sometimes even checking three times if she felt something was particularly creepy or disturbing in the air.

She pulled on it one more time and walked away from her dorm, following the call of the machine.

# MAREK

ALL MAREK EVER wanted was to write the great American novel. He dreamed of the fame and, if being honest with himself, the fortune that followed. He imagined literary classes and groups discussing his novel and, of course, his brilliance. He would be revered for decades or even centuries as the quintessential novelist of the twenty-first century. Maybe his name would even become synonymous with brilliant writing. Professors would say that some other writer was very "Marekesque" in tone.

Therefore, Marek left the world of Wall Street brokerage firms and began to write. He would sit at his desk, staring at the street below. He would watch people living their lives, hoping for a glimpse into a story, a character. After weeks of this, Marek discovered that he had nothing to write, nothing to say. He would just sit in cafes and parks, staring at the blank pages of his notebook. He bought different colored paper and pens, hoping for the inspiration that makes great writers. Nothing worked. His pages stayed blank.

He continued to live off his savings, moving into a small studio apartment to help save money. He still couldn't write. Eventually his money ran out and he had to get a job to pay the bills. He found a job pumping gas, praying that it would help him find inspiration. He hoped to meet someone, anyone, who would inspire him to write. But it didn't happen.

Years went by and Marek grew older; the smell of gasoline had permeated his skin. But still he wrote nothing. He began to blame his life in a small town. How could he write an inspirational novel living an uninspired life in an uninspired town? He needed something exciting to happen, an adventure to write about.

Marek noticed Charlotte while pumping her gas. She smiled at him with a cheery hello. Charlotte had acknowledged his existence more than anyone else had since he had left the brokerage firm and lost all his friends.

He saw her name on her credit card and thought it was the perfect name for his heroine. Maybe it was finally time to write. He needed to know more about her, so he could tell her story.

. . .

CHARLOTTE HAD BARELY NOTICED THE MAN PUMPING GAS into her car, but she had been raised to always be polite, so she greeted everyone cheerfully and said please and thank you regularly. For her, it was almost as robotic as saying bless you when someone sneezes.

The machine had been more talkative lately, crying insistently for food; it was as if It was on the verge of a temper tantrum. Charlotte had to find it someone soon, so when Marek asked her if she would like to grab coffee that afternoon, with a quick glimpse at his left ring finger, she said yes.

Marek arrived at the dentist's office to pick up Charlotte; he entered the building, closing the door gently behind him. He had gone home first and tried to wash the smell of gasoline out of his pores. But it didn't work; he now smelled of cheap soap *and* gasoline.

. . .

CHARLOTTE CAUGHT A WHIFF OF MAREK before he came into the room. She straightened herself in her chair. Donning her work smile and demeanor she said, "Hi, I'll be ready in one moment." The pulsing in her head quickened with excitement. "I just have to check on the rooms and then I can lock up. Why don't you come with me, so we can talk while I lock up the practice?"

Marek nodded and followed Charlotte to the examination rooms. She moved into room 5.

"Is it hard working here? I mean, no one really likes the dentist."

"Oh, no," Charlotte replied, glad that Marek was making small talk. It helped to muffle the quickening desperation of the pulse. "I like it here. Good dental health is important. I feel like I'm a small part of that."

As she pretended to straighten the counter, he felt the impulse to sit in the exam chair. Within a few minutes, Marek had reached over and placed the suction straw in his mouth. He didn't know why he had done it, only that he was compelled to do so.

Marek had finally met a truly interesting character and was on his adventure. He had something to write about, only he would never have the opportunity to write his book.

# LYRA

Lyra tried to leave it alone; she tried to let Annie deal with her own problems—namely Nathan. When Annie first introduced Nathan to Lyra, she thought he was great. But lately, something had changed; Nathan had changed. He was no longer the funny, sweet guy she had originally met. He had become moody and distant. The man who doted on his girlfriend had become morose.

She had told Annie to walk away, but she wouldn't and now Annie was acting strange herself. She was skipping classes, not eating properly, and basically neglecting herself.

Once Annie stopped coming back to their dorm room until very late at night, Lyra started to panic. She decided that she needed to follow Annie; she needed to find out what was happening to her friend. But first, she had to find Annie.

Nathan was her first stop. As she knocked on his apartment door, her mind raced with what she would say to Nathan when he answered.

"Lyra, hi," Nathan said as he opened his door. "Come in, I guess." As Lyra walked into his living room, she noticed how disheveled his life had become. Books, papers, and clothes were strewn all over the floor and furniture. She remembered Annie praising how neat and organized

Nathan had been; she was shocked to see how much things had changed. What had happened that had caused such a change in both Nathan and Annie?

"Um," Nathan uttered as he knocked some books off of a chair, "sit."

As Lyra sat, she sighed audibly. "About Annie … " she started. She noticed that Nathan was staring straight ahead as if in a trance. "Nathan, about Annie," Lyra yelled forcibly.

"What?" he stammered, shaking his head.

"I'm worried about her. She went to see that dentist and hasn't been the same since. What happens there, Nathan?"

"What dentist?" Nathan sputtered. His eyes widened.

"The one you went to."

"Why? Why did she go there?"

"For you. You've changed since seeing that dentist, and she wanted to know why, so she went there too. And now she is skipping classes, not sleeping well, not eating. What happens in that place?"

"I … I … Where is she now?"

"I don't know," Lyra said, "she was gone before I woke up today. She took her backpack, but her books are on her desk. Nathan, what is happening to her?"

"I can't explain it, but Lyra, stay away from that office. Don't go there. I'll check on Annie; I'll help her."

Lyra stood up, looked at Nathan, opened her mouth to say something, but then thought better of it and walked out of his apartment, shaking her head.

. . .

NATHAN KNEW HE NEEDED A PLAN TO HELP ANNIE. He needed to find out what Annie heard when she was in the office. If she was changing, she must have heard it also, or at least heard something.

. . .

Annie spent another day sitting on a bench outside of the dentist's office. After she left to get something to eat and returned, she noticed that the parking lot had emptied except for one car—the receptionist's car was still there. She decided to look around the building.

As she walked the perimeter of the building, she felt the cry get louder. She followed the cry to a window and peered inside. It was an examination room. The room looked old, out-of-date. Annie wondered if the room was ever used for patients' care. Annie quietly hoped not, as the room did not seem to be hygienic. The desperation of the cries through the window were growing louder and more plaintive.

She walked back toward the parking lot just in time to see Charlotte entering her car.

Annie waited for her to drive away and then went back to the window. She tried to open the window, but it was stuck or locked; Annie didn't know which.

The cry was getting more desperate and Annie knew that she had to get inside the building if she was going to help the piteous creature.

She looked around and saw a rock that looked large enough. She lifted the rock and threw it at the window, shattering the large pane of glass. Using her sweatshirt, she pulled the extra pieces of glass out of the pane and then climbed through the window.

The cry was becoming unbearable in its intensity. Annie tried to locate the creature from which the cry emanated.

. . .

Lyra finished her classes and walked into town so she could find the dentist's office. She was not going to leave Annie's future to Nathan; she would try to help her herself.

Lyra found the office and walked up to the front door. It was locked. She looked around the building's exterior and saw the broken window. She gingerly pulled herself up and peered inside. There, she saw Annie.

Lyra immediately realized that Annie must have broken into the building. She couldn't believe that the dentist would leave a window broken, so Annie must have done it. But why? Did dentists have narcotics in their offices? Could Annie be trying to steal drugs, or even a script pad?

Lyra had to stop her; she had to get her out of the building. What if there was a silent alarm? The police could be on their way. Leaning toward the window, Lyra whispered, "Annie. Annie!"

Annie slowly turned around and saw Lyra. "What are you doing here?"

"That was my question. Annie, what are you doing in a locked dentist's office? One with a broken window?"

The machine started to talk to Annie.

"Did you hear that?" Even as she asked, she knew that Lyra didn't hear the machine.

"Hear what? Annie, come out here. You're going to be in trouble. What if the police come?"

"Come in here. I need your help."

"What? With what?"

"Just come in, please. Help me and then we can leave. I promise."

Lyra exhaled slowly and pulled herself through the window. "What do you need?"

"Just come over here."

Lyra moved across the room. She suddenly felt a strange impulse; it was as if something had entered her brain and was trying to take over. Lyra struggled against it.

"Annie, let's leave. I don't … something isn't right. Let's just go."

"Don't fight It."

"What? How do you …

"It says," Annie interrupted, "that you should just relax. Listen to It."

"Who?" Lyra started to back toward the window. But even as she moved, she was finding it more difficult to resist.

"I don't know. But It needs you. It will stop crying if you help It. Please make It stop crying; I can't stand hearing the crying anymore."

"What are you talking about?" Lyra found herself moving forward again; no matter how hard she tried to leave, she was compelled to move toward Annie. "Annie, what is going on? Help me, please."

Annie stood next to the suction straw and watched as Lyra reached out and grasped the straw. Tears flowed down Lyra's cheeks as she placed the suction straw in her mouth.

Lyra felt the machine whir on and begin to suck the moisture from her. She leaned against the wall as she felt her mouth become cotton, her lips dry and crack. Within a few minutes, her eyes were too dry to tear anymore, and she felt the room start to spin.

As her brain dried out, she began to imagine herself in class, on a run, anywhere but slowly, painfully dying in a dentist's office. She pictured herself on the stage, receiving accolades for some achievement. She saw herself dressed in a beaded gown, shaking hands with important people. Her organs were failing, and she was finding it more difficult to breathe as her lungs began to crumble into dust.

Annie stood and watched as Lyra died. The machine was finally quiet. Annie felt only relief.

But then the machine began to talk again; It gave her instructions to remove the straw from Lyra's mouth and to bring her corpse into the basement to join the others.

. . .

ANNIE LEFT THE DENTAL PRACTICE IN A STATE OF FUGUE, covered with dirt and sweat. The machine was happily humming in her mind, keeping her from regretting what she had just done.

She walked down the streets of her college town, heading back to her dorm. The streetlights illuminated the dirt on her clothes, her face and hands. She realized that other people were moving away from her, shying away from the dirt. She began to move furtively, turning down deserted streets. She didn't want people to remember seeing a dirt-covered girl walking down the street away from the dental practice. She had to remain just another anonymous person on the street. She had to keep the secret from ever being discovered; she had to make sure no one ever found out about the machine.

When she arrived at her door, she quietly slipped her key into the lock and turned it gently to the right, listening for the click. She opened the door, removed her shoes—she didn't want to disturb her dorm mates; it was after midnight now—and headed to her room.

She grabbed her towel and headed to the showers so she could wash the dirt off herself. She hid her dirt-covered clothes in the bottom of her hamper. She would do her laundry later that afternoon, when everyone else was in class, so the evidence would be washed away. The machine was already removing any guilt she may have felt.

After showering, she quickly dressed and headed to the cafeteria for breakfast. She glanced around the room, located Nathan, and smiled. After picking up a tray and some food, Annie made her way through the noisy, crowded room and sat down next to Nathan—her Nathan.

. . .

NATHAN LOOKED AT ANNIE. SOMETHING WAS DIFFERENT, wrong. Annie had somehow changed. It was barely perceivable, probably only noticeable to one who loved her, but it was there. A change.

"Hi, Annie. How are … you? Where's Lyra? You guys always have breakfast together," Nathan said, looking past Annie, scanning for Lyra.

"Oh, um … she went to the library for some last-minute cramming—big test today." Annie smiled at Nathan. She quickly ate her toast and headed out to her first class, her mind racing to find as many excuses for Lyra's absence as possible.

She sat in her next few classes, recording the lectures as she thought of how she would explain Lyra's disappearance. She didn't have to worry about her family, for like Annie, Lyra was basically alone in the world. Her parents were somewhere in Europe—Lyra never knew exactly where, or when she would see them again. No one would look for her and notice she was missing, no one except dorm mates and friends from here., at least not for a while.By the end of her second class, she knew the story she would tell. She would use the fact that Lyra was a stereotypical Type A personality. After spending the early morning cramming for a test—she must keep her initial lie intact—Lyra realized that she was not ready for the test, that she didn't know the material well enough to pass the test, let alone get her usual A. Lyra couldn't handle that, so she left school.

It was believable, she hoped. Everyone knew that Lyra was a high-strung perfectionist, that anything less than an A was unacceptable to her. In fact, there were floor jokes about it. This would—it should—work.

But now, Annie had to get rid of Lyra's stuff. That became the problem. Lyra would have never just left it all behind for good, but she wouldn't have taken it with her right away—it would be too methodical. Lyra had to be distraught when she left. However, if Lyra were to send for her things, then Annie would have to invent an address for Lyra, and then everyone else would want it also. That wouldn't work. If floor mates tried to contact her and never got a response, they would become suspicious. Annie needed a better solution. She had to come up with something, and come up with it soon.

# SUSAN

Susan reached the edge of town and pulled her car over to think. She had not come up with any ideas on how to destroy the machine. She feared that if she got close to it, she would be compelled to do one of two things—either kill for it again or put the suction straw in her own mouth. Neither of these acts would end the machine or stop its evil.

Susan had no idea where to begin. She started her engine and drove into town, hoping for inspiration. She arrived at her old apartment, slipped her key in, and entered. The odor of misuse hit her first, then the smell of rotting food. She quickly began to clean and air out her home. She first disposed of the food in the refrigerator and then carried the garbage down to the complex's dumpster.

As she cleaned under the kitchen sink, she saw the evidence of small rodents and cockroaches. She went into her utility closet and retrieved a box of rat poison. She generously sprinkled the powder under her sink and around the borders of the rooms, hoping it would end this particular issue. Then she went into her bedroom, opened the windows, lay on her bed, and slept.

When she awoke, she thought about the rat poison. *What if I somehow poison the machine? I could treat it like any other vermin. There's a poison for everything; I'll just have to find the right one. And then figure out how to get it to take the poison.*

She had her first idea; she just needed to know how to execute it. She could think of only one way to insure the machine received the poison. She would have to ingest the poison herself and then place the straw in her own mouth. It was the only way. *I deserve this. I deserve to die this way after all I have done.*

Now she needed to learn what poison would kill the machine.

# DAVID

With Susan and Keith gone, missing without a word on when they planned to return, if ever, David was left trying to hold their practice together. Just as they were before agreeing to work with Keith and Susan, David's hours had become unbearable. He worked ten-hour days, six, sometimes seven days a week, caring for his patients as well as Keith's and Susan's. It was becoming unbearable. He knew it was time. He placed ads in various dental magazines and periodicals. He needed new partners.

When he told Charlotte of his decision, she blanched at the idea.

"Charlotte, it will be fine. The new partners will be fine. You're a great employee. Believe me; it will be fine."

Charlotte gave him a small smile and nodded, "Of course; I'm sure it will be."

. . .

That night, though her mind reeled with thoughts of all the things that could possibly go wrong, Charlotte slept. The machine was quieter, just a slight drone in the back recesses of her mind. When she woke, she felt better than she had in weeks. As she sat, sipping her coffee, she began to wonder why. Why wasn't It screaming for food?

It had been screaming for weeks now, ever since Drs. Andres and Caine had left for their tryst. Now It was quiet. She was grateful for the silence but desired to understand why It was quiet. Exhaling slowly, she walked down to room 5 and placed her right hand on the knob. Turning the knob slowly, she once again, began to hear Its thrum.

A small smile played on her lips for a second, replaced by a look of concern. She placed one foot inside the room and felt a strange feeling creep into her mind. It was like an itch deep within her brain tissue. She knew the only thing that would stop the itch was in this room. She felt herself being pulled toward the machine. The desire to place the suction straw in her mouth grew within her.

She exhaled quickly as she stepped out of the room, slamming the door behind her. She stood there, frozen, betrayed. She once again placed her hand on the doorknob. She knew what this meant; she knew what would happen to her, but she still couldn't move away from the door.

"Charlotte," David yelled. "Where are you?" The sound of his voice resonated within her, pulling her out of the trance.

"I'm, I'm here. I'll be right with you," Charlotte replied as she slid the key into the door and turned it. Charlotte walked away from room 5, knowing that if she returned, it would be her last trip there.

# ANNIE

ANNIE WAS DIFFERENT. Nathan wanted to believe that it was Lyra's sudden departure that was affecting her. He wanted to be able to agree with her floor mates, but he suspected that it wasn't true. Annie no longer ate in the cafeteria, choosing instead to eat alone in her room. When Nathan questioned her about it, she tried to explain that she had so much work to complete this term that she studied while eating. If that had been the only change, he might have believed it, but it wasn't. Annie was out late most nights and refused to tell Nathan where she had been. She was obviously tired, worn out, but insisted that she was fine, even when the circles under her eyes showed otherwise. Nathan knew that Annie was not acting like the Annie he loved.

Annie had been to the dental practice. Lyra had followed her there. Now Lyra was gone, and Annie was ... different. Nathan had to find out what had happened. First, he would talk to Annie, and if she still wouldn't tell him what had happened, he would find Lyra.

Annie was in class for the next few hours, so Nathan decided to go the dentist's office. As he walked toward the building, he noticed a car driving slowly behind him. It turned when he did and stopped when he stopped. He told himself that he was being paranoid, that no one was following him. He could not think of any reason for anyone to follow him.

Just as he decided that the driver was probably a dental patient, the car pulled up next to him.

"Excuse me, you're Nathan, right?" Dr. Andres said, looking at Nathan.

"Yes, and you're Dr. Andres. You fixed my tooth."

"Get in; I need to talk to you."

"Um, yeah, no. I … erm … I don't think so."

"Believe me, I understand. Look, meet me at the diner at the next corner. It's a public place."

"Um, okay, I guess."

. . .

Leaving Nathan to walk, Susan pulled into the diner's parking lot and parked her car. By the time Nathan arrived, she was seated at a corner booth, sipping coffee. Nathan walked over and slid into the bench opposite her. He signaled the waitress that he would like some coffee and then looked at Susan.

"So, what do you want?" he asked.

Susan exhaled, "Just some honesty. And I promise I won't think you're crazy. Tell me about your time in Room 5."

Nathan looked at her for a few seconds, was about to speak, when the waitress appeared with his coffee and two menus.

"Thanks," Nathan sputtered. Then, looking at Susan, he remarked, "I don't know what you mean."

"What happened to you in room 5?"

"Look, um, the receptionist put me in the room, I waited

for a while, then you came running in all frazzled and yelling for me to go to a different room. That's all."

"There has to be more?"

"What? Why does there have to be more?"

"What about after? Any weird dreams or thoughts? Anything?" Susan inquired, desperately looking to find something, a reason why Nathan wasn't dead and buried in the cellar.

"Weird dreams? Oh, I mean, well, sure. But they were drug induced. You had me on some strong stuff," Nathan said, awkwardly smiling at her.

"No, I didn't. It was only triple strength Tylenol. That shouldn't induce wild dreams. What did you dream about?"

"I don't remember."

"It. The machine." Susan whispered hoarsely, her eyes pleading to be understood.

Looking around the diner, Nathan whispered to Susan, "Where did you find the mummy?"

"The mummy?" Susan asked, wondering how Nathan knew about the condition of the bodies but not the machine.

"The one you buried in the woods."

"How do you know about that?"

"Well, I kind of … followed you that night."

"Why did you follow me?" Susan asked as the waitress made her way back over to their table. "Look, Nathan, let's get out of here and go somewhere private. We need to talk." They quickly paid their bill and left the diner together. They climbed into Susan's car and drove to Susan's apartment.

# CHARLOTTE

CHARLOTTE SPENT THE day, quietly working. It was the first time in weeks that she had worked in total silence. There was no constant humming sound accented by the occasional pang of desperation and hunger.

As she filed patient files and organized the billings, her mind occasionally wandered. Why was the machine quiet to her now? Was someone else feeding it? And if so, who? Charlotte needed to find out.

First, she would check appointments from the past few days. Maybe a new patient had heard the call from the machine. There had been five new patients during the time between its last known feeding and its noticeable absence. But how could she determine which patient was now feeding the machine? She vaguely remembered someone, maybe a girl, trying to get into room 5. But something was blocking the memory, something did not want her to remember.

She exhaled slowly, touching the patients' files, hoping one would jump out at her, but it didn't. Glancing around, she saw David, his back turned to her, entering a room down the hall. She slipped the files into her bag so she could read through them quietly at home.

After tidying up her work station, Charlotte walked out of the office while the sun was still in the sky for the first time in a while; she smiled as she felt the sun's rays on her face. She got into her car, opened the windows, and drove home, thankful that she hadn't sublet her apartment.

Once there, she heated up her last TV dinner, noting that she was going to have to go food shopping the next day. She then sat down, took the files out of her bag, and began to read through them, hoping to find a clue as to who the machine's newest helper was, who was hearing the call to feed.

# SUSAN AND NATHAN

SUSAN UNLOCKED HER apartment door and led Nathan into her living room. They both sat down and exhaled simultaneously. Susan stretched herself across a floral love seat as Nathan perched himself on her chocolate colored couch.

"Let's talk," Susan said.

"Okay. Tell me where you got that mummy?" Nathan asked.

Susan breathed deeply. "No, first I need to know what you heard. How did you survive room 5?"

"Survive? What do you mean?" Nathan asked.

"Nobody, I mean *nobody*, survives room 5. How did you? Did you hear anything? Feel anything?"

"Well, I heard something. Kinda like a low thrumming. I don't know. I just figured it was a truck or something outside."

"Okay, but you didn't feel a need to … to … " Susan looked away from Nathan. Then she stood up and walked across the floor toward her window. Nathan heard the clicking of her shoes on the hardwood floor.

"To what?" Nathan asked.

"To put the suction straw in your mouth?" Susan said hesitantly.

At first Nathan scoffed at Susan's suggestion, but then he began to remember something. "I … don't … think so."

"What is it?"

"I don't know, it's just ... like I'm trying to remember a dream. There was this strange feeling, almost like a pulling sensation. It's hard to describe. It felt like something was trying to force its way into my head, trying to make me do what it wanted."

"How did you resist it? No one else has, at least I don't know of anyone."

"It never got fully in; I just felt a gnawing presence. Wait, you mean, it's real? Not just a weird feeling or a dream? What does it make people do?"

"Die, or kill. It makes some people die and others basically kill for it."

"How? I don't understand. What did it do to you?"

"It somehow—" Susan said, choking back tears as she looked out of her window, "forced me to bring it people. So those poor souls, those people, would kill themselves, and it could grow stronger."

"What? How? I don't understand," Nathan replied. He walked across the room, handing Susan a tissue.

Dabbing at her eyes, Susan slowly whispered, "It would dehydrate them."

"What? Is that what ... who was the mummy in the woods? Did it do that? What is it?"

"I'm not sure what it is, but it is somehow linked to the old suction straw I found in the building's basement. As for the mummy ... " Susan started to cry again, as she walked over to a table covered in photos. She picked one up and traced the image with her finger. "He was Keith. My partner in the practice and the man I ... " Susan dropped to the floor of her apartment, her body shaking. She just sat there, clutching her photo of Keith, crying uncontrollably as the truth of what she'd done fully impacted her.

No more Keith.

As soon as Susan calmed down, she took a deep, shuddering breath and said, "I'm going to start at the beginning." After a short pause, she continued. "From the very beginning, I felt the pull. I came to the office looking for a place for David, Keith, and me to open a practice together. I saw the suction straw and touched it. It was like it woke up when I did. It started to quietly hum. It was hardly discernible. I left with pictures of the place and a gnawing feeling that I had to return.

"It wasn't hard convincing David and Keith to come here, Keith already knew the area, his family owns a cabin not too far from here. Once we had settled in and our practice began to grow, so did its voice. It started as a slight hum, like a fluorescent bulb, but within a few months, the hum had grown into a scream; it was awful. It sounded how I would imagine an injured animal would sound. It took no time in taking over my consciousness, in making me respond to its hunger. It taught me how to stop the screams. I tried to ignore it, to pretend that it wasn't happening. I even tried to leave once, with Keith, but I felt so sick. Keith wanted to go to the emergency room, but I knew what would make me feel better. It was as if being away from the machine was poisoning me.

"I didn't know what to do or what it wanted at first. I just knew that I wanted to get away from it but couldn't leave it. Whenever I was away from it, I can't describe the headaches I would get. It felt as if something was squeezing my head in a vise. I thought the pain would make me pass out. So I moved into the office one night. I just started sleeping in my office. Although I was still controlled by it and I could still hear its cries of hunger, I no longer had the headaches.

"We hadn't finished renovating, and room 5 was left unfinished. The room was so far away from the other rooms that I figured that I could store it safely there, until I could decide what to do.

"Once it was set into a room with a dental chair next to it, it began to tell me what it needed. Everything I tried to do to stop it made it worse. Now I knew what it wanted from me. I still resisted, but it became more demanding, more insistent. I tried to fight it; I tried to deny it, its request, but eventually it became so desperate. I couldn't rebel against its demands.

"But how was I going to do it? I was a healer and vehemently non-violent. How was I, Susan Andres, going to kill someone? But it told me how.

"The next question I had to find an answer to was who. I realized that it had to be someone that no one would miss or look for. But how could I find someone like that?

"But as luck would have it—well, lucky for the machine, I guess—an elderly patient came in. She needed to have a procedure done and as per usual I inquired as to whom would be picking her up. When she told me that she had no one, that we would have to call her a cab for after the procedure, I knew that I had the perfect victim. She had already lived a full life, and no one would be looking for her. I had her placed in room 5 and then left for a few minutes—following the directions of the machine.

"I sat in my office, fidgeting, not knowing what was happening in room 5. Then the machine came back into my mind and sent me back to room 5. At first, I was confused; she seemed to be exactly as I left her, sitting back in the dental chair, but then I walked around the chair and saw her.

It took every ounce of my resolve to not run from that room screaming, but once again, the machine knew what to do. It told me to lock the door and to continue with my day. So that's what I did. Then later that night, after having dinner, I came back to the office. The machine told me how to find the small room beyond the cellar—a place where it would be safe to bury the remains of the victims."

"Wait," Nathan interrupted, "you saw what the machine does, what it's capable of, and you still fed it?"

"It's more complicated than that. You can't understand the compulsion, the need to feed the machine. It's uncontrollable; nobody can resist its pull to kill or be killed."

"Except me. I resisted the pull. Somehow I resisted the machine," Nathan replied.

"That's the question. How did you do it?"

"It was like it never fully got in. It was more like an annoying gnat, buzzing right outside the peripheral. I must have somehow blocked it."

"Okay, the next question is can we use that to stop the machine?"

"Wait, what? Stop the machine? How?"

"I don't know, but there has to be a way. Who is feeding it now?"

"I don't know, obviously. But how do we find out?"

"Research time, college boy."

"Research? Where? Under evil dentistry?"

Turning on her laptop, she calmly said, "Let's start by looking for missing people, paranormal events, anything odd or unusual. Get started." Susan handed her laptop to Nathan.

"What are you going to do?" Nathan asked.

Susan smiled. "Go back to work."

"But the machine?"

"I can't hear it anymore. I should be safe, but if I hear even a slight thrum, I'll leave town again."

After Susan left, Nathan started searching for information on evil dental instruments. He came upon an article about a Doctor Robert Elizabeth and his wife, Lori Elizabeth, who had been missing for more than fifty years. It was rumored that she played with the occult while running a tea and candle shop adjacent to her husband's dental practice. At first, he only planned on scanning the article—he assumed that it would be about an unskilled dentist and his wife—but a photo caught his eye. Dr. Robert Elizabeth ran his dental practice out of and lived at the same location as Susan's dental practice.

He settled back on the sofa and began to studiously read.

*The Chronicle August 1, 1958*

*Philipsburg—Dozens of bodies, which appeared to be mummified, were found in the basement of a neighborhood dental practice on Wednesday. Police were called to the residence of Robert (deceased) and Lori Elizabeth. Robert Elizabeth was a respected dentist in the town and practiced out of their house, with his wife, Lori, aiding him as his dental assistant. Neighbors had reported that they had not seen Lori Elizabeth in over a month. Neighbors said that Robert and Lori Elizabeth had been excellent neighbors. They also reported that after Robert died, a strange man was witnessed spending time in the residence.*

*After entering the residence, police discovered*

*the bodies buried in the root cellar of the home. Local men volunteered to help remove the bodies from the house. A local professor has been asked to help identify the bodies, using similar techniques as those employed by paleoanthropologists. If you know anyone who has visited the practice of Robert Elizabeth and has gone missing, please contact the police.*

*The police have requested that anyone who has knowledge of the whereabouts of Lori Elizabeth please call the department.*

. . .

NATHAN REREAD THE ARTICLE AND THEN BEGAN A WEB search for more information. Unfortunately, all the other articles that he found contained the same information as the original. Nathan quickly called Susan's cell and filled her in on the new information.

# SUSAN

SUSAN HAD PULLED her car over to take Nathan's call. After hanging up the phone, she eased her car back onto the road and drove to her dental practice. She parked her car and entered the building.

She stood outside the reception area and took a deep breath. So far, she heard nothing, not even a low hum. Sighing with relief, Susan stepped into the waiting room.

"Susan ... I mean, Dr. Andres?" said Charlotte, shaking her head with confusion. "When did you get back? Are you back? Where's Dr. Caine?"

Susan just smiled at Charlotte, quickly inhaled and walked back to her office. It was there that she saw David speaking with two strangers.

"Susan?" David asked incredulously. "Is Keith with you?"

"No," she said, glancing at the two strangers in her office, "But we can discuss that later." She extended her hand to the two men. "Hello, I'm Dr. Susan Andres. And you are ... ?"

The two men looked at David, who quickly jumped in to introduce them. "Oh, sorry, this is Dr. Jameson and Dr. Simons. Let me walk them out and then we'll talk."

David left with the men, only to return few minutes later. He walked into the office. "What the fuck, Susan? You can't just walk back in as if nothing happened."

Susan stood there, looking intensely at the wall. Finally turning her head toward David, she said, "I'm sorry, David. I screwed up. I have no excuse. But I'm back; I promise. I'll start tomorrow."

"And Keith? Where is Keith? Is he coming back soon?"

"I don't know. He's gone. I last saw him on the day we left. We had a major, um, difference of opinion. I haven't seen or heard from him since. David, I think he's gone."

Exhaling, David said, "Okay, well, look. This practice has gotten too big for just one—or even two of us," he quickly added, noticing a twitch in Susan's mouth as he said one. "I've been working ten to twelve hours days for six days a week. I can't remember the last time I spent time with my family or friends. It's too much. I think we need to bring in new partners."

Susan desperately searched her mind to come up with a reason not to. A new person shouldn't be exposed to the machine, but nothing was coming to mind. She was beginning to realize how dependent she had become on having the machine think for her.

"I agree," she said, quickly thinking, "but it must be someone we both agree to; someone who we both feel will be an asset to our business." She hoped this would allow her the time she needed to destroy the machine before approving of a new candidate.

"Agreed."

"Let's both write down qualities that we want in a partner and then discuss them later."

"Sounds great. Oh, and Susan—welcome back."

David left to see to a patient.

Susan sat at her desk and glanced at her cell phone. She thought about what Nathan had told her about the building.

Maybe somewhere in this building, she would find a clue, a hint indicating what the machine was and maybe even a way to stop it from killing.

She began to search her office first, looking for any loose boards. She knew that most of the main floor of the building had been renovated, including most of the drywall, so she doubted that anything was hidden in these walls or any of the examination rooms. As she crawled around on her office floor, she heard the door open.

"Dr. Andres?" Charlotte asked, watching with a perplexed look as Susan crawled across the floor pushing on planks.

"Oh, hi Charlotte. How are you?"

"I'm fine, but, um, what are you doing? Did you lose something? Can I help you look?" Charlotte asked, beginning to lower herself to the floor.

"Oh. Thank you but no," replied Susan as she stood, brushing dirt off her pants. "Did you need to see me?"

"I have tomorrow's schedule for you."

"Great. Just leave it on my desk. Thanks."

Charlotte laid the paper on Susan's desk and then walked out of her office with one last curious glance.

Susan looked at the schedule from Charlotte and saw how many patients she would be seeing tomorrow. David was right; they needed a partner to help ease the load. But right now, she had more exploring to do.

After searching her office, she went to Keith's and placed her hand on the doorknob. She questioned whether she had a right to go in there. Was she being disrespectful to Keith and his memory? But then she realized that Keith would want the machine to be stopped. So she exhaled slowly, telling herself that this was to stop the machine, to avenge Keith's death.

She quietly entered his office and began to explore his space. She looked over the walls and floors. It was in the fireplace that she found her first clue: an old key hidden behind a loose brick. One that looked like it would open a small trunk or jewelry box. She was inspired to look further into the house.

By the time she finished looking through hers and then Keith's offices, the practice was closing for the day. This would be her opportunity to look in David's office and the floor above. If she was caught upstairs, she only had to say that she was thinking about expanding the practice onto the upper floor. With their busy schedule, this would be a viable excuse.

After everyone had left for the evening, Susan called Nathan. "Nathan, I found a key. It was hidden in a fireplace. I'm going to stay here and search some more. Now that the offices are empty, I'm going to see about David's office and the upstairs."

"Let me pack up here and then I'll come and help you."

"No, I don't think that's a good idea. We don't know what will happen if you're too close to the machine. No, don't come here. I'll let you know if I find anything else."

"Okay, I understand. But let me know if you need help."

She started in David's office, searching as before, looking for loose floorboards or loose bricks. She found nothing there and knew it was time to head upstairs.

As she walked toward the stairs, she had to pass by room 5. She calmly walked by the room, assuming she was now numb to its call.

But she was wrong. As soon as she was outside the door, she felt it. A slight tug in the recesses of her brain ... but this time it was different. Before the pull had instructed her to kill for it, but now she felt a pull to enter the room and to sit in the chair.

Susan picked up her pace and then ran up the stairs. She realized that the machine wanted her dead; it wanted her to join the others in the cellar.

Once upstairs, Susan settled down and regained her purpose—to find the box that would be opened by the mysterious key.

She went through each room, imagining what they must have looked like during the time of Lori Elizabeth. Old pieces of furniture were still in place, covered with a thick layer of dust. Susan tried to picture a couple living here, dreaming of their life together. She didn't hear the front door open or Charlotte calling her name. She just continued to search for the box that she knew had to be somewhere. No one would hide just a key; there had to be a box.

# NATHAN AND ANNIE

Nathan left Susan's apartment and headed back to campus. He had planned on going straight to bed, as exhaustion had suddenly overtaken him, but when he walked onto campus, he turned in the direction of Annie's dorm.

He knocked on Annie's door and waited for her to answer. As he stood there, he began to drift off to sleep. He could feel his eyes getting heavier and heavier. He soon slipped down the wall, falling asleep while sitting on the floor.

. . .

An hour later, Annie quietly stepped over Nathan, entered her room, grabbed her toiletry bag, and left for a shower. She couldn't let Nathan see her covered with dirt—he would have too many questions. She blow-dried her hair, put on clean clothes, and snuck back down the hall, once again stepping over Nathan, sleeping prone on the floor. She put her toiletries in her room and grabbed her backpack. She closed and re-locked the door.

Taking a few steps backward down the hall, she whispered, "Nathan?" She moved closer to him, kneeling next to him, "Nathan, why are you sleeping on the floor?"

"To see you. I miss seeing you, Annie; I miss talking to you, walking with you, eating with you. I miss you."

Annie blushed slightly, reached out her hand, and helped Nathan get up off the floor. "Come inside."

. . .

As they lay in bed, sleeping, curled in each other's arms, Annie moaned in her sleep, pushing herself away from Nathan. Nathan awoke from sleep and groggily asked, "Annie, what's wrong? Honey?"

Annie moaned louder, tossing herself across the bed. "Annie, wake up," Nathan called.

Annie continued to sleep, moaning ever more loudly, "No, no, no, please don't make me, please."

Nathan shook her, begging her to wake up. After fifteen minutes, Annie's eyes opened wide as she let out a long scream.

. . .

Annie looked at Nathan shocked. "What happened?" she asked.

"You tell me, Annie. That must have been some dream—or nightmare."

"Um, yeah, I guess so, but I don't really remember it," Annie lied, pushing away the images of Lyra's last moments that filled her mind. Looking at the clock, Annie realized that she had to get up and get dressed.

"Where are you going?"

"Oh, um, I have to study some more. Back to the library for me."

"Annie, you need to get some sleep," Nathan replied, stretching out on his side, propped on his elbow.

"I will, just ... after my test. Oh, and um, Lyra left her key to the room. It's on her desk. Can you lock up when you leave? Thanks, Nathan." Annie threw on a pair of jeans and an old tee shirt, then hurriedly left the room with her book bag thrown over her back.

Annie didn't know what to do. She could feel the pull of the machine begging her for more food. She had no idea as to where she could get It food, what kind of food It wanted, or how she would give it food.

She went to the library, found a quiet table and began to study. But within minutes she could no longer push the sounds out of her mind. What had been a low-grade hum had become a deafening scream. Every second she tried to ignore it, it grew louder and more incessant.

Within a few hours, she knew what she had to do. If she wanted to placate it, to end the never-ceasing noise in her head, she would have to feed the machine. But how? She needed to figure out not only what to feed the machine, but how she would get the food to it. She had no legitimate reason to go back to the practice, so there was also that problem.

Annie had to come up with a plan. She sat through her classes, half listening, half thinking. She couldn't think of a way to get back in. She couldn't break in again; it was too risky. She had to find a way to feed the machine without breaking into the practice, without calling attention to herself.

...

Nathan was watching Annie. She was becoming more and more distracted. She was sleeping less and less. And when she did sleep, it was erratic and disturbed. She was in a constant state of confusion, and yet seemed obsessed by something. She wouldn't tell him what she was thinking about, but it had obviously captivated her.

The next night, Nathan woke to the sound of Annie talking in her sleep. He couldn't understand all she was saying, but he could tell that she was not just agitated; she was scared.

# SUSAN

Susan continued to scour the upper floor's rooms, looking for the locked box. She had just begun to walk up the attic stairs when she heard Charlotte talking downstairs. "What is she doing here so late?" Susan whispered out loud as she continued up the stairs. She turned on the overhead light and continued to search, remembering to stay as quiet as possible so Charlotte wouldn't hear her.

Susan walked through the dust- and cobweb-filled room, glancing around for any place where a box might be hidden. As she headed to the northern end of the attic, she saw something—a patch on the wall where the boards didn't quite match up.

*Could this be it?* she wondered as she headed to the spot. Squatting on the ground, she pushed on the center of the patch—nothing happened. Her heart sank. *Maybe there is no box*, she thought. *Maybe there is no way to stop it*. She started to stand, leaning her right hand against the wall. She felt it move. Looking over, she saw a gap opening between the patch and the regular wall.

Smiling, she continued to push on the patch, watching the wall open. Reaching into the dark abyss behind the wall, Susan felt around. There it was. She reached in and grabbed the box with both hands, lifting it out of its hiding spot behind the wall.

She blew the dust off the box and looked for a lock. Once she found it, she removed the key from her pocket and put it in the lock. She turned the key, exhaling from the anticipation. She lifted the lid and looked inside. There she saw a book. Removing it from the box, she held the book in her hands as she left the attic.

She quietly went down the stairs and entered her office. Closing the door behind her, she sat at her desk and opened the book. It Lori Elizabeth's diary.

As she opened the book, she heard a knock on her door. "Come in," she called, closing the book and placing it on her lap.

. . .

CHARLOTTE OPENED THE DOOR AND POKED HER HEAD into Susan's office. "Dr. Anders, what are you doing here so late?" Charlotte asked.

"Oh, just, going over patient files for tomorrow; I want to be on top of my game. And you? What are you here so late?"

"Oh, just catching up on filing and billing."

"This late? How often do you stay this late?"

"Oh, not that often," Charlotte responded, whispering inaudibly, "anymore."

"What? I'm sorry, I missed that last word."

"Oh, it was ... nothing," replied Charlotte, as she turned to leave. "Good night, Dr. Andres. It's nice to have you back with us."

"Thank you, Charlotte. Good night to you."

Charlotte went into the hallway, wondering what book Susan had hidden from her view when she entered.

. . .

SHAKING, SUSAN PACKED THE DIARY INTO HER BAG AND left the practice. Had Charlotte seen anything? What, if anything, did Charlotte know? Susan would read the diary at home. As she drove home, she began to think about Charlotte. Could she be the one who had been feeding the machine in Susan's absence? Susan would have to investigate it, watch Charlotte's behavior. Someone was feeding it; Charlotte would be a good and obvious choice.

Susan headed home, after stopping for a pizza and beer. She entered her apartment, placing the pizza and beer on her coffee table, kicked off her shoes, and settled on the couch. Flipping open the pizza box lid, she grabbed a slice and bit into it. Washing it down with a gulp of beer, she opened the diary and started to read.

> *I've never kept a journal before, but friends have recommended it to help me deal with my grief, so here it goes. My devoted Robert died two weeks ago but it feels like it only happened earlier today. My grief is so strong, my misery so powerful. I fear I will never know happiness again.*
>
> *I have tried to talk to him; have brought in clairvoyants, reputed to be even more powerful than I am. But to no avail. No one seems to be powerful enough to bring him back. My coven has agreed to meet with me, each of us specializing in a different area. We will find a way to reach him. We have to for I fear that I cannot live without him.*

Susan read through the next few pages, which were filled with variations on the same information. Lori wrote of her devotion to Robert, of her deep mourning for him. Susan started to read a few pages in.

> *We have been working hard together. We've researched so many different spells and potions. We are now collecting the elements and ingredients that we will need to contact Robert. It shouldn't be too much longer and I will be talking with him again. Of course, in the ideal world, I will be able to bring Robert back to me completely, as a whole person again. But I fear that is just a fantasy I now hold dear.*

Susan stopped reading. Her clock read 11:00 and she knew she had to go to sleep so she could work tomorrow. She laid the book on her coffee table and got ready for bed.

# CHARLOTTE

CHARLOTTE FINISHED CLEANING up her desk, filing papers, and making sure all billings were up-to-date. She heard the back door close and then Susan's car pulling out of the parking lot.

Although she was curious to see what Susan had been doing in the practice so late at night, she had other things she had to investigate first. She hesitantly walked down to room 5 and rested her hand on the doorknob. She stood there, listening for instructions, humming, anything to know it was still there.

She heard nothing but silence. She decided to go down to the cellar, to where the bodies were buried. Maybe she would hear it there.

Charlotte walked back to her desk and removed the antique key from her center drawer. She didn't remember putting the key in the pencil slot of her drawer; she usually kept it in the tray on the left. She knew that nobody would have moved it to a different spot in her desk. She rationalized that she must have put it there the last time she'd used it.

She went to the back of the building, put her key in the lock, and then opened the door. She turned on the light and went down the stairs.

Charlotte stood in the secret chamber, her mouth gaping open in shock and dismay. There in front of her was a fresh mound of dirt. Someone new had joined the graveyard; someone Charlotte knew nothing about. She now knew that she had not put the key in the wrong place; someone else had. The machine had found a new supplier; Charlotte was done.

She left the room slowly, plodding up the stairs. She locked the door and then left the building. Charlotte thought about Susan as she drove home, wondering what Susan knew about the machine. By the time she got home, she had decided to find out exactly what Susan knew about the machine and what had truly happened to Keith.

Charlotte slept soundly that night, waking the next morning feeling refreshed for the first time in a while. Out of habit, she made herself coffee and then realized that she didn't need it. She left it sitting on the counter as she went to work.

On her drive to the office, Charlotte began to plan her next move. Part of her was contemplating just leaving town, fleeing from this life and starting over somewhere else. Her mother had done it, so she could too. As she pulled up to a traffic light, she felt her hand begin to move toward the turn signal. She could turn right and head out of town, the machine no longer a part of her life.

As the light turned green, Charlotte began to turn right when she suddenly and unexpectedly realigned the car and went straight instead. Charlotte, always reliable, dutifully went to work.

Charlotte pulled into the parking lot, noting the presence of Susan's car. *She's here early*, Charlotte thought. *Maybe I should ask her now.*

Deciding on her course of action, Charlotte walked into the office and placed her purse and coat in the back room. She turned on her computer, turned on the lights, and unlocked the front door. She logged in to the computer and checked the day's schedule—just another day for Charlotte.

As she checked in patients, her mind began to replay the day before. What was Susan doing in the attic? The whole thing was just strange. Susan and Keith leave together; only Susan returns after silence for weeks. She then begins exploring the building. *What is going on with her?*

Charlotte decided that she would go into the attic during the office lunch hour, so she could try to figure out what Susan had been doing up there the other night. Charlotte waited until everyone had left for lunch and then headed up the stairs.

She followed Susan's footprints on the dusty floor, trying to determine why Susan had come up here. As she walked to the far corner, she saw a niche in the wall. In front of the niche, on the floor, lay a box. The box was open and dust-free. Charlotte knew that whatever Susan had been looking for, she had found it in this box.

Bringing the box downstairs with her, she again paused in front of room 5 and listened—nothing.

"What are you doing?" Susan asked, looking at Charlotte from down the hallway.

Jumping slightly, Charlotte stammered, "Um, um, nothing."

"Why are you touching the doorknob like that?" Susan asked, walking closer to Charlotte.

"Oh, I didn't realize I was—no reason." Charlotte started to walk back to her office, clutching the box in her hands.

# SUSAN

SUSAN, SEEING THE diary's box in Charlotte's hands, began to devise a plan—how she would approach Charlotte later that afternoon. Charlotte knew something—why else would she have that box in her hands, and why would she be standing outside room 5? It was time to find out exactly what Charlotte knew.

After seeing her last patient, Susan approached Charlotte's desk. "I need to speak to you in my office. Come down as soon as you're done here."

"Okay," Charlotte said cheerfully.

. . .

CHARLOTTE FINISHED ORGANIZING HER DESK FOR THE next morning's appointments. She walked to Susan's office and knocked tentatively on the open door, her mind trying to determine what, if anything, Susan knew about room 5.

Susan turned around in her chair and looked at Charlotte. "Come in and close the door."

Charlotte entered the office and sat down across from Susan, looking at her employer with curiosity.

"So, I need to talk to you about something odd," Susan said. "I'm not sure how to begin. Well, um ... you had a strange look on your face when you were touching room 5's doorknob. Did you hear something coming from the room?"

Charlotte was unable to hide her surprise. "What? Noise?" She looked away from Susan, trying to hide her eyes as she lied. She realized that Susan knew. How much, Charlotte wasn't sure. Did Susan know that Charlotte had helped the machine feed? Was Susan planning on calling the police? Charlotte's pulse raced as images of her trial and time in prison careened through her mind.

"Maybe a humming sound ... " Susan encouraged. Charlotte's eyes grew larger and her breathing quickened. Susan *did* know. But how? Had Susan dug the earlier graves? Charlotte couldn't reconcile this image of Dr. Susan Andres with the one she had known. It seemed so out of character. But then, who would believe that Charlotte was capable of such atrocities, yet she had killed, or at least helped to kill, innocent people. Maybe Susan was the chosen one before Charlotte was.

"Humming? Well, I mean ... " Charlotte stammered, desperately trying to find the exact right words to use. She didn't want to say more than Susan already knew, but what did Susan know? She exhaled and quickly whispered, "It started quietly. Just in the back of my mind, but it quickly grew." Suddenly she felt a searing pain in the center of her skull. She grabbed her head, fell to her knees, and screamed.

Susan stood, frozen at first, watching Charlotte as she writhed in pain on the floor. Then she, too, felt something. It was small, like an itch in her brain. She quickly grabbed Charlotte and headed for the door. She ran, dragging Charlotte with her, down the hall and out of the building. She could feel the itch growing stronger; she knew that she would soon be incapacitated, much like Charlotte now was.

Laying Charlotte in the back seat of her car, Susan quickly drove out of the parking lot and headed out of town.

. . .

Charlotte continued screaming, clutching her head in both hands. She felt a fire-hot pain searing into her brain, as if something had placed a red-hot piece of coal in the center of her skull.

As Susan navigated them away from the practice, the pain lessened. Within 20 minutes, the pain had ceased, and Charlotte slowly began to sit up.

"Lie back down," Susan ordered, "you'll feel sick otherwise." Charlotte, feeling her stomach lurch, obeyed and lay back down. Susan stopped driving when she reached a diner. She pulled into the lot and parked her car. Opening the back door, she helped Charlotte out of the car. "Let's get some coffee," Susan said as she led Charlotte into the diner.

Susan requested a seat in the back corner of the diner and ordered coffee for them both, as Charlotte headed to the restroom. Charlotte splashed cold water on her face and quickly fixed her makeup, which was smeared. She left the ladies' room and went to find Susan. Sitting across from Susan, Charlotte stirred sugar and cream into her coffee and took a sip.

Sighing deeply, she said to Susan, "You too, huh? It had you too."

Susan nodded, "What is it? Do you have any ideas?"

"No, but if it set us both free, it must have someone else under its power. Who? Who feeds it now?"

"We need to find out. We need to stop it from continuing. We need to kill it," Susan whispered vehemently.

Charlotte nodded. "Not to change the subject, but what was in that box from the attic?"

"A diary. Nathan, the young man whose teeth I worked on—"

"I remember him," Charlotte interrupted, recalling how he had been in room 5 but left alive.

"He did some research for me. He found an article mentioning a dental assistant who worked with her husband, a licensed dentist. She was in our building and was rumored to be into the occult. Mummified bodies were found on the premises; she had disappeared, and as far as Nathan has been able to determine, was never found. I found her diary."

"How does Nathan know about the machine?"

"He hears it, but some reason, he is able to resist its call."

"Huh," Charlotte responded. "Then we need him to retrieve our things from the office. I can't go back there." Charlotte rubbed her temples gingerly.

Susan reached into her coat pocket and pulled out her phone. She found Nathan's number and dialed.

# NATHAN AND ANNIE

NATHAN WAS LYING in bed, watching Annie. She was in the midst of a nightmarish sleep; she was tossing herself all over the bed while moaning painfully. As he lay there, hoping for a discernible word—anything that might help him understand what was happening to her—he heard the light buzz of his phone vibrating. He picked it up from the floor and quietly got up. He went into the hallway and answered.

"Hello," he whispered, not recognizing the number.

"Hi, Nathan. It's Susan Andres."

"Oh, hi."

"I need your help. I'm at the diner on Dundridge Road with Charlotte, the office manager from my practice. Please, come meet us here. We have a lot to discuss."

"I would, but I don't have a car right now and I can't borrow one right now"

"Oh, okay. I'll pick you up, then. I need to go to my apartment and to Charlotte's apartment to pick up a few things. But it seems that the machine, the evil thing, does not want Charlotte and me to compare notes. I need someone to help me in case I become incapacitated, or worse, fall back under its spell."

"Yeah, sure. I'll meet you at the campus's main entrance."

"Great. I should be there within an hour." Susan hung up the phone and headed to her car. Charlotte was staying at the diner, afraid to go back to town—afraid of what the machine might do to her.

Nathan checked on Annie; she was breathing normally and appeared to be finally sleeping soundly and undisturbed. He grabbed his jacket and backpack, closed the door, and left. Walking across campus, everything seemed so quiet and peaceful. It was hard to believe that the evil he knew existed was in this idyllic town. He arrived at the front gate just as Susan pulled up. Climbing in, Nathan fastened his seatbelt as Susan pulled the car back onto the road.

"I need to go to my apartment and then to Charlotte's." Susan navigated the dark streets as she headed to her home. She parked her car and headed through the front door. Once inside she grabbed a small carry-on suitcase and threw a few essentials into it. She then grabbed the diary and left. She ran down the sidewalk and jumped into her car, tossing the bag onto the back seat.

"Now to Charlotte's."

. . .

SUSAN ENTERED CHARLOTTE'S APARTMENT AND TURNED on the light. Glancing around, she noticed how organized Charlotte was. Everything was spotless and in its proper place. She opened the front closet and grabbed the duffel bag from its labeled hook. She went into Charlotte's bedroom and grabbed what Charlotte had asked for. Then she left, pausing only to again admire the organization and neatness of Charlotte's world.

Locking the door behind her, Susan headed back to her car. She tossed the bag into the back seat and headed back to the diner, where Charlotte was patiently waiting for them.

As soon as Susan and Nathan sat down, Susan removed the diary from her purse and placed it on the table. "Here's the diary I found in the attic."

"And here's what I found out about the practice online," Nathan added, pulling out a stack of papers. "I found out more about her after we talked," he told Susan.

Charlotte reached over, removed the top sheet and began to read the article from a local newspaper.

*The Chronicle July 23, 1958*

*Philipsburg—On July 29, police were called to the house of Dr. Robert Elizabeth (deceased) and his wife, Lori Elizabeth. Neighbors had reported that they had not seen Lori Elizabeth or any signs of activity for at least one month. Upon inspection of said property, detectives discovered that the house has been abandoned for at least that long. The whereabouts of Lori Elizabeth remain unknown. The police are waiting for a search warrant so they can enter the residence, as no sign of a disturbance was noted on the structure or its property.*

*The Chronicle August 2, 1958*

*Philipsburg—Twenty-five bodies have been recovered from the cellar of the dental practice and home of Dr. Robert Elizabeth (deceased) and his wife, Lori. The bodies appeared to be drained of all liq-*

uids and were mummified beyond recognition. The identities of the victims remain a mystery.

The whereabouts of Lori Elizabeth is still unknown. Neighbors claim that in the months after Dr. Robert Elizabeth's death, strange people were seen coming and going at all hours of the day and night. Lori Elizabeth had been considered eccentric, as she was the proprietor of what neighbors called a "Witch Shop." The shop was advertised as a tea and candle store. Neighbors were quick to add that Lori Elizabeth had always been friendly and helpful, even giving help to those in need at no cost.

Police are becoming suspicious that one of the many visitors may have done something evil to Lori Elizabeth and that her fate rests as one of the mummified.

They are asking for any information about the whereabouts of Lori Elizabeth.

*The Chronicle August 4, 1958*

Philipsburg—Police have discovered the disappearance of the body of Dr. Robert Elizabeth. It is another grisly turn of events in the strange occurrences at the Elizabeths' home and practice.

After discovering twenty-five mummified bodies in the basement of the home/practice of Dr. Elizabeth, and the subsequent disappearance of his wife, Lori, police were issued a warrant for the exhumation of Dr. Robert Elizabeth's corpse. The coffin was found to be empty. The funeral home where the body was prepared for burial claims that the body was in

> the coffin when it was placed in their hearse.
>
> Police are again asking that if anyone knows the whereabouts of Lori Elizabeth, please contact the police immediately. She is considered a person of interest and may be dangerous.

"From what I've read in the diary, Lori was, well, obsessed with finding her dead husband's soul and being reunited with it," Susan said.

Nathan reached into the stack of papers, scanned through them, and handed Susan a copy. "Read this one."

"Oh my God," Charlotte muttered, "Oh my fucking God. Do you think it's her ghost? Is that humming sound, well, her?" her eyes were wide open with fear.

"Maybe," Nathan said.

"I don't know, but I think not," Susan replied.

"Why not?"

"I read a lot of her diary. I don't think she would haunt like this. She doesn't appear to be evil or even bad, just desperate—desperate to be reunited with her husband."

"What? All those bodies in the cellar, only having one ghost would be a miracle! That place is probably riddled with angry ghosts," Charlotte exclaimed as Nathan shook his head in disbelief.

"So, you can believe in a haunted suction straw but not—" Susan stopped talking as the waitress came over to refill their coffee cups and take their order for food. After she walked away with their order, Susan continued, defeated, "I don't know what else to believe." Shaking her head, she muttered, "When did demon possession become the most viable option in my life?"

"We have to stop this thing. It's our only chance of redemption!" Charlotte exclaimed.

Susan looked at her barely touched coffee, *Redemption?* she thought. *Do I deserve redemption?* Aloud she only said, "I'll finish reading the diary tonight, or at least I'll try to."

"I'm going to continue searching for more information," Nathan said.

"Anything could help," Susan agreed, checking her watch and then looking at Charlotte. "Let's get a hotel room and get some rest."

"What about David?" Charlotte asked.

"What about him?"

"Should we warn him?"

"He's never shown any sign of, well, of ... I don't know what to call it ... but he's never shown any indication of a response or reaction to it."

"I think I'll go look at the cemetery. Maybe there will be a clue in the names of the people," Charlotte. "I need to feel useful, and I can *not* go back to the practice."

"I'm not sure what those names will provide, but it can't hurt. Maybe there's a reason why some people react differently to its call then others," Susan mused. "I'm tired. Let's go."

As Susan and Charlotte drove Nathan back to campus, they both began to feel the pull of the machine—but this time it wasn't trying to make them bring it food. It was trying to make them food, to influence them to sacrifice themselves for its insatiable appetite.

"Do you feel that?" Charlotte whispered.

"Feel what?" Nathan asked shakily, looking from Susan to Charlotte.

"Yes, but it's different from before," Susan replied, "More of a humming, almost hypnotic, almost pleasant."

"That must be why. Why they do it, voluntarily. It's almost relaxing."

"What are you two talking about?"

"You don't hear it, then?"

"No. Watch out!" Nathan yelled, as the car began to swerve.

Susan blinked and pulled the car back into her lane. "Oh my God, I'm sorry. I just felt so relaxed that I began to fall asleep."

"Drop me off here. My apartment is close enough. Get yourselves out of town. Now."

Susan pulled the car over, Nathan jumped out.

"We'll be in touch," Susan said as she pulled away and drove out of town.

Once settled in her room, Susan removed the diary from her bag and opened to a dog-eared page.

### Day 17

*So, I have the plan written out. I've contacted many of the white witches in the area, asking for any advice on how to contact Robert. I cannot take any chances of failure. I must succeed in speaking to my beloved. There must be a way— maybe a potion to enhance my powers. It is time for me to research other alternatives.*

### Day 21

*I have arranged for others, who like me are able to see into other realms, to come over tonight so we can try to pool our powers. I have the mugwort for tea and cinnamon sticks to enhance our powers. I'm very hopeful that we will be able to reach him. I spent so much time researching how to strengthen my reach into the realm of the dead. Hopefully, with the addition of herbs, teas, spices, and crystals, I will be able to find Robert.*

*I need to finish setting up the séance room and let the tea steep, but otherwise I am ready, so ready to speak to Robert again. Now I need to lay out the quartz crystals and hematite. I pray that this works as I will have run out of recourses if it fails.*

*I am going to use my purple velvet table cloth with the embroidered stars on the table. It was Robert's favorite—maybe it will entice him to return to me again. I have laid out all that we will need, I hope. Now I need to get dressed. I will wear my blue dress (another of Robert's favorite things), my hair up, and Robert's favorite pieces of jewelry.*

*Day 22*

*Last night, myself and five other witches from around the area met at my store. We burned the cinnamon sticks in hopes that it would increase our combined psychic vibration frequencies, and then each of us drank the mugwort tea. We will each continue this until we are ready to call to him, our intertwined powers uniting in the hopes of reaching him, of bringing him back to me.*

*I spent last night, and will spend the next nights, sleeping with anise in my pillowcase. I'm taking no chances and trying all methods I can to find my Robert.*

*Day 25*

*We spent hours, into the early morning, trying to reach Robert's spirit. The smell of the burning cinnamon stick is still lingering in my hair. We tried so hard. By the end of the session we were all covered in sweat and exhausted, both physically and spiritually. Each of us felt drained of all power. We had spent the entire night swaying and chanting. We tried every spell we knew. We held hands and danced around the fire made from the wood of a cedar tree, all while burning cinnamon sticks and drinking mugwort tea.*

*But no matter what we tried, we could not reach my beloved. He is still unattainable. I am so tired. I need desperately to sleep so I can think of a new approach. I am coming to find my Robert. I truly am. No matter how hard it is, no matter how dangerous, I will find a way to Robert once again.*

*Day 33*

*It's been over a week since I last tried to contact Robert. Don't worry, journal; I'm not giving up. I've been researching other methods, other ways to contact spirits. I'm still burning cinnamon sticks throughout the day and only drinking mugwort tea. I am going to be seeing a different practitioner this week. He is known as a great ceremonial priest and is called simply Dr. Z. He is known to practice both white and black magic. Many in my coven have warned me not to meet with him, for they fear he will be my undoing, but I cannot turn back. My hope rests with his advice and knowledge. I can only pray that he knows of a way to connect with the dead, one which I have yet to try for myself.*

*Day 40*

*I've spent many hours over countless days talking with Dr. Z. I've learned more than I ever could have imagined. Of course, he has warned me against using dark magic, against what he called "perde son Âme," losing one's soul in French. I do understand his fears, I truly do, but my need for Robert has grown and become almost unbearable. I accept the risk to my person and soul if it means I can talk to my Robert again.*

*I've agreed to wear a talisman, to protect myself, to take every precaution that I can. Before I can try again, I must gather the necessary ingredients and of course find my perfect talisman.*

*Dr. Z says I will know my talisman when I get near it. It must be not only strong enough to protect me from harm, but it must compliment and attach itself to my spiritual self. I don't know how long it will take to find the right one, but I will begin the journey today. I will begin by visiting all other magic shops, both light and dark, in this area. From there, I will move outward until I find it. I'm off now in search of my ideal talisman.*

*Day 50*

*A new problem has arisen. I'm running low on money. Robert always brought in enough money for us to live on, but with him gone, I am going broke. My shop has always been more of a hobby, a pastime in which stayed busy during my days. I'm going to have to find a way to bring in more, and not just for living expenses, but enough to fund my search for my talisman and Robert's return to me. I may need to find a job in another practice. I am a dental hygienist, after all. I will have to spend my weekends looking for my talisman, but it is still possible.*

*Day 52*

*Money will no longer be a problem. One of Robert's patients came by. He was in desperate shape—a tooth was rotting, causing him excruciating pain. I have assisted Robert enough times to be able to take care of a rotten tooth, so I did. He paid me what he would have paid Robert. I have decided to reopen our practice. When I don't have a patient on schedule, I will run my shop. It should not take very long to earn enough money to buy what I need to perform the ritual—to bring Robert back to me.*

*Day 55*

*Word has spread of my search for my perfect talisman. Now merchants are coming to me to show me their wares. Which is perfect; I no longer need to travel to find it. I can now stay at home, working either in my shop or the dental practice.*

*This new arrangement has also allowed me to meet other practitioners, some of whom have known of rituals I have yet to try. I have let it be known that I will only deal with white magic, so I have no fear of darkness entering my home.*

*Day 65*

*I have it. I have all that I require to perform the ritual. Robert will be back with me soon, very soon. I must tell you how I have obtained all I need to succeed. The other day, I met a man who, although not a practitioner himself, deals exclusively with objects of unknown powers. He had heard of my quest through his journeys and had in his possession an object he believed would be of interest to me.*

*He came to my store just before closing, quietly slipping in. He stood, silent, in a corner as I helped my final customer with her selection.*

*As I walked her to the door. I turned the lock so I could close for the evening. Upon turning around, I started. There he was, just standing in the shadows, waiting patiently for me to notice him. He approached me, speaking quietly. Once he explained why he was here, I saw it—my perfect talisman. The minute I saw it, I suspected that it was the right one. As soon as I held it in my hand, I knew.*

*It is a beautiful necklace, made of clear quartz and hematite. Its power should to protect me from any harm. It cost me more than I had anticipated, but when all this works, it will surely be money well spent.*

*Day 70*

*I've spent the past five days preparing. Gathering supplies to replace those I depleted with my earlier failed attempts. I finally have all the ingredients that are necessary to contact Robert. The only way this could fail is if I am not strong enough. I only pray that I am; that I have the power within me to carry on. The salesman gave me a chant to say over the talisman just as I summon Robert's ghost. If all works, then Robert should be with me for days on end.*

*I've sent letters to my coven and asked for them to come and help me. Hope, plus God's will, we will be strong enough in combination to make this work. For now, I shall have to test my patience and wait for a time when we can get together and once again call for my beloved's return.*

*Day 71*

*It's scheduled for tomorrow night. I am so excited. I keep checking and rechecking my supplies.*

*Five green candles, red roses for their petals, and a sharp knife for the ritual. Cinnamon sticks, mugwort tea, and crystals for enhancements, and of course my talisman for protection.*

Only the strongest of witches are coming to help me, and each of those has a talisman of her own.

Tonight, I sleep on anise pillows and hope to dream-walk to Robert.

### Day 75

I truly don't know how to describe the other night, but I will do my best to try.

By the time the others had arrived, I had set the candles out and placed the bronze bowl in the center of the circle. The ceremonial knife was placed near my chair, as were my matches. I wore my finest silk dress and had pinned my hair up in Robert's favorite style. My newly acquired talisman hung on my neck. I had adorned my fingers with powerful stones and wore bangles of hematite on each wrist. Never one for taking unnecessary risk, I had made a cleansing incense with frankincense resin, rosemary, bay leaves, mugwort, St. John's wort, angelica, and basil.

Right before the others arrived, I held my talisman and chanted, "Contra obsecro hoc spitum justa ad facientem voluntatom may hem." With the protection spell in place, I was ready to begin summoning Robert's spirit.

After the strongest members of my coven arrived, we began our ritual. Everyone was dressed in their best silk, wearing their talismans.

We sat in a circle, hands held in commune, as I lit the ceremonial candles. I then placed five *red rose petals in the bowl, burning them. Using the ceremonial knife and without hesitation, I cut my palm. I held my hand over the candles' flames and dripped blood onto each candle.*

*As my blood dripped, we chanted, "God of my World and the next, lend me your sight; give me the power to see things that can give people fright; too long they've been trapped in the dark, but now let them in the light."*

*The candles started to flicker as the chanting finished. Then we saw him. At first, he was a shadow, but slowly he materialized into a full corporeal spirit. My Robert was standing before me. My heart was beating so fast I could hardly catch my breath. He was here, standing in the shadows. At first, I wasn't sure what I was seeing. He was a faint, quivering light. He was unable to even speak at first. As we continued chanting, he grew fuller and more corporeal. Within the hour, Robert was standing in front of me.*

*For these past three days, I've had my Robert here to talk to, but that is all. I know that I should be happy with that, but I want more. I need more. I want more than just his soul back; I want him.*

*Day 77*

*I am researching again. Now that I've had my Robert back here with me for those three days, I know that I need him back, fully back. Not just his soul but his body too. I don't know how to do it; I don't even know if it is possible, but I will do whatever I can to make it happen. I will revisit all the shops, talk to all the practitioners. Maybe I can find a way; a way to be reunited fully with him.*

*My first task will be to find Dr. Z. He helped me before, so I will ask again. If there is a way, he will be the most likely to know it. I will go today to find him.*

*I spent today visiting my practitioner friends, but no one has any ideas on how to truly bring back the dead. Even through the use of voodoo, my task seems unreachable.*

*I've had no luck in locating Dr. Z, nor have I found any information on the man who sold me the talisman. I will keep looking for them both; I have left messages for them at all the shops I have frequented. I feel that they are my best chance.*

*I must confess that the day of the funeral—of Robert's funeral—I absconded with his body. I pulled my car next to the hearse and, after tricking the driver into leaving me alone with the coffin, I removed his body from the coffin (with the help of a friend) and placed it in my car. After the funeral, I returned home with his corpse. It is being kept, hidden, in my basement until I can bring him back. I soaked the body in honey in order to preserve it. I've kept the body in case I was able to return his spirit to his corporeal body. I have never known of the spirit returning but I must remain hopeful that I can reunite with him one day.*

*Day 85*

*I have been working tirelessly for the past week. Between my two businesses and my search for Dr. Z and the mysterious salesman, I've had no time for rest. But I know that once I have been reunited with my Robert, it will all be worth it.*

*I have messages out there, begging him to contact me. For now, I must have more patience than I've ever had. For now, I will try to contact Robert again.*

*Day 93*

*Just one hour ago, a miracle happened. The mysterious salesman, as before, suddenly appeared in the recesses of my store. It had been a quiet, uneventful day and then there he was, no warning. I nearly jumped out of my own skin.*

*He told me that he'd heard a rumor that I had been looking for him. He reaffirmed that he would do anything and everything he could to help me on my quest.*

*I made some tea, put out a plate of biscuits, and sat with him. We talked until late in the evening, discussing any and all options. So many ideas were debated only to be thrown out as impossible.*

*Finally, at around one in the morning, he jumped up and began to pace the room, mumbling to himself with every step. He then turned and looked at me, smiling proudly.*

"It's a risk," he said, "but it could work." I could feel excitement for the first time since I learned of Robert's death.

"I must go check something first. I'll be back soon, very soon; I promise." And then he left. All I can do now is wait.

*Day 98*

Last night, right after I locked the doors to the shop, I saw him standing in the shadows again. Only this time, he wasn't alone. Standing next to him was a strange man. He was very short, maybe five feet tall but probably not quite; he was dressed in the most gentlemanly fashion. He wore a diamond on his breast pocket, carried a carved walking stick, and tipped his fedora as I walked over.

Introductions were made, and then we sat down around my table with some tea and biscuits. As our discussion progressed, I came to learn that this unusual little man was quite powerful. He had been born with the gift of not only talking to the dead but also of conjuring and resurrecting the departed. I could feel excitement grow inside of me. Here was a man who could bring Robert back to me. My joy was quickly becoming uncontrollable. I could feel my body trembling throughout, and I quite believe that these two men could feel the vibration in the air.

And then I deflated. His powers only worked if the departed had only been dead for a week or *less. He could not resurrect a body that had been decomposing. I had lost my Robert, yet again. My despair is growing anew.*

*As they left, he pressed his hands around mine and looked deeply, probingly into my eyes. He then quietly said that he may have another way, that he would contact me in another week. And then he left.*

*I am trying to stay positive, trying to be hopeful. I will do whatever I can to bring him back to me; no matter how difficult it is, I will endeavor through it.*

*Day 105*

*I'm not sure if I made the right decision, but I did what must be done. I have made a deal to bring back my Robert. I've signed the papers, in my own blood, and am ready to begin the process. Tomorrow, I shall meet the man who contains the power needed to return my beloved Robert to me. Regardless of my trepidation, the deal has been made. I must uphold my side of the bargain or I will never see Robert again—not even in my own death. And that is something that I could not bear.*

*Day 125*

*I know now that this was a mistake; a horrible, grave mistake. I've made a deal with the devil. In my desperation, I have literally sold my soul to the devil. I will do my best to describe the past twenty days, but I fear for my very life and have been walking through a fog from lack of sleep.*

*The mysterious salesman and his short friend manipulated me into believing that Robert would be returned to me if I signed the contract, in my own blood, with them. The contract was written in an ancient language and I knew not what I had signed. You are always warned to read what you sign, but I was so desperate I signed anyway.*

*Two days after signing, my first payments (of many) came due. The horrors of what that entailed is truly indescribable. I was required to bring my patients to them. I don't know what happened next, for I left the patient with them in a closed room. I could hear the patient struggle, for only a moment or two, and then all I could hear was silence. Then after they were finished, I was required to remove the "husk" (for I know of no other way to describe what was left of this person) and bury it in the root cellar.*

*I don't know how long this can continue; eventually someone will notice that men come into my practice and do not ever leave. What is to be done then, I don't know.*

*Day 150*

*I have been overwhelmed this past month; the guilt has all but consumed me. I can't recall the last time I have eaten nor slept. All I see before me are the remains of these poor men and women, their bodies drained of all liquids. I don't know if I can go on. The only thing that keeps me living is the thought that one day I will be reunited with my beloved.*

## Day 170

*No more. I can do this no longer. I must find a way to end this horrible deal. I just don't know how. I don't want to involve my coven, to endanger them with my foolishness. I must keep them safe. I need to find someone powerful enough to help me, someone with whom I share no attachments.*

*I've heard of a witch. I am not going to include her name or identity, in case the wrong person finds this journal. She lives in a gypsy camp outside of town. She is young, but from what I have heard, she is most powerful in the dark arts as well as the light. I will try to sneak over to see her soon. I just pray that she can help me.*

## Day 175

*I may have found a way to end this deal. I met with Her, out in the gypsy camp. I have explained my situation, and with her guidance and expertise, we have come up with a plan. I will need to construct a spirit trap and trick this demon into it. Then I will have to trap it inside. I must quickly gather the necessary herbs and find a hollow tube in which to trap him. Everything must be carefully prepared, myself included, or I do not have a chance of success.*

*She has agreed to advise me but has refused any involvement in the actual fight. I can't blame her. She is young and has a full life to live; the last thing she needs is to become intrinsically connected to a demon, especially for a stranger.*

*Day 182*

*It is set. I have purchased a hollow piece of wood made from a sacred tree. I will trap the demon inside it and then bury it with its own victims. I have blessed my athame and have completed the ritual of the pentagram. Using the blessed athame, I carved a seal onto the trap that will hold him inside for all eternity. I shall say the spell tonight. With all hope and luck, this nightmare in which I now reside will be over soon.*

*Day 183*

*It is done. I have trapped him, but not in the sacred tube. I am going to once again attempt to describe what happened, but I am not sure how much I remember or how accurate my memories are.*

*I had set up all that I needed to complete the task. I then called for him to come to me. As soon as he appeared in my room, I started chanting while mixing the herbs.*

*I cannot begin to describe the anger that contorted his face as he realized what I was doing. His eyes grew small, shining a blood red in their intensity. His mouth grimaced at first but then opened as if his jaw had become unhinged, baring rows upon rows of hollow-tubed teeth. His ten-inch talons clawed at the air. The sound he made ... I cannot even begin to describe the horror of it. It was as if thousands of animals were reaching out in pain, screaming from the deepest of abysses. But I continued with my mission. I* held the hollow tube in my hands above my head. I could see him contort as his spirit began to leave the body in which it was housed. As grey smoke left his body, I pointed the tube at him, continuing to chant the trapping spell.

He then yelled, "You will never see Robert again." And I hesitated, for just a second, but it was enough. The spirit, now in the form of smoke, did not go into the tube I had prepared. It instead flew from the room as I gave chase.

I was able to once again trap it, in the dental office. I am so thankful that I had the foresight to place trapping seals throughout the house. His spirit ended up inside my newly purchased suction straw. I quickly drew seals on it, trapping him inside.

Then I sat on the floor. My body was drained and exhausted. But I knew that I could not rest for long. I had much to accomplish if I was going to keep this evil thing trapped. The next thing I did was grab a sharp tool and carve the seals into the suction straw, trapping him for all eternity. I said a blessing over the straw, and then redrew the seals with my athame dipped in my own blood.

I carried it down to the root cellar. I will bury it, tomorrow, for now I must finally rest. I am exhausted beyond anything I have ever felt before.

Day 184

I got no sleep last night. Every time I started to fall asleep, a terrible humming sound entered my *brain. I'm sure it is from exhaustion; I will take a sleeping draught for tonight.*

*In the meantime, I need to go down to the cellar and bury that machine, so it can do evil no more.*

*And then I must advertise for a new dentist to take over this practice. It is time that I leave and never return.*

*Day 186*

*The buzzing sound won't stop. It now haunts me day and night. It is time that I leave and start my life anew. I shall place this book in the attic and pray that no one ever needs use of it. I wish luck to this world, for I now know that true evil does in fact exist.*

# DAVID

David dialed Susan's cell in a rage. She picked up after several rings, sounding sleep-addled.

"Hello?"

"Susan? Where are you?"

"Oh God, David. I'm so sorry. I can't come in."

"Now? Today?"

"Well, maybe for a few days."

"Seriously? Susan, you just came back after being gone for weeks and now you need a few days off? Great." David slammed down the phone, exhaled loudly, and stormed out of his office. His day had just become busier.

"Charlotte, where is today's schedule? Charlotte?" David said as he approached the receptionist's desk. David looked around the front of the office and realized that there was no sign of Charlotte—no coat, no purse, the morning's coffee had not been made. "Great," David muttered, "first no Susan, now no Charlotte."

He looked at Charlotte's desk and found the day's calendar. It was filled. Both David and Susan had full schedules. Now what was he going to do? If he cancelled on half of the scheduled patients, he could very well risk losing their business. He needed a better solution. He went back to his office and found the phone numbers of the partner candidates, the ones whom he had met with so far. It was time to give them a trial run—check out their skills not only as dentists, but their rapport with patients as well. With the day's workload, he needed the help.

David looked at the cards and dialed the number of his top choice, Dr. Rachel DeNeuve. She agreed to come in for the day, in hopes of gaining the partnership. David then called a local temp agency for a secretary for the day. Once that was settled, David went to prep the examination rooms and the procedure rooms for the day's patients.

The temp arrived just in time for the first patient's arrival and quickly began to admit them, placing them into exam rooms.

As David and Rachel worked on patients in need of fillings and various dental surgeries, the hygienists completed routine checkups. But still, the waiting room teemed with patients.

. . .

RIGHT BEFORE LEAVING FOR LUNCH, THE TEMP HAD FILLED all the patient rooms. As she walked back to the waiting room, grateful that David had told her to take her lunch hour now, she glanced down an unused, dark hallway. She turned down the hallway and found herself standing in front of a door, room number 5. She put her hand on the doorknob. She felt It—a low, pleasant thrum. The stress of the day began to fade away; a sensation of relief washed over her as she turned the knob and opened the door. She had never felt such a pleasurable sensation before. She entered the room as if she was walking on warm sand gently molding to her feet. The pinch of her high-heeled shoes faded away, her feet feeling as if she had had the greatest pedicure ever. She heard the quiet click of the door closing behind her, but she didn't bother to look. All she could sense was a perfect day—the warm sun cascading over her. She could smell the salt air as the sound of waves licking the shoreline numbed her thoughts. She sat in the chair, reaching over for the suction straw. As she placed it in her mouth, a small part of her brain tried to scream out, but it was too late and too quiet. She laid back, soaking up the sun's warmth as the machine drained her.

. . .

By two o'clock, David had realized that the temp was not returning from lunch. As soon as he had the chance, he planned on calling the agency so he could let them know how disappointed he was.

At the end of the day, David and Rachel closed the practice and left for the night. They had both decided that Rachel would return the next morning.

# ANNIE

ANNIE WOKE UP and reached over for Nathan, but found the bed empty. She looked over, noticed that Nathan's backpack was gone, and crawled out of bed. As she headed to her closet, she heard it—a low, slight thrum. She immediately knew that the machine was calling her; that she would need to go to It, or It would become agitated and the noise in her brain would become louder until she would not be able to stand it. She threw on some clothes and headed out to the dental practice.

When she arrived at the practice, she immediately knew to go to the back of the house and slide open the window to room 5. Grabbing the window sill, she pulled herself into the room. Annie stood frozen, her jaw agape. A mummified woman sat in the chair, the suction straw dangling from her lower lip.

Annie could tell that this victim had been a young woman and was dressed in professional clothing. Who was this? How did this happen? Why had she been summoned to dispose of this body? She quietly peered out of the room and realized that the office was empty; it must be before hours. How much time did she have before someone arrived?

Annie walked quietly to the cellar door and inserted the key she had found lying in the grass. She opened the door and walked down the stairs. Once at the bottom, she grabbed the shovel, found an open spot, and started to dig a new grave.

When she had finished digging, she returned upstairs to retrieve the body. She lifted it into her arms, thankful that the process had lightened the body's weight, and carried it down the stairs.

She carefully lowered it into the ground and began to cover it with dirt. She suddenly froze; did she hear something? She moved toward the door and opened it slightly. She noticed that the overhead lights had been turned on. The practice had opened while she was disposing of the body.

Her heart raced as she closed the door and quietly went back down the stairs. She finished burying the body, making sure the dirt was patted down.

She then crept back up the stairs and peered through a crack in the door. She had to find a way to get out of the building without anyone seeing her. How was she going to do that? If she was found, how would she explain her presence in the practice? She watched through the door's crack, waiting for her moment to escape.

As soon as it got quiet, she inched her way out of the cellar. She slowly moved against the wall, creeping toward room 5. Each time she heard a footfall or voice, she froze, catching her breath. As soon as she was confident that the person was not heading in her direction, she continued.

When she arrived at room 5 she opened the door, noticing its creak for the first time, and stepped inside.

Annie grabbed her backpack, which she had left under the window, and climbed out the window. She stealthily moved past the building and onto the street.

Looking around her, Annie headed back to campus and her dorm room.

Annie sat on her bed, wondering who the mummified body was and who had brought it to the machine in the first place. Why had she been summoned to clean up someone else's mess?

Shaking her head, Annie looked at the clock as she realized how hungry she had become. She glanced around and noticed that she had no food in her dorm room, so she picked up her ID card and headed down to the school's coffee shop for a sandwich.

# NATHAN

NATHAN GLANCED THOUGH the coffee shop window as he was walking to class. Inside he saw Annie sitting at a table, casually eating a grilled cheese sandwich. He put his hand on the door, ready to surprise her, when he saw his watch. He only had five minutes to get to class. Sighing, he removed his hand from the knob and headed to his chemistry lab.

He went from chemistry lab to criminology. But no matter how hard he tried, he just couldn't fully focus on the lectures. His mind kept wandering over the recent information they had gathered. He couldn't understand what was happening but more importantly, how he had gotten involved in not just a murder, but a supernatural serial killing spree. *Of course*, he thought, *how do I know, truly know, what is happening? I mean, I don't know these people. Maybe they're crazy. They could be making the whole thing up. But then, what was that sound? I know I heard it. It pulled me to itself. No, they are telling the truth. I just know it; I feel it.*

Nathan sat there, his mind reeling. He began to question his own sanity.

Suddenly he felt the urge to flee, to go home to his parents. He wanted to see his parents, to go back to the normalcy of his childhood. A time where killer machines were only found in horror movies or nightmares.

He ran across campus to his apartment and quickly packed a bag. He grabbed his emergency money as he ran out the door. He ran until he was standing, panting, in front to the ticket window of the bus depot. As he was ordering his ticket, he felt a presence in his mind. Someone, or something, was calling to him. He stood there, slack jawed. Was this it? *Is this what Charlotte and Dr. Andres hear?*

He stood there, frozen. Listening as the hum grew louder, beckoning him to come to the dental office. For the first time, he truly understood how Charlotte and Dr. Andres could fall under its influence so easily. Nathan suddenly realized that he had to stay; he had to help stop the machine. It had become an imperative.

He shouldered his backpack and walked out of the depot. He slowly turned right, exhaled, and walked back to campus. He had work to do. Nathan went to the campus library, logged on to a computer, and continued his search from the other day. There had to be a clue, a hint, about how to stop this, this evil, from continuing. And he had to find it, soon.

Nathan sat in front of the computer screen and stared at the blankness. He had no idea as to what he should look up or where to find any help. After staring for ten minutes, he decided to begin by finding more information on Lori Elizabeth. Maybe he would be able to figure out a solution. He knew it was a long shot, but he couldn't think of another solution. After Nathan had searched the internet for hours, the college's librarian suggested that he try the local library's microfiche machines and old newspaper room.

Nathan packed his papers into his backpack and headed into town. He walked to the town's library and approached the front desk.

"Hi, um, I'm looking for old newspaper articles from the late nineteen fifties through the early sixties."

"Any topic in particular?"

"Well, yes. I'm looking for information on the, um, the disappearance of Lori Elizabeth and the strange occurrences in her house."

"Okay. I don't know who that is, but if you have a date and a location, I may be able to help."

"Yeah, um, the summer of 1958 here in Philipsburg."

"Here? Well, then, it's the local paper that you want. Let's go back to the newspaper room and see what we can find. Unfortunately, the papers from back then are not in the computer." She led Nathan to a back room and then awkwardly pulled the large portfolio off the shelf. Opening it to the middle, she told Nathan that he should start there and then went back to the front desk, leaving Nathan alone in the dusty room.

Nathan began to gingerly look through the portfolio, scanning the text for any mention of Lori Elizabeth. He came to one of the articles he had found online and reread it, and then continued to scan the papers. A few papers later, he came to another article.

*The Chronicle August 6, 1958*

*Philipsburg*—*Of the twenty-five bodies that have been recovered from the cellar of the dental practice and home of Dr. Robert Elizabeth (deceased) and his wife, Lori, five have been positively identified. Police, with the help of a forensic specialist, used the victims' clothing as a means of identification. The bodies appeared to be drained of all liquids and were mummified beyond recognition. The identities of the rest of the victims remain a mystery.*

*Police have been unable to locate Lori Elizabeth and have yet to identify one of the mummified corpses as her. Using eyewitness accounts and a forensic artist's rendering, an all-points bulletin has been issued for the two men whom neighbors claim to have seen outside of the Elizabeth's residence.*

*Police are again asking that if anyone knows anything about the whereabouts of Lori Elizabeth, please contact them. Experts are still working on identifying the remaining mummies and are optimistic that they will be able to give a name to each.*

Nathan read the article through multiple times before he made a copy. As he waited for the copy, he began to wonder if any of Lori Elizabeth's neighbors could possibly still be alive. If so, would they remember anything useful? He picked up his copy and walked over to a computer. Using house numbers close to that of the dental practice, Nathan began to google addresses, looking for the names of the residents from the 1950s. After compiling his list of names, Nathan then set out to see if any of them were still alive.

After an extensive search, Nathan managed to locate two of the neighbors. Both were in their eighties now, but Nathan knew he had to be optimistic; he had to believe that he would find information he could use to help stop the machine.

He walked out of the library and headed to the first name on his list. His mind raced with questions. What would he ask them? Would they remember anything from so long ago?

Nathan stood outside the single-story building, staring at the front door. He had just realized that he didn't have a legitimate reason to visit the nursing home. He would need to find a reason for being there. He reached for his phone when her remembered what Susan had said. They were not to use their personal phones—leave no evidence that you are connected to any of this madness. He put his phone away and quickly turned around and headed back to the library. More research was needed.

Nathan sat in front of the computer screen once again. He searched for "Wedding Announcement for Robert Elizabeth." As the pages loaded, Nathan wrote questions—questions that he desperately needed answered—on a sheet of paper. He would spend his free time finding out the answers in the hope of learning how to stop the evil.

. . .

SUSAN SAT IN THE BACK BOOTH OF THE DINER, LORI Elizabeth's diary in her hand. She had read through it and was now taking notes on the spells and potions used in the rituals performed when conjuring the evil. She needed to find a counter spell, or at the very least garner a better understanding of the powers Lori Elizabeth had unleashed. She had made an appointment with a local psychic in the hopes that she would be able to make sense of Lori Elizabeth's tale.

Just as Susan was standing, getting ready to leave for her appointment, her cell phone rang, the screen stating the Nathan was calling.

"Nathan, are you okay?" Susan breathed.

"What? Yes, I'm fine. But I have found some very interesting stuff on Lori Elizabeth. Can we meet up?"

"Yes, let's do that. I have an interesting appointment to go to now, but let's meet in the diner in, say, four hours. Does that work?"

"Okay. I'm going to keep digging."

"See you then." Susan dropped her cell phone into her bag, left her hotel room, climbed into her car, and headed south, out of town. When Susan arrived at the psychic's, she felt herself growing nervous. She climbed out of her car and walked to the door, gently knocking. There was no response. She looked around and saw a small note on the ground in front of the door. Opening the note, Susan read,

> *Please go away. I will not, can not be part of the evil you face.*

Susan sighed as she walked away. She climbed into her car and slowly drove away, the note crumpled in her pocket.

. . .

CHARLOTTE LAY ON HER HOTEL BED, HER HANDS WRAPPED around her head. She could only make a small whimpering sound as she writhed in pain. The machine was calling her, more plaintively than ever before. She wasn't sure how much longer she would be able to withstand its call. She knew she had to resist, but it was getting harder each passing moment.

# HELEN

THE NURSING HOME sat on the corner of two residential streets. It was a large ranch-style building that stretched from one edge of the property to the next. The front was impeccably gardened, with red and white flowers littering the flower boxes positioned under each of the front windows. Hedges, immaculately manicured into rectangles of green leaves, ran the length of the sidewalk in front of the house. Two oak trees stood sentry on either side of the brick-paved front path. The building itself was an eggshell color with burgundy shutters and doors. A curved driveway of interlocking brick—a tessellation of reddish brown—only further enhanced the look of the place. The backyard, as seen from the side street, was a plethora of colors and smells arising from the gardens it contained. Nathan walked up the driveway, looking at the building as he planned his approach toward not only Helen McAdams but the nurses and possibly even the security guards.

Nathan walked into the nursing home's entrance and approached the front desk. The receptionist looked up. "Hi. How can I help you?"

"Hi. I'm here to see Helen McAdams."

"Is she a relative of yours?"

"Not exactly ... well, really not at all. Is there any way I can speak to her? It's really important."

"I'll have to check with her doctor. Please wait here."

"Okay," Nathan said, hopeful, as the receptionist walked away. *At least she didn't just kick me out; this is good.* The receptionist went through a series of locked doors and disappeared from his sight.

Nathan sat in the lobby, looking at the Norman Rockwell reprints hanging over the flowery wallpaper—large white roses cascading on a field of light brown, a color that Annie would probably call some fancy name, one he had never heard of himself. The Naugahyde-covered chairs moaned as he shifted his weight. He glanced at the titles on the magazines fanned out on the oval coffee table. They were the same titles that one would find in a doctor's office—innocuous periodicals meant to entertain but not inform.

He glanced at the analog clock on the wall and realized that he had been sitting, waiting, for over half an hour. *She's not coming back*, Nathan thought. *Another dead end.* Just as he stood to get ready to leave, the door opened and a woman in a white coat walked over.

"Excuse me, are you looking for Helen McAdams?"

"Erm, yes. Can I see her?"

"Well, first I need to know why. You're not a relative, so how do you know her?"

"My name is Nathan, and I'm a college student. I'm doing a research paper on the life of Lori Elizabeth—kind of an exposé on what happened at her husband's dental practice. Anyway, Helen McAdams was her neighbor during the time of the disappearances, and I was hoping that she might remember something from that time."

"Okay, I will bring you to her, but I will warn you that she gets confused frequently so her memory might not be as vivid as you are hoping. She has early onset dementia; from all accounts, she is having a lucid day today, so you may be in luck." She led Nathan down a hallway papered with the same floral print as the waiting room.

"I know this is a long shot but I'm hoping for a first-person account—something that will be more than just regurgitating newspaper articles."

The doctor smiled at Nathan, "Well here she is. Helen, this is the young man we talked about. He is here to talk to you. Can you talk to him?"

Helen smiled crookedly and said, "But of course I will. Sit, young man; let's chat."

Nathan sank into the overstuffed floral wing chair and smiled back at Helen. He cleared his throat. "First, I need to ask you, is it okay if I record this conversation so I can focus on you and not on taking notes?"

Helen nodded, "Of course. That'll be fine."

Nathan turned on his recorder. "I wanted to ask you about an old neighbor of yours, from when you were a child. Do you remember Lori Elizabeth? She lived in the house next door to yours."

"Now, which one? We had neighbors on both sides, you know."

"She lived in the large Victorian."

"They were all Victorians. It was an old street."

Chuckling to himself, Nathan replied, "Right. Of course. I don't know what color it was back then, but she and her husband ran a dental office out of their home."

She nodded. "Oh, you mean … " moving closer to Nathan, Helen whispered, "… the witch's house."

Nathan looked at her, shocked, "Well, yes, I guess one could call her that—Lori Elizabeth. What do you remember?"

Helen leaned her head back, staring at the ceiling, "A lot. I remember a lot. Although some of it seems to be a dream, or maybe more of a nightmare."

"Can you tell me what you remember? It's really important."

Helen sighed. "Well, let me see. Lori Elizabeth was a very interesting person. She ran a tea and candle shop out of their house." Leaning toward Nathan, Helen whispered covertly, "But I overheard my mother talking to some friends once. They referred to it as a witch shop." She then continued talking in a normal volume, "I wasn't allowed inside. Back then, children listened to their parents, so I never did go inside. But I saw who did and, well … " Helen again leaned forward and whispered, " … pretty much every woman in the neighborhood would sneak over there, but few of them would ever acknowledge it. They wouldn't even say hi to her; hell, they—my mother included—would turn their backs when they saw her coming down the street and then whisper horrible things about her. Even as a child I felt badly for her. But she never seemed lonely or upset about it; even when a neighbor would throw a party and she was the only house not invited she would smile. It was as if she knew some secret to happiness. Maybe she did; she was a witch, after all, maybe she had a magic potion." Helen smiled in a self-satisfied way.

"Really? Huh, I just assumed that she would be scary or at least mean. You know, the neighbor who would yell at all the kids to get off their lawn."

"Oh, no. When my mother was out, at the store or at a Tupperware party, I would sneak to the fence with the hope that she would be in her garden, and if she was, I would talk to her. She was very friendly and nice. She would tell me stories of her childhood on the farm, all the things she learned about plants and medicine. She showed me how to identify different herbs and how they helped you heal. You know, I still use some of her cures. At least I did until I came here. They work, and why pay the pharmaceutical companies when I can just as easily pick up some teas or herbs and feel better, just as effectively as modern medicine? Anyway, I liked her." Chuckling to herself, Helen grinned as if sharing a secret. "Oh, and her clothes. Now of course, when she helped her husband—she was a certified dental assistant, after all—she wore respectable clothing, but when she was in her shop or just out in the neighborhood, she wore the most outrageous outfits. Nothing like any other women in the area. I'm not even sure if the other women would have worn her clothes as a costume."

"How did she dress?" Nathan asked.

Once again Helen smiled. "You have to remember that she was much younger than the other women on our block. Oh, well, the other women called them Gypsy clothes. They said it with disdain, but I thought they were beautiful. Long flowing dresses with so many shiny bracelets. Oh, and she had pierced ears and wore large hoop earrings. She was so colorful and sparkly—just how a young girl dreams of dressing. She seemed to float through life. She was magical. But then … " Helen grew sad, her voice taking on a forlorn quality, "… her husband died, and she changed. It was as if she lost her spark when he died. I've lost a husband, and I loved my husband, but her grief—well, it was something I have, thankfully, never known. It was as if she died with him. She just, well … it seemed like she just disappeared for a while. I mean, no one saw her at all. There was some gossip that she may have hurt herself so she could be with him; others thought that maybe she had left—gone back to the family farm or something. Then a few months later, she reemerged. She was reopening his practice and her tea and candle shop. But she was not the same woman. She didn't smile easily, and when she did it seemed, well, it seemed strained."

Helen stopped talking for a minute as if lost in her memories. Exhaling loudly, she ran her hands over her face and continued. "It wasn't too much longer before her friends, I guess they would be her coven, began to come around. I mean, they were always in the area, but now they were there all the time. She also began to take small trips—gone for a day or two and then she would return invigorated. But again, it lasted only a day, and the sadness, the overwhelming grief would return."

Nathan interrupted, "Do you remember who any of the women from her coven were?"

"Hmm." Helen thought for a few minutes, "I don't, except for maybe one. I'm not sure, but I think the woman who owned the candy shop was one of them. I remember a very tall woman, and she was tall. Definitely over six feet tall. Which was unheard of for a woman."

"Her name? Do you remember her name?" Nathan could hear the frantic tone in his voice. He took a breath. He knew that he could not alarm Helen. She had to believe that this was a school paper, and not something else.

"I don't. I'm not even sure I ever knew her name, but her shop was called Sweet Tooth, if that helps at all. I do remember that on more than one occasion her shop, I mean Lori Elizabeth's shop, was open well past midnight. Sometimes the coven was there, but a few times they weren't. I saw a man leave once. All I remember was that he was small of stature and, well, something about him creeped me out. I had nightmares after I saw him—I mean sweat-drenched, screaming-out nightmares for weeks. It was strange because I was never prone to nightmares before that, but for a few months I had one or two a night. And then just as suddenly they stopped. I haven't had one since—not like those, anyway." Helen yawned and stretched her back.

A nurse walked over. "It's time to go, Helen. You have your art class now."

Helen stood to leave. She turned to Nathan. "If I remember anything else, I'll call you."

Nathan wrote his number on a slip of paper, "Thank you Helen. You've been a great help." He shook her hand and left the nursing home. He had more research to do, but first he had to meet Susan and Charlotte at the diner so he could tell them what he had learned.

# CHARLOTTE

Charlotte was sitting, knees drawn to her chin, in the corner of her hotel room. She was trembling, drenched in sweat. She tried to get up when she heard a knock on the door, but was unable to. The room started spinning around her as if she was on an amusement park ride. Someone knocked on the door again. As Charlotte crawled across the rug toward the door, she thought that the knocks sounded frantic, almost in hurried desperation. Charlotte made it to the door, pulled herself into a standing position, and opened it.

"My God, Charlotte. Are you okay?" Susan exclaimed.

"No; I don't know how much longer I can do this." Charlotte swayed, and Susan reached out to stabilize her. "I don't know how much longer I can resist. How do you do it? How are you functioning?" Tears rolled down Charlotte's face.

"I don't know, except I left the area. I went far away from here and broke its connection. Maybe that's why. Nathan is on his way to the diner. Let's get some coffee and food. We will find a way to help you. You just have to stay strong."

Charlotte nodded, smiling slightly. "Right, stay strong."

"Let's get you cleaned up. I bet some food will help you feel better."

Charlotte tentatively stood and headed toward the bathroom. She turned on the hot water and gingerly stepped out of her pajamas. She stood under the hot stream of water, her eyes closed. She could still feel the slight pulse in the back of her skull. She turned around, letting the water cascade over her face, trying to block the sound.

She stepped out of the shower, wrapping the towel around herself. She quickly dried off and got dressed. The more she thought about having some food and coffee the hungrier she became. She grabbed her purse and the hotel room key, closed the door, and followed Susan to the diner.

When they entered the diner, they both scanned the room, looking for Nathan. They located him in the back corner booth and sat down across from him in the back corner booth. Charlotte sighed. "Have either of you guys found out anything new?"

Nathan started. "I talked to the next-door neighbor of Lori Elizabeth. She remembered the identity of one of the women from Lori Elizabeth's coven, hopefully one of the witches who helped her try to find Robert. I'm going to spend this afternoon meeting with her. Hopefully, she will remember who the others were. One of them might be able to help us; at the very least, we might gain more insight into how this happened. Susan, can I borrow the journal? Seeing the spells that they used may help jog her memory."

Susan looked at Nathan. An unwillingness to give the book to him grew inside of her.

Susan reached into her bag and carefully removed the journal. The feel of its leather cover filled her with a level of joy that seemed unnatural. "Maybe we can make copies of the pages." She motioned for the waitress to come to their table, allowing for Charlotte to order a cup of coffee and some eggs and for her to ask for the nearest copy place.

As soon as the waitress left, Susan looked at Nathan. "Okay. I'm going to go make two copies of the journal. One for you to use with the witches and one for Charlotte to study. The diary may still give us clues not only to what is happening but also to how to stop it." Susan stood and left the diner.

"Sounds like we have a plan." Nathan picked up his fork and was about to take a bite of his pancakes when he stopped and looked at Charlotte, "Um, are you okay?"

"What? Err, yeah, I guess." Charlotte stammered as she reached for her eggs.

"You don't look okay," Nathan responded. "I mean like ... I'm sorry, but you are really pale, and you look so tired, so amazingly tired."

Charlotte slowly nodded. "I am." Then she whispered, "It's the machine. It keeps talking to me, humming in my brain. I can't sleep or eat or anything. This is the first food I've eaten in days." Charlotte bit into her eggs and began to chew.

# ANNIE

Annie lay sprawled on her dorm bed, her eyelids fluttering. She moaned, drawing her knees into her chest. It had been calling her, screaming into her consciousness. It was hungry; It was begging her for Its food.

"I don't know how," Annie mentally cried. "How do I get into the office with another person there? How? Please, I want to help you, but I don't know what to do."

Suddenly, her mind went silent. For the first time in weeks, she couldn't hear the machine's pleas, whines, or demands for food. Her head instantly stopped hurting. *It's over*, she thought, and she fell asleep.

When she awoke, it was dark outside. She exhaled deeply and began to roll over in her bed. She couldn't. Quickly she realized that she wasn't in her bed, she was with It—the machine. She was sitting, reclined, in the dental chair. She tried to stand but was not able to move her legs. Panic rose in her. Her brain pushed for her legs to move, but she could not control any part of herself. Her body was frozen.

Her heart raced faster with each passing second. Her body became covered with sweat, the sting of it burning her eyes. She was unable to wipe it away, unable to break whatever was holding her down. She could feel that she wasn't strapped to the chair; it was as if she had been immobilized—perhaps by a drug. She tried to slow down her breathing, forcing herself to take deep breaths, slower and deeper each time. She could feel it working; her heart slowed down as she gained more control.

Moving only her eyes, she scanned the dark room, looking for a glimpse of light on which to focus. But she couldn't see any. She continued to breathe slowly, trying to get her heart to beat slower. As she worked on her breathing she began to listen for sounds, any indication of life outside this room. But she heard nothing save the pulsing of her own heart. She tried to open her mouth, tried to scream for help, but she was unable to move her jaw.

She waited. She knew that the machine had brought her here for a reason, although she didn't know how. She had no memory of coming to the office.

She remembered the silence and then falling asleep. She just didn't know how she had ended up in this chair.

Then she heard It. A slow pulsing sound began to play in her brain. It was very subtle at first, almost imperceptible. But she knew It would grow louder, more pronounced. She knew It would, somehow, convince her to put It in her mouth; she knew she was going to be Its next meal. She knew how horribly she was going to die.

"Please, no," she thought, "Just tell me how to bring you food. How can I get people in here? Please don't kill me."

The pulsing changed tempo and pitch suddenly. The machine had a plan. It gave the plan to Annie slowly and meticulously. She now understood what she had to do; she knew how to bring It Its food.

And then she was able to move again. At first it was just her fingers and toes, but then she was able to shift herself out of the chair, climb out the window, and began to equip herself for the plan. Tomorrow she would go hunting.

# NATHAN

Nathan walked up to the large red door, reached out his hand, and grasped the lion-head knocker. He raised the knocker and brought it down onto the door. He could hear the sound resonate throughout the house. He stood and waited.

Within a short time, he heard footsteps on a hard floor coming toward the door. The door swung open and there stood Barbara. She was a stately, tall woman. An obvious elegance hung around her. Even well into her eighties, Barbara stood with perfectly erect posture. She graciously welcomed Nathan into her grand home. Her house had been built at the turn of the last century but had been obviously updated in the subsequent years. The foyer was large and open to the floor above it. A beautifully carved banister wound itself up the side wall, coiling around the hardwood staircase. Nathan stepped onto the white marble floor and carefully slipped off his sneakers. He followed Barbara into the sitting room and sat on the settee where she gestured.

Barbara poured him a cup of tea from a gleaming silver teapot and handed him the porcelain cup. "Sugar and cream are on the tray. Please help yourself."

"Thank you"

Barbara made her own cup of tea, whispered a prayer over it, and took a sip. Smiling, she sat back and looked at Nathan. "So, how can I help you?"

Swallowing his tea, Nathan took out his recorder and his copy of the journal. He looked at Barbara and began, "Well, first, do you mind if I record this conversation? It would ensure that I am as accurate as possible."

"Well, of course, darling. Record away," Barbara stated, moving her hand in the air dismissively.

"As I told you on the phone, I am doing a college project on the disappearance of Lori Elizabeth. I've been researching the events that led up to her disappearance, from the death of her husband to the discovery of the mummified corpses in their basement."

Barbara snuffed in disgust, "Awful business, that was. Just awful."

"Yes, it was. Before I ask anything, do you have any ideas or theories as to what happened?"

"Well, not for the bodies. I don't know what that was about, unless … " Barbara drifted off, staring out the floor-to-ceiling window.

Nathan turned to look too. "Unless what?"

"Unless she did it. I don't know. Could she have conjured up something? I don't remember her being that powerful of a witch. And how would that have brought Robert back to her? I don't know. We tried everything that we knew." Shaking her head, Barbara continued, "We were so young and naïve, so innocent. We were messing with things that we did not, could not, possibly understand. Maybe she went too far. We were just five children, really; I think the oldest of us was twenty-six. But oh," Barbara sighed, "we thought we knew so much, enough to mess with the natural order of life. Trying to resurrect the dead—we were fools."

"Who else was there? Do you remember the rest of the coven?"

"Of course I do. Let's see. There were six of us in total—Lori Elizabeth, myself, Edith Pilaffe, Judy Cross, Patricia Scotts, and Sheri Duvane. Now let me think—Edith died young, in her thirties. Judy died just a few years ago. But Patricia and Sheri are still with us. At least they were last week. At our age, a week ... well, can make the difference. Anyway, I saw them both at the club. I could call them, see if they can meet with us. Would that help you?"

Nathan looked at her with disbelief. Could he be this lucky? To be able to talk with them all, together and now? "That would be great."

Barbara stood and left the room. Nathan heard her dialing a phone, talking, and then dialing again. She came back into the room. "They will be here tonight for dinner. Join us then, say six o'clock. Bring your recorder." Barbara moved to exit the room, with Nathan following. "I look forward to seeing you tonight," Barbara said as she closed the door behind him. Nathan walked down to the street. He looked back at the house and saw Barbara watching him from behind a curtain in the front window.

Nathan stepped into his roommate's car (which he frequently borrowed) and drove back to campus. He ran to Annie's dorm room, grabbed his books, and left for his afternoon class. He sat in class, trying to focus on the day's lecture. He found his mind constantly drifting to his dinner tonight. He kept wondering what the women would be like. What new information might he discover? He left class at the end of the lecture, realizing that he had not truly heard anything his professor had said. He sighed and went to his next class, determined to pay attention in this one.

His next lecture was his criminal justice class. His professor was teaching about serial killers and the pathology behind them. He sat in the front row, center seat; he had to force himself to focus and take notes. His mind began to wander again. He wondered how Susan or Charlotte fit the description the professor was teaching; would they be considered serial killers? They both had been involved in the deaths of multiple people, even if they didn't do the actual killing themselves. How would society view them—as killers or as the unwitting victims of a maniacal machine? But were they truly unwitting, and why didn't he have the same affliction? He'd heard the machine, too, and yet felt no need to "feed the machine." Why? What made him different; what allowed him to resist the call?

By the time class ended, Nathan had heard maybe a third of the day's lecture. He would have to borrow notes from a classmate again.

Nathan headed back to his apartment and began to get ready for dinner. He showered—for what seemed to be the first time in days, maybe weeks—and changed into clean clothes. He then headed off campus and returned to Barbara's home.

Nathan pulled up, parked his roommate's car, and then retraced his steps back up to Barbara's front door. He knocked on the door and waited for Barbara to answer. Barbara ushered Nathan into the house and down to the dining room, where the other women were sitting. Each turned her head and smiled as Nathan entered the room. Barbara gestured toward a chair and then moved to the head of the table.

Nathan sat in the appointed seat and looked around the cavernous room. The walls were covered in a cornflower-blue paper on the top, with white wainscoting on the bottom half. The furniture was a dark wood, obviously expensive. On the table lay an elegant china set with sterling silver flatware framing it. Nathan looked at it all, thinking that this room alone would finance his education. He reached for a crystal goblet filled with water and took a sip.

"Okay, everyone. Let me first make introductions; then we can reminisce about the past in a few minutes. Sheri and Patricia, this is Nathan. He is researching, well, Lori Elizabeth. I was hoping that we could tell him some of our stories about her, especially around the time of her disappearance. He is going to record us. It will make it easier for him to recall information for his paper. So," Barbara smiled, "who would like to begin?"

Sheri and Patricia looked at each other for a moment and then at Nathan. "Well, I haven't thought of that time in a long while," Patricia began, "but let me see what I remember. Lori Elizabeth was one of the kindest souls I had ever met. She was so generous with herself and her time. Do you ladies remember when Edith had her first baby? Lori Elizabeth was a treasure to her. You see, Nathan, Edith's husband was in Korea, a medic there I believe. Anyway, Edith had the baby near her parent's home in, now where was it, I believe Minnesota. So, Edith moved here with her husband and their new baby and then he was sent overseas to Korea. We had just met her—Edith, that is—and what does Lori do? She knits and sews clothes for the new baby, helps to watch the baby when Edith needed to sleep or just needed a break. That was Lori—selfless. Always concerned for others."

"If Lori had been around when Edith died, the baby wouldn't have been put up for adoption—that is a guarantee. She would have taken her in. No questions asked."

"Wait," Nathan interrupted. "What about Edith's husband?"

"Oh," Patricia continued, "He died. He came home for furlough, what was it, about a month? Anyway, when he went back to Korea, well, if Edith wasn't pregnant again. He died a few months later, shot while trying to rescue some injured men. Edith was inconsolable for a while. But we all chipped in to help her, and she rallied herself for the sake of her children." A tear rolled down Patricia's face. "But poor Edith, she died having that baby. The poor baby," Patricia sighed, "he didn't make it either. Eclampsia. It was awful. Her daughter was adopted, a nice family from Northvale, I believe."

"Northvale?" Nathan asked. "I think my mom grew up in Northvale—in fact, she was also adopted. That's strange." Before Patricia could continue, he hastily added, "I thought there were six of you, including Lori Elizabeth?"

"Yes. We lost Poor Edith long ago and then Judy, oh what, about a decade ago." The three women became quiet. "Judy was an amazing, strong woman," Sheri said. "She was a fabulous artist. That's a picture of hers over the buffet. She ran a local art gallery for at least forty years. It was so sad to see it shuttered right after her funeral.

"She had no family to take it over?" Nathan asked.

"Just more sadness. She had a daughter. Humff, so uptight that one was. She never knew how to love life, how to embrace the beauty."

"So much like her father. I've never been so happy to see a marriage end. He just sucked all the joy out of a room." Patricia interjected as Sheri and Barbara nodded.

Sheri continued almost in a whisper, as if what she was about to confide was a secret instead of known to the other two women. "Remember how happy Judy was the morning after Victoria stayed out all night? She must have called me by ten that morning. It seems that she came home in the wee hours of the morning with her hair and clothes disheveled. Judy was ecstatic. Her daughter was finally having fun. Six weeks later, she disappeared. Judy never saw her again. She was devastated. Victoria had spent any free time she had in church during the last six weeks and then left. Judy must have cried trillions of tears over the years for that girl."

The women grew quiet as they ate their meal. Nathan wasn't sure if it was out of sadness or because they were comfortable enough with each other that they didn't need to talk.

When they had finished with the main course, they cleared the table and then sat back down. "But you want to know about before Lori disappeared. Are there any specific times that you are interested in knowing?"

"Well, actually I was interested in the witchcraft part."

"Wiccan. We were Wiccan. Some of us still are practicing," Sheri corrected.

"Sorry, but you see, that's the problem. I don't know much about this stuff, and I would like to better understand it, so I can present a clearer picture and provide a more sophisticated analysis of the events. I really need to get a good grade on this; it's critical."

"Okay, well we were a—I guess it could be called a coven, but we didn't think about it that way, at least not at first. We were just a group of friends who had similar interests. I never considered us a coven until after Robert died. That is when we really began to use our abilities for something other than helping others—mainly through the use of healing herbs. But after Robert died, we began to experiment with other powers. We began to study and search for ways to contact the dead beyond the usual séances." Sheri picked up a piece of strawberry pie with a dollop of whipped cream and began to chew. She nodded to Patricia.

"Let me think," Patricia began. "I know that I focused on which herbs could enhance powers and could be used to contact the dead. Edith was looking into stones and gems."

Barbara interjected, "I was charged with getting the supplies. Whatever we found out we needed, I went out to procure it. I must have visited dozens of shops over those months. I spent a fortune on herbs and spices, plus the stones and gems. But we would have moved the earth if we thought it would have helped Lori. She wouldn't have hesitated to do that for any one of us."

As the women continued eating their desserts, Nathan inquired, "Do any of you remember the two men who helped Lori? I believe that one of them may have been a ceremonial priest?"

Barbara and Patricia glanced at each other with a look of disbelief, "A ceremonial priest?" Barbara asked. "What was she thinking? Are you sure? Where did you get that information? Patricia, did you know about this?" Patricia shook her head.

Sheri looked down at her food for a minute and then audibly sighed. "She told me that she had met him while shopping at a store out of state. He had given her some new ideas to try and then stayed in contact."

Barbara and Patricia stared at Sheri. Patricia stammered, "Why didn't we know? Why was this kept from us?"

"Lori wasn't sure how she felt about it and, well, she didn't want to get us involved in case things went wrong. I found out by mistake. I overheard her talking to someone late one night. I had gone over, it must have been after midnight, to check on her. She had been having a particularly rough time, what with all the failures in trying to contact Robert, and I was worried about her. Anyway, I heard her talking to someone in her shop. I waited until he left and then went in to speak to her."

Nathan was confused. Nowhere in the journal did Lori mention that Sheri had paid her a visit during the night, nor did she mention that Sheri knew about the ceremonial priest. Why did she leave that out of her story? "What did she tell you? What about the second man? Did she tell you about him too?"

"A second man? No, I never heard about a second man. How do you know about a second man?"

"Full disclosure—I am in possession of a copy of Lori Elizabeth's journal. The first man, the ceremonial priest, brought another man to see her. He, the second man, promised to reunite her with Robert. She later regretted her arrangement with him, but it was too late."

"Seems like you may know more than we do. Why did you need our help?" Patricia asked.

"I want to know some of the background information. To try to understand how she did it, and why."

"Well, the why is easy," Barbara said. "She was desperate to get Robert back. I know that lots of women have lost their husbands—hell, I've lost three of them. But this was different. It was as if she had stopped being able to function. I don't want to say that she loved her husband more than the rest of the widows in the world, but her reaction was the most intense I have ever seen."

Patricia and Sheri nodded as Barbara spoke. Sheri added, "I loved Lori—we all did—but she was, well, almost unstable, maybe even insane with grief."

"Um, can we see it?" Patricia asked.

"What?" Nathan responded.

"The journal. Can we see the journal? Maybe it will jar a memory. Please."

Nathan nodded as he pulled out his copy and laid it on the table. Patricia reached for it and began to read it aloud to the others. She hesitated only when Barbara and the others cleared the dessert dishes and brought out decaf coffee. It was almost midnight when she had finished reading. Nathan looked at the three women. Each face glistened with tears for the friend who had been so tormented, their eyes showing the dismay they felt over the distress that had plagued her, that caused their Lori—their sweet, giving friend—to unleash such an unnatural horror.

"Where did you find this? Is this why you are interested in Lori Elizabeth?"

"Umm, well, a friend found it. I'm not sure where exactly."

"Nathan, what is really going on? What class are you writing this paper for? Tell us the truth."

"I can't, not yet. But I will soon. We may need your help; are you willing to help us?"

"Of course! At least, I am. I can't speak for the others," Barbara replied, looking at Sheri and Patricia pointedly.

Sheri and Patricia looked at each other and then at Nathan. Sighing, Sheri relied, "We will help. Remember, we are not as young as we would like. But I'm sure we can be used for something."

Nathan thanked Barbara for the meal and then thanked the women for their promise of help. He climbed into his borrowed car and pulled away from the house. As he wove through the dark streets, he played the recording, listening to the conversation again, trying to find anything that could help them. When heard that at least Sheri was still a practicing Wiccan, he began to formulate an idea. Maybe she could be a good resource for him; maybe she would know how to stop the machine. Maybe she would be able to find the spell needed to end this nightmare for them. He had her contact information. After he spoke to Charlotte and Susan, he would call her. Maybe set up a meeting between Sheri and the others. Between them, maybe—just maybe—they would be able to destroy the machine, finish what Lori Elizabeth had tried but failed to do.

. . .

NATHAN AROSE THE NEXT MORNING, DETERMINED TO FIND out more information about Lori Elizabeth. He took out his notes and located the name of another woman who grew up on the same street as Helen. He was going to visit her. As he climbed into his roommate's car, he wondered if Sarah, this woman who knew Lori Elizabeth, would remember her in the same way as Helen.

He pulled up in front of a small cottage. Its postage-stamp yard was covered with flowers, interspersed with bird feeders and yard decorations. In the middle of the yard stood a bistro table with two ornate chairs. In the center of the table sat a small floral teapot.

Nathan walked up a slate walkway to the yellow door. He raised his hand and knocked soundly on the door.

The door creaked open. Nathan smiled at the small, plump woman who was standing before him.

"Hello," she tentatively said, "How can I help you?"

"Hi, my name is Nathan. I'm a student at the University; I'm researching and writing a paper on the disappearance of Lori Elizabeth. During my research, I found that you once lived on the same street as Lori, at the time of her disappearance."

"Why, yes, I did."

"I was wondering what you remember about her and if you are willing to share any memories you may have of her."

"Of course, dear. I'll tell you what, my house is a mess. Why don't I meet you in the garden, there. Go sit and I'll be right out."

Nathan looked over at the bistro table, nodded his assent. He walked over to the table, took out his phone and notebooks, and readied himself for the interview.

Sarah appeared, carrying a tray of cookies, a teapot, and two teacups. She placed the tray on the table and sat down opposite Nathan.

Nathan held up his phone, asking, "Is it okay if I record our conversation? It would make it easier if I don't have to focus on taking accurate notes."

"Not a problem. Now, you wanted to know about Lori Elizabeth. I do remember her from when I was a girl. She was a larger-than-normal person on our block. Of course, I don't mean her size; she was physically rather small. But she ... her spirit was so large, she filled a room by herself. I can still vividly see her walking down the street, her clothes flowing around her. She was an abnormality in our town. No other married women wore her hair down, flowing in the air, or clothes that floated around her. She was a free spirit, before anyone knew what that meant. But even with all of her, um ... how do I put this ... all her flamboyance, she was well-liked."

"I spoke to another woman who grew up next door to her; she said that most of the women in the neighborhood wouldn't speak to her in public but would visit her shop alone. Is that what you remember as well?"

"Yes and no. It depended on the woman and her need for, hmmm, respectability. My mother didn't care about others' opinions very much, so she did speak to her in public. She also took me to her shop with her regularly. Thinking about it now as an adult, my mother was really brave. It was definitely social suicide—well maybe not suicide, but not recommended—to speak to her in public."

"You went to her shop? What was that like?"

"It was wonderful. I most remember the smells. Such wonderful smells—teas, herbs, and candles all mingling together. The colors, too. She must have had a candle in every conceivable color lining one wall of the shop. She also had a gift, a knack, for knowing exactly what a client needed. She knew what color candle would help you or what kind of tea you should drink to fix whatever was bothering you. And she was right, always right. My mother left with exactly what she needed every time—not always what she came in for but what she needed. Lori Elizabeth was truly gifted."

"What was she like, though, as a person?"

"Oh, she was kind, gentle, with laughing eyes and quick to smile. She was nothing but kind to me, loving even. I was so sad, as sad as a child can be for someone else's suffering, when her husband died. She just seemed so deflated, like the light that had shone so brightly in her had died with him. My mom thought that perhaps he'd put the light in her to begin with, so when he died, he took it with him."

"Do you remember anything strange happening right before she disappeared?"

"Her friends, five women, came by more, especially at night. And then there were the two strange men. They only came at night, late at night. There was something about them that scared me as a child, just made me uncomfortable. The first time I saw the small man I had nightmares for a week. He didn't look scary, but he just ... I don't know how to describe it; he terrified me. It was like I was looking at evil. I still don't like thinking about him."

"Have you felt that way any other time?"

Sarah thought about her answer while nibbling on a cookie, "Yes. One other time. I needed to have some dental work done. I made an appointment with a new practice; it was in Lori Elizabeth's old house. I got as far as the lobby, and there it was. That feeling, like I was gazing upon evil incarnate. I fled the building and found another dentist. I'm sure it was just memories flooding back but it felt so real. I won't even walk down that street. There are always ways around it—just may take a little longer, but I'll spend the time if it means that I can avoid that evil feeling."

"Is there anything else you remember?"

"Not right now, but if you give me your number, I'll let you know if any memories come back to me." Sarah stood, placed her tea set onto the tray. She put the slip of paper with Nathan's phone number on it into her front pocket and carried everything into the house.

Nathan returned to his car and drove back to his apartment. He needed to talk to Susan, Charlotte, and the others. Sarah had seen the demon; she'd felt his presence. He needed to know if she was safe.

# CHARLOTTE

Charlotte had packed her bags and was getting ready to leave the area. She wasn't sure how long she would be gone, but it had to be long enough to break the hold the machine had on her. She left the hotel and stepped into her car, grateful that Nathan had picked it up for her the day before.

She had never been on the campus, but somehow, she knew exactly where she needed to go. She parked her car and climbed the steps that led to a dorm. She waited outside until she saw a group of college-aged kids walk toward the door. She quickly walked over and slid through the door as they entered the dorm. She went up four flights of steps. She tentatively opened the door and then walked down the hallway to room 407. She reached into her purse and removed her keychain. She slid a key off and slid it under the door. She then walked back down the stairs and strolled out of the building. She returned to her car and left campus.

She drove. Through the night and the next day. She didn't stop until the screaming in her brain had turned to a pulse. She ate a burger and drove more. Soon the pulse disappeared, and her brain was quiet. Charlotte had no idea where she was, and she didn't care. It was quiet. Now she had to wait for it to forget about her. She found a hotel, booked a room, and settled in for the week.

As soon as she stepped out of the shower, she took her phone off the charger and dialed Susan's number.

"Hi, Susan. Just wanted to let you know that I'm far enough away. I don't hear It calling anymore. It's actually kinda weird—I haven't been alone in such a long time that I don't know how to react. But it is nice and quiet. Anyway, I'll let you know when I'm heading back. I have my cell phone turned on."

She left her room and headed to the lobby to find out if there was a place to get food nearby, preferably something hot.

# ANNIE

ANNIE RETURNED TO her dorm room, exhausted. She had planned on going to her psychology lecture that afternoon but now she wasn't sure if she would be able to stay awake through it. She was determined to go to the lecture. She grabbed her books, which were sitting on the floor atop her braided rag rug. She saw something metallic shining on the floor. She reached over and picked up the errant key. She realized that she had never seen this key before, it must have wound up under her door by accident. She left her room and walked to her nearest neighbor. As she raised her hand to knock on the door, a thought entered her mind.

She instantly knew what this key was for and why she had it. She quickly dropped it into her pocket and headed to her psych lecture. The professor stood in front of the class, his arms resting on his podium. He had pushed his shirt sleeves above his elbows and had loosened the knot in his tie. His jacket lay askew on a small table where he kept papers that his teaching assistant would hand back at the end of the night's lecture.

He stared intensely at his captive audience, picked up the remote for the slide show, clicked the button, and began the lecture with a picture of a woman in bondage. Annie had forgotten that this night's lecture was on sexual mores.

As she sat, diligently taking notes, she could hear someone behind her whispering to others around him. At first, she couldn't make out what was being said, but eventually she heard the misogynistic comments. She turned around, along with at least half a dozen other women, and stared at the man. He just smiled and then jammed his tongue into the inside of his cheek.

Annie turned back around, red-faced. Just then she began to hear the machine. It started as a pulsing but quickly escalated to a throbbing sensation. Annie could no longer focus on anything but the call of the machine. It was pleading for her to bring It food, threatening her if she did not comply. Annie stood to leave at the end of the lecture and began to walk out the door.

She suddenly felt a hand squeeze her shoulder as a deep voice whispered huskily, "What's wrong, baby? You didn't like my joke?"

She turned her head and looked at the face, maybe ten inches from hers. She moved away as quickly as she could. She found herself fleeing through a throng of students, weaving through them as if she was moving through a crowded dance floor. As she escaped the crowd, she looked behind her. No one was following her. The machine was screaming, and she was not able to block It from her mind.

She hurried toward the dental practice, the newfound key in her pocket. She scoured the streets, looking for someone, anyone, whom she could feed to the machine. She saw many people, but no one who was right for her needs. After arriving at the dental practice, she moved to the back of the building and waited for the doctors to leave. The sun went down as she sat there, reading through her textbook. She would have to go hunting now; she had to find someone. She crept out of her hiding spot and walked down the street.

She would continue this ritual of hunting for someone, anyone to feed to the machine. She didn't care who she took to It as long as she was able to bring It food, to lessen Its cries. Then one night, as she walked the darkened streets, she turned a corner and headed down the next block. As she walked past a diner, she heard a voice, "Hey, look, its that girl from class."

"Just leave her alone, Jared," his friend said, and started to walk in the opposite direction from Annie. But Jared couldn't stop. He followed her down the street, subjecting her to his sexual come-ons and harassment. Annie's pulse quickened. She wondered if he was planning on attacking her and how would she react if he did. She made a mental note of what she had in her bag, trying to decide what she could use as a weapon, how she could defend herself.

Annie imagined what horrors he could visit upon her. She pictured him violently raping her, pushing her to the ground as he tore off her clothing. She wondered if he had a weapon. She saw him slamming into her, hurting her in ways that she was unable to truly comprehend. She felt terrifying fear for the first time since her father died and she had found herself alone and homeless. Panic was rising in her, threatening to drown her in fear. Then the machine took over. Annie's fear dissipated as the machine buzzed gently in her head, calming her, giving her strength that she did not normally have.

As she moved down the street, she realized that she was leading him to the dental practice, the place where she had brought others before; she believed that she had fed the machine five times, including Lyra. This would be her sixth meal. She continued walking until she came to the practice. Using the key she'd found on her dorm floor, she unlocked the front door.

She left the door open and went inside. She continued through the lobby, past reception, and down the hallway to room 5. She turned the doorknob and found the door was locked. Panic rose in her, but she suddenly, inexplicitly knew where to find the key. She backtracked to reception, opened Charlotte's desk, and removed a key. She could see, from the corner of her eye, that Jared was standing in the dark lobby. She then returned to the hallway and walked back to room 5. She could hear soft footfalls following her. She entered room 5 and walked to the window.

She stared out the window, listening as Jared entered the room.

. . .

JARED SAW ANNIE STANDING IN THE WINDOW. He approached her but suddenly felt a compulsion to sit in the examination chair. He couldn't understand why, but he needed to sit there. He sat. He felt the overwhelming need to place the suction straw in his mouth. He reached for It and placed It in his mouth.

Annie turned around, looked at Jared, and smiled. He panicked as he felt the suction straw begin the process of dehydrating him. His brain screamed for him to remove the straw, but he was unable to move. He was paralyzed. He looked at Annie, his eyes pleading for help, but she just smiled at him and walked out of the room. "I'll be back later." Annie closed the door as Jared realized he was dying.

Jared could feel himself becoming dizzy and light-headed. His thoughts were becoming muddled; they dulled so much that he was unable to recall the most basic facts. He sat there as his mouth grew cottony and his lips cracked. His tongue swelled and his eyes started to blink compulsively, attempting, but failing, to create tears. He could feel his nasal passageways and cavities become dry and itchy. Slowly the feeling travelled down his body. His lungs struggled to draw in oxygen as each of his organs shut down and then atrophied and died. Jared died, not understanding what was happening or why. He died knowing only fear.

# SUSAN

Susan left Charlotte and Nathan eating in the diner as she headed two blocks away to a place where she could make copies of the journal. As she was walking, she began to formulate a theory in her mind. Perhaps the fact that Charlotte was suffering so much while she wasn't had to do with the fact that she had left town. She left the area and went far enough away that the machine was unable to contact her anymore. Maybe the machine had a radius in which it could summon its victims, and she had in fact moved beyond its reach. If that was true, then perhaps Charlotte could go far enough away to break its bond with her, thus freeing herself from its grasp.

Susan entered the storefront convinced that this was the solution— they had to get Charlotte out from under its power or risk losing her to its evilness. And they needed all the manpower that they could muster.

Susan made the copies and hurried back to the diner just as Nathan and Charlotte were finishing their food. She handed them their copies and then started to talk to them about her epiphany. It was agreed that Charlotte should immediately leave town and return in a week. Nathan would interview what was left of the coven, and Susan would talk to other local practitioners about the spells contained within the journal.

The three of them left the diner and went to each of their cars. Nathan headed back to his apartment to get ready for his evening, Charlotte headed back to the hotel to pack her things and then leave town, and Susan headed to the nearest hotspot—she needed to find all the wiccan shops in the area.

Susan typed in her internet search and wrote down the names, phone numbers, and addresses of various shops in a sixty-mile radius. She went through the list and deciphered a route that would hopefully be the most convenient, and walked back to her car. After climbing behind the wheel she headed off toward the first shop on her list.

She pulled up to the shop and looked at the store. It looked like any shop in the plaza. Susan wasn't sure what she had expected, but it wasn't this. She wondered if this was the right kind of shop.

She strolled up to the store and opened the door, the tinkling of bells alerting the proprietor that a potential customer was in the shop. Susan browsed through the shop, idly looking at the candles, spices, herbs, and stones. She picked up a pink quartz crystal and ran her fingers over it. She realized that she loved the way it felt cold in her hand, the jaggedness of the edges playing against the tenderness of her palm. Even the weight of the stone made her feel more relaxed.

"How can I help you? Ah, that stone speaks to you."

Susan looked at the woman and smiled, "I guess it kinda does. What is it?"

"That is rose quartz. Wonderful, isn't it?"

"Yes. I have to admit, I had doubts about all of this stuff but this rock—" "Stone."

"Yeah, right, stone. This stone really, I don't know … "

"So, how may I help you today?"

"Well, I found an old journal and was wondering if any of the spells it contains are real."

"Oh, well let me see it and I'll let you know."

Susan removed the journal from her purse and handed it to the shopkeeper. The shopkeeper motioned for Susan to follow her and disappeared behind a beaded curtain. Susan walked through the curtain, noticing the way the beads clinked against each other as they cascaded over her. She entered a small room, a niche in the store. In the center of the room was a small, round table covered in a black velvet tablecloth. The room was lit only by candles and smelled of burning incense. Susan wrinkled her nose; she felt a slight tickle in her nasal passageway as the smoke from the room enveloped her.

"Please, sit." The woman motioned for Susan to sit as she moved a candle onto the table. She sat down and opened the journal. "Well now, let's see." She began to read. Minutes passed in silence. Susan sat, trying not to cough, watching as the woman read the journal. She glanced around the room, noticing all the paraphernalia one would associate with a fortune teller—a tarot card deck sat on a sideboard; next to it was a crystal ball. There were sheer curtains hanging on the walls, giving the room an otherworldly appearance.

Normally, Susan would laugh at all this. She would have found it mildly entertaining but now, after all she had witnessed, she just hoped that this woman was real. She had become a believer in all things dark and dangerous. She knew that true evil existed; she only hoped that true goodness also did. It was imperative to her only feelings of well-being.

The room's darkness prevented Susan from seeing the color leaving the woman's face, but she heard a change in her breathing. "What is it? What's wrong?"

"I ... I ... I can't help you. Please take your journal and leave my shop at once." She slid the journal back to Susan using only her fingertips, as if she was afraid to touch it any more than necessary.

Susan picked up the book, placed it back in her purse, and began to leave. She turned around and asked one last question. "Who can help me? Please, I need help."

The woman looked at Susan. "There is evil in that book."

"I know," Susan replied, "that's why I need help. Please. We have to end this, and end it now."

"There is one—Rose Adams."

"Rose Adams? I didn't find that name when I researched places to check."

"You wouldn't. She doesn't own a shop. She is a powerful witch. If I give you her number, will you please leave here and not return."

"Yes. Thank you. Thank you." Susan took the paper with the phone number and left the shop. She looked at her watch and saw that it had gotten late, so she went back to the hotel. On her way, she stopped at a fast food restaurant and bought herself dinner. She sat in her room, munching on fries, trying to decide what she should do next.

She knew that in the morning she would call Rose and try to get an appointment to see her. Until then, Susan decided to just rest. She took a long, hot shower, curled up in the bed, and flipped through the TV channels, looking for anything mindless and entertaining. While she watched a home repair show, she fell asleep. It was one of the last deep sleep she would have.

. . .

When she awoke the next morning, she felt refreshed and ready to tackle the day. After showering and getting dressed, she walked to the diner and ordered coffee and pancakes. She ate her breakfast and then went back to her hotel room. She grabbed her phone and the slip of paper with Rose's number on it. She dialed the number and then waited nervously for an answer. Her mind vacillated between making an appointment and then showing her the journal or just being honest and explaining her problem. By the third ring she had decided on making an appointment and then begging for help.

"Hello?" A voice slightly tinged with an exotic-sounding accent echoed in the phone.

"Oh, yes, um, hello. Is this Rose?"

"Yes, I am Rose. How can I help you today?"

"I need to make an appointment, for as soon as possible."

"Of course; I have time this afternoon. Say around three o'clock."

"I'll be there. What's the address?"

Rose gave Susan her address and then hung up.

Susan checked the time and realized that she had about four hours until she had to be at Rose's. She decided to reread the journal and to make a list of the herbs and spices that Lori Elizabeth had used. She was going to research the powers that they supposedly had and determine how they had helped to unleash the unspeakable evil.

She wrote her list and looked up the reported powers of each of them. She noticed that a majority of the items could easily be found in most kitchens, but some of them Susan did not recognize. She would have to ask Rose about them also. She opened her notebook to a fresh page and began to write down questions that she needed Rose to answer and explain.

Susan got into her car and drove to the address that Rose gave her. A sign hung in the doorway, reading "Palms read. Fortunes told." She knocked on the door, looking around. The door creaked open. A small, frail-looking woman stood in the doorway. Her long black hair hung down her back. She was wearing a long, flowered dress with flowing scarves draped over her.

"Ah, Susan, come in." she said as she dramatically waved her hand into the darkness behind her. Susan followed her into the darkened room, listening to the jingle of Rose's bangles. They entered an inner room and sat down at a table. "Now, how can I help you?"

Susan exhaled and started, "I actually have a few questions for you. Can we turn on some lights?" Susan blinked in the dark room, trying to make out Rose's form.

Rose, her voice sounding shocked, stumbled for a light. "Um, okay. But may I ask why?"

"I need to talk to you, not get a reading. I was told that you are the real thing and quite knowledgeable about these things."

"What kind of things?"

"Well, I found a journal, written by a practitioner, and it is full of spells and witchcraft. I was just wondering if it could be, well, true."

"Let me see it."

Susan handed over the journal, the pages with the spells and incantations clearly marked for Rose to read, and once again sat in quiet while someone read the journal. She felt the usual jealousy and rage over the idea that someone other than she was touching the book, but she breathed through the feelings and sat as still and quiet as possible. When Rose finished reading, she put the pages down and looked at Susan.

"You don't like anyone other than yourself touching this book, do you?"

"No, but I don't know why. I just feel very protective over it."

"So, what is it that you want me to explain to you?"

"Honestly, all of it. I mean, is this even possible? Are demons real? Can they be summoned and if so, how can we banish it?"

"I thought it was banished? That's what the journal says. She trapped it inside a spirit trap. It cannot escape that. She did everything correctly. She must be very powerful."

"But what if it is trapped but has found a way to, I don't know, communicate with certain people and to influence them to do things, out-of-character things."

"Unlikely, but anything is possible. Why? Tell me what is happening."

"I will, but the last woman I visited, the one who gave me your name, acted terrified. She read the journal and couldn't get me out fast enough. Why aren't you scared?"

"I am. I am terrified, but if this demon is still able to possess people, he must be stopped permanently."

"He is." Susan proceeded to tell part of the story to Rose, leaving out her own culpability and crimes.

Rose asked, "Can I keep a copy of the various spells and incantations that she used? I will be able to construct counterspells that way."

"Of course, but I don't have a copy. I can bring one by later today?"

"That will be fine. Until then."

Susan stood to leave. "Thank you and, um, how much do I owe you?"

"For now, nothing. Let's just stop this evil."

Susan smiled and left. She walked back to her car and headed back to the hotel. As soon as she got there, she planned to call Nathan and then Charlotte and fill them in on the latest discovery.

# ANNIE

Annie left Jared in the office. She now knew how long the procedure would take and therefore how much time she had before she had to return and bury the mummy. She never referred to the person as anything but food before and the mummy after. It was the only way that she could detach from what she is doing; what horrors she was bringing to the lives of others.

She went to a coffee shop and ordered an everything bagel and a cup of coffee. She sat at a small bistro table in the corner, listening to the Indie music while glancing through a local newspaper. She had started to read through the local papers, looking for any missing persons reports. She needed to make sure that she was protected; that she was not leaving a trail.

After finishing the paper, she reached into her backpack, removed a textbook, and began to study for her classes. She knew that she had to keep her grades up and go to class—had to keep up appearances so no one would suspect anything was different about her. She checked her watch and realized that it was time to finish. She packed up her things and walked out of the coffee house, like any other college student. She idly walked down the street before slipping down an alleyway that led to the back of the dental practice.

She used the key that she had found under her dorm door and entered the darkened building. She went down the hall and entered room 5. There she found the withered husk that had once been Jared. She carefully removed the suction straw from his mouth and placed It into Its holder. She then lifted what was left of Jared and carried him into the basement, where she dug a hole and dropped the body. She buried the body and walked back up the stairs. After double-checking that the lights were turned off, she locked up and started back to her dorm.

. . .

SATURDAY MORNING, ANNIE WENT INTO THE DORM'S shower, where she ran into her neighbor, Stacey. Stacey excitedly whispered, "Did you hear?"

"No, what?"

"Some frat boy has gone missing."

"What?"

"Yeah, missing. He had had problems with some other students during a lecture on Monday night. A few day's later, he went for a late night diner run and never returned to his frat house or dorm. No one has heard from him. Crazy, right?"

Stacey started to leave but turned back. "Aren't you in Dr. Epstein's psychology lecture on Monday night?"

"Um, yeah, why?"

"He got into an argument with some girls during class, after the lecture ended some of the other students were heard saying that he should be expelled. He must have really been out of control. Anyway, everyone left for the night. The next day, someone reported him to a dean. It was being investigated. Then he went into town a few days later. He was never seen again."

"Wow. That is scary. Guess I won't be walking across campus alone at night anymore."

"The college is arranging escorts for any student who wants one."

"That is great, except how would one know if the escort is someone safe?"

"Oh, I never thought of that. Maybe I will never leave this dorm at night again."

"But it could be someone here!" Annie tried not to smile, enjoying watching Stacey squirm at the thought that someone living near her could be evil, could want to harm her or someone else.

After Stacey left the bathroom, Annie looked at her reflection in the mirror. She wasn't quite sure if she recognized herself anymore or if she really cared that she didn't. She brushed her teeth and entered the showers. As the tepid water ran over her, she thought about Nathan. She tried to remember when she had last seen him but was unable to pinpoint exactly when it was.

She realized that if she was to behave normally, she would need to either publicly break up with him or start spending time with him again. She would have to weigh the pros and cons of both and decide. After rinsing off she wrapped her towel around herself, picked up her toiletry basket, and left the stall. She went back to her room, debating with herself about her Nathan problem.

By the time she was dressed and had brushed her hair she knew what she had to do. She and Nathan would have to break up. She didn't have time to pretend to be in a relationship, not with school and the machine's extensive feeding schedule. Plus, the expected mourning period would allow her the freedom she needed to find her prey and to dispose of the remains. Now all she had to do was figure out how to end things with Nathan.

The first thing she needed to do was find Nathan. Since she hadn't seen him in at least a week, she wasn't sure where he would be. She decided to check his apartment first. If he wasn't there, she would leave him a note asking him to meet her later that day.

# ROSE

AFTER SUSAN LEFT for the second time that day, Rose closed and locked the door to her shop. She went into the back of her shop and sat in her favorite soft chair. As she reread the journal, she recalled some of the facts. It slowly dawned on her that she knew who had written this journal; she had just never known her name, at least not her real name.

She laid her head back and closed her eyes. She let her mind wander back over the years, trying to remember the details of that night. The loud, desperate knocking at her door in the middle of the night, the look on the face of the woman who stood on her doorstep. The woman was disheveled, her clothes covered with sweat and dirt. But it was the look on the woman's face that she most remembered; it was the visage of someone who has seen true evil and lived.

Her eyes were almost closed, as if she was walking while half-asleep. Her hair was half in a loose chignon, half hanging down around her head. Her shirt was partially unbuttoned; her skirt's hem was torn as if it had been caught as she ran. Dirt was streaked down her cheeks and a drop of blood sat on her bottom lip.

"How can I help you?" Rose asked the stranger, as she

gestured for her to enter. The woman entered the building after looking over her shoulder, as if checking to see if someone was following her. She came in and locked the door behind her. She then sighed, sat down, and began to cry.

Rose placed a hand on her shoulder, gently squeezed, and then walked over to the sideboard. She lifted a tea tray and carried it back to the small table. She poured a cup of tea and handed it to the woman. "Just breathe for a few minutes."

The woman took a sip of the tea and told Rose a strange tale: one filled with a dead husband, witches, a powerful gypsy who advised her on how to construct a demon trap, a ceremonial priest, and a demon—a demon who was now trapped in something called a suction straw. Rose had her describe exactly how the seals were drawn on the suction straw and felt assured that she had completed the task correctly. She then advised her to run, to leave the area and never to return or have contact with her prior life. Giving the troubled woman her phone number, Rose told her to call if any trouble arises.

Rose reopened her eyes and looked at the journal. She was reading a story that matched the tale from all those years ago. She sighed, and then she rose and walked into the kitchen. She picked up her phone and opened an old phone book. She flipped through the pages and stopped past the halfway point. She dialed a number and waited for the other phone to answer.

When she heard the other line pick up, she said, "It's back."

The line went dead.

Rose went back into the front room and unlocked her door. She flipped the sign on her door and sat down at the table. She waited for her next customer.

. . .

The machine sensed that a new power was coming. It felt fear for the first time in many years. It was going to have to end this power. It had to find a way. This new power could not be killed the regular way; it was too powerful. The machine was going to have to find a different way to eliminate it. It would have to think on this, and if It was going to think properly and efficiently, It needed to feed. It had to call for Annie, Its source for food.

. . .

Annie felt the pulsing grow in the back of her mind. It got louder and more desperate much faster than usual. Annie knew that she had to find It food quickly or the pain would increase exponentially. She closed her book and looked around the library, but there was no one there alone save herself. She left the building and began to walk toward the dental practice. She saw Nathan walking toward her. *Perfect*, she thought. *This will be much easier than breaking up.*

"Hey, Annie," Nathan said, approaching her. He kissed her quickly. "Where are you going now?"

"Just for a walk. I need to clear my mind. Do you want to join me?"

"Sure."

Nathan and Annie began to walk away from campus. They talked about their past week and how busy they had been. Annie carefully and discreetly led Nathan toward the dental practice as they walked and talked.

As they turned the final corner, Nathan suddenly

realized where Annie was leading them. He knew what she was planning on doing, knew who had taken over for Charlotte. He had to get away from her now. "Um, Annie. I just realized the time. I have a big test tomorrow so I'm going to head back to campus. Are you ready to head back?"

"No; I guess I'll walk alone for a while," she said, disappointment echoing in her voice. Nathan quickly walked back toward campus, peeking over his shoulder as he went. Every noise he heard seemed to be Annie stalking behind him. He felt an intensity of fear like he never had before. Every molecule in his body felt like electricity was shooting through it.

As soon as he got to his apartment, he locked the door and went to his room. He moved furniture in front of his door. He then picked up his phone and called Susan.

"I know who is feeding the machine now."

"Nathan? Wait, what? Who, and how did you find out?"

"It's my ... girlfriend ... Annie. She just tried to feed me to it. I guess I should say ex-girlfriend, huh?"

"Oh God, Nathan. I am so sorry. Does she know where you are now?"

"Probably. I mean, she was my girlfriend, so, yes she knows where I live. Why? You don't think that I'm really in danger?"

"I don't know, just please be careful. And if you hear anything in the base of your skull, call me immediately."

"Okay. I just can't believe that it's Annie. It just ... well ... doesn't make sense. She has always been a caregiver. This doesn't fit."

"I'm more interested in finding out how she was called by it. Did she have any dental work done? And how is she getting in the building?"

"Oh God, it's my fault," Nathan said, sadness reverberating in his voice. "She went there to find out what happened to me; why I was having such awful nightmares after my surgery. This happened to her because of me."

"No. If anyone is to blame, put it on me. I unearthed it. I brought it back. I fed it and helped it grow."

"Lyra," Nathan uttered.

"Who?"

"Annie's roommate. Annie claims that she freaked out over the stress of midterms, but that doesn't seem like Lyra. You don't think that Annie killed her?"

"Nathan, anything is possible. I … " Susan audibly gulped, "… killed the man I loved for it. Once it takes over, you are no longer able to control yourself; it completely takes you over."

"Not completely; you and Charlotte both broke away. Maybe we can still save Annie too. What changed it for you?"

"Keith. When I realized that Keith was gone and I was the reason why, I became horrified and fled. It was just that. And I don't know what changed for Charlotte, except that Annie started to kill. Maybe the machine felt a better connection with her and left Charlotte. I don't know. Listen, I got some more information today. I met someone who may be able to help us with the whole magic part. But I am so tired right now. Let's meet for breakfast tomorrow. When are you free?"

"After ten o'clock."

"Great. I'll see you at ten thirty in the diner."

"See you then."

"Please call me if you need help tonight."

"I will. I'm done being brave. I'll take help wherever I can get it."

"Night, then."

Susan hung up the phone and got ready for bed. She was asleep within seconds of laying her head on the pillow, only to awaken throughout the night.

Nathan didn't sleep that night. He just lay there waiting to hear either from Annie or from the machine. There was no contact, but he still didn't sleep.

# ROSE

SOMETHING WAS TRYING to contact her; she could feel it in the base of her skull. She quickly stood up and placed her most powerful talisman around her neck. She burned sage and other incenses to help ward off the evil. She sat at her table, chanting to the goddesses for their protection. The humming stopped. Sighing with relief, Rose looked up just in time to see a young woman standing in her doorway.

Rose began to lay out Tarot cards, already beginning to see the future. The cards filled her with dread. She knew now that this young woman was not here for a reading; she knew to be careful around her. She felt an impulse to flee, yet she stayed, fastened to her wooden chair. Her destiny must be met; this she knew.

As the young woman entered the room, Rose sensed a stronger evil. She held her talisman in her hand as she said, "How may I help you? What do you want me to foresee?"

"Tell me my future" the young woman answered. "Tell me all."

Rose caressed the crystal ball, which sat on a pedestal on the circular table. "I see nothing of you," she replied. "The ball tells nothing. I am sorry, perhaps you could come back another time. My powers seem drained this evening."

"Please, I need to know tonight. Try the cards; they say the cards always know," said the young woman.

"I am tired; the cards will not behave as long as I am tired. Come back another night," Rose pleaded. She sensed mana in the visitor; she again grabbed her talisman and held it in her gnarled hand.

"The cards will behave," replied the visitor. "Just try. I need the answers."

Rose shuffled the cards and laid them on the table. "You must separate the cards into four piles; then I will try. But I can't promise. I am very tired."

The young woman divided the deck. Rose turned over the top card of each pile, her bangles chiming against her twitching arm.

"Read the cards to me," demanded the young woman, as she slipped her hand into her purse. "What does my future hold?"

Rose gazed at the cards and knew them to be right. She believed in the powers they held. "I cannot feel the cards; my powers are weak. I am an old woman and I am tired. Please come back another time," replied Rose.

The young visitor stood. "I shall return tomorrow night, then. Please be able to tell my fortune then." As she turned to leave, she whirled back toward Rose. And with flashing metal, Rose fell in a pool of her own blood. The young woman walked into the dark night. As she rounded the first corner, Annie looked down at her hands and saw that they were covered in blood. She wasn't sure why.

# CHARLOTTE

She hadn't heard a single sound from the machine in days now. She was finally getting used to the quiet again. She was not sure when she would be safe to return. But she was torn between her desire to stay away, to be able to live her own life again, and her responsibility in helping to end the horror of the machine. She ultimately knew that she would return, that she would help to end it. She would have to do penance for her crimes. That could only be done by helping to kill the demon and free everyone from its hypnotic power.

She would call Susan later and then decide when and how to return.

# SUSAN

Susan climbed out of bed early that next morning. She planned on seeing Rose before meeting Nathan for breakfast. She got ready, jumped into her car and headed back to Rose's. As she turned the final corner, she found herself unable to drive the rest of the way to Rose's shop. She pulled her car over and got out. She sauntered down the street and entered the alleyway. As soon as she entered the darkness of the shadowed alley, she realized that it was teeming with official vehicles. Two police cars, an ambulance, and the morgue van blocked the entrance to Rose's shop.

She stood in the shadows and watched as two men dressed in blue suits wheeled a gurney out of the shop. On it lay a black bag. Susan knew that Rose lay in that bag, that she was dead. She left the alley and slowly walked back to her car, her mind trying to wrap itself around what she had just witnessed.

Rose was dead. Their only help, the only way they had to stop this evil from continuing. Now they had lost their most important ally, the only one who truly understood the magic at play. Susan was beginning to believe that this would never end, that they had lost any chance of winning this battle.

Susan drove to the diner, parked her car, and walked inside. She scanned the room and located Nathan scrunched down in a back booth. He was staring forlornly at the table, his fingers idly tracing the lip of his coffee cup. She nodded to the hostess and walked over to Nathan's table. She signaled the waitress for a cup of coffee, sighed audibly, and sat down, exhausted. The weight of all that she had seen pushed her deeper into the pleather seat.

"What happened?" Nathan asked her.

"Everything, just everything," Susan whispered. She exhaled and then said, "I met a powerful witch. She was willing to help us. She was getting potions and spells ready; we were going to win." Susan took a large gulp of hot coffee as soon as the waitress brought it.

"That's great. I met with what's left of Lori Elizabeth's coven. With their help plus the witch you met, we might just stand a chance."

"No," Susan said. "She's dead. I stopped by there again today, to get more answers. The police and EMTs were there."

"Maybe she isn't dead."

"I saw the body bag."

"But do you know that it was her? Maybe someone else died."

"No, it was her. I feel it; I know it. The bag was the right size for her. She was very petite. It was her. Who are these women that you met with? And are they truly willing to help us"

"Yes, they have willingly, almost happily, agreed to help us. They were dismayed to learn that Lori used a ceremonial priest and had conjured up a demon. They want to put it right for her. They want to expunge the demon, to resurrect her—Lori's—reputation. They don't want their friend remembered like this; they don't want this to be her legacy. They will help."

"Um, not to be insensitive, but how old are they? Do you really think they can help?"

"Yes, I think they can. They are still powerful witches—they only use it for good, to help those in need—but they want to help, and I think they can."

"Well, I hope so. They might just be our only hope."

"There is one more thing—I mean it might be nothing, but it is a strange coincidence. The women started to reminisce about their families and those of the other members of their coven. One of the stories sounded a lot like my mother's story. From what I remember, her birth mother died while giving birth to her brother, who was stillborn. Her father had died in a war, so she was put up for adoption in Northvale. Even the time period fits."

"That is interesting, but does it help us?"

"Well, what if I hear it humming because I'm related to one of the witches in the coven?"

"If that were true, then we would all have to be related to one of them. What are the chances of that being true?"

"Yeah, I guess it is unlikely."

"Let's call Charlotte. We can have her look into any familial connections between those of us who are affected by the machine and members of the original coven. Maybe there is something to your theory. Maybe that's why we can hear the machine and others can't. I don't know how this will help us, but…"

Susan picked up her phone and dialed Charlotte's number. She waited through five rings and then hung up. "She's not answering. I hope she's okay. I hope she isn't … I don't know."

Nathan nodded and said, "Let's give her some time and then call again. She could be in the shower or something. Or maybe she needs to charge her phone. Let's give her a chance before panicking."

# ANNIE

ANNIE WAITED UNTIL well after midnight before returning to her dorm room. She still didn't know why there was blood covering her, but she did know that no one could see her like this. She skulked into the dorm and walked as quietly as possible down the hall to her room. She slipped off her blood-soaked clothes and placed them carefully into a garbage bag. She then put on her robe, grabbed her shower caddy, put on her shower shoes, and headed down the hallway to the showers.

She swung open the outside door and stepped onto the white tiled floor. She stood in front of the large mirror that hung over the four sinks that lined one wall. Her face was streaked with blood; stripes of red dyed her hair. The red ended where her clothes had begun. Where there had been no clothes, her body was painted.

She turned around and walked to the back of the room, where the shower stalls stood. She went to the very last one, stepped in, and turned on the water. Her robe hung on a hook right outside the curtain. She could see it as the force of the water moved the shower curtain. Her mind flickered to the shower scene in *Psycho* as she watched the blood circle the drain. She continued to wash the flecks of blood from her skin and hair. Once she was certain that she was clean, she dried off while letting the water continue running, hoping that the blood would wash far down the drain.

She then put her robe back on and walked back to her room. As soon as she lay down, she heard the humming sound. "No," she whispered, too tired to speak louder. The machine began to grow louder. "I said no," Annie said. "I'm too tired. I just can't tonight. Please." The machine issued one loud piercing shrill and then quieted for the rest of the night. Annie gasped in pain, which quickly receded. Her mind quieted down and she fell asleep.

When she awoke the next morning, she felt better than she had since before her first kill.. She stretched out of her bed and went to brush her teeth. The humming started. It began as a slow throbbing but quickly grew in intensity. She knew that she had to bring It food today, as soon as possible. It had given her a reprieve the night before, but that would not happen again. She knew that she would suffer greatly if she did not bring It food.

# CHARLOTTE

CHARLOTTE WOKE UP late that morning. She wiped her eyes and stumbled out of bed. This had been the first night that she had slept all the way through without being awoken by the machine. The quiet had been disconcerting at first but had already become her norm. After she finished getting ready for the day, she checked her phone. She quickly found that she had missed many phone calls from both Susan and Nathan. Fearing the worst, she dialed Susan's number first.

"Susan, is everything okay?"

"Yes and no. How are you? We were worried that something had happened to you. I'm glad that it didn't."

"Oh, I'm sorry. I overslept, for the first time in weeks. I slept so deeply that I didn't hear the phone ring. So, anything new happen?"

"A lot. I'll give you a brief synopsis. I met a witch who thought that she would be able to help us."

"That's great."

"She died. I met her yesterday and she died last night. Seems a little coincidental to me. I'm going to look into what the police know and try to piece together what happened."

"Oh my God, this is getting more and more insane."

"Wait. Nathan met with Lori Elizabeth's old coven—or at least, the ones who are still alive. They are willing to help us. Nathan believes that they will be an asset to us."

"Wow, that's great. How did he find them?"

"Internet. He's a college kid; they're all computer geeks. But listen, there is one weird thing. The women of the coven told him about some of their families. Anyway, he thinks that his mother may be the daughter of one of the coven members. She died in childbirth, and her older child was put up for adoption. The date and place line up with his mother's adoption."

"That's ... just ... wow."

"So, we began to wonder, what if the reason that he can hear the machine is because he is related to one of the original witches? If so, then why can we hear it?"

"Well, that gives me something to do then. I am going to research all our ancestry. Maybe I can find a biological reason that has enabled each of us to hear it while the others can't."

"That sounds great. I'll talk to Nathan and get as much information as I can and text you."

"Get Annie's information too. I need to find out about her too. I'll go back a few generations in hope that I can find a connection. Do you think that we may have inherited some kind of witchy power? A way to stop this thing? Because I have never done anything that would indicate any special kind of power."

Susan laughed. "I haven't either, but it is worth looking into. Who knows, maybe we just have to be taught how to use it. It's a long shot but worth looking into. Any help we can get."

Charlotte left her hotel headed to the county library to start her job researching. She felt happy to have a reason to get up and a way to help.

She walked into the library and asked the library assistant where she could find the public computers. She went up the winding staircase, turned left at the periodicals, and walked straight into the computer room. She sat down at the computer farthest in the back and logged on to the internet. She picked up her phone and checked for the text that Susan had promised her. Nothing had been sent yet.

She decided to start on her own genealogy. She found one of the genealogy sites, but then quickly realized that if she signed up for one of their programs, it would be traceable. If she was only looking for her family it would be okay but she was going to be researching a lot of other people. Sighing, she left the site and began to look for the information on her own. Her own knowledge only went back to her parents' generation; she could only hope that she would be able to find out the rest, that somehow the internet would be able to fill in blanks that her mother had always refused to tell her.

She entered her birthdate and her mother's. She filled in her father's name, but that was all she could. She didn't remember his birthdate, or if he had even told her any information about his family. She had killed him so quickly she never got a chance to find out anything about him or his—and her—family.

She was amazed at how quickly information was filling her requests. She began to take notes on the information she was finding. . She couldn't believe that she was finally learning about her extended family. She wondered why she hadn't done this before now. Was it out of respect for her mother? She hadn't spoken to her mother in years, so why? When the data stopped appearing on the screen, she looked at her cell phone again. She still didn't have a text from Susan.

She typed, "Susan, I need the information about you, Nathan, and Annie. Also, can you provide me with the names of the witches in the original coven, so I can compare. Thanks"

While she was waiting for the information from Susan, she began to read over the notes she had just taken. It was the first time she had seen the names of any of her relatives. She felt a desire to call them, to contact family.

Within an hour, Susan had sent Charlotte her own information. Charlotte began her next search. She inputted the data into the computer and began a search of Susan's family's heritage. Within a few hours, she had Susan's family mapped out for multiple generations. Charlotte began to compare their trees, looking for a common ancestor.

She glanced at her watch and realized that she had been in the library for six hours and was desperately hungry. Charlotte packed up her papers and research and headed out of the building in search of a place to eat.

Later that night, Susan sent Charlotte the information for both Nathan and Annie, plus the list of the members of Lori Elizabeth's coven. Charlotte put the list together and planned her next day's activity. More research was in her immediate future.

# ROSE

A SMALL FIGURE stood outside Rose's shop. She had stood there, hidden in the shadows, for the past several hours waiting for the police to leave. By the time they had left, the crime scene tape wrapped around the shop's perimeter, she had grown tired and hungry. But she had no time for sleep or food; she had too much to do, too much to take care of.

She silently stooped under the crime scene tape and entered the shop's interior. She looked around in astonishment at the shop. Nothing had changed, at least not perceptibly, since she had last been here. She began to mentally compute how long it had been since she had last visited Rose, amazed that it had been over fifty years.

She lit a candle and walked around, admiring the collection of herbs, spices, crystals, and other magical items that Rose had acquired over the years. She sidestepped past the pool of blood that had puddled on the floor and continued her surveillance of the room.

She went into the back room and looked around. She had hoped to find out why Rose had contacted her after all these years.

She saw it. It was sitting on a side table, next to a floral chair. She picked it up and glanced through the pages. She didn't know how Rose had acquired a copy of the journal, but it didn't bode well. Something must have happened for someone to have found this.

She left the shop and headed into town. She had to go to her old house. She had to make sure that it was truly back and killing again. She had to know what she was up against this time, if she was to stop it. And she would stop it, for good this time. This was ending now.

As she moved closer to the house, she began to feel a deep, resonating humming form in the back of her head. She remembered that sound—a desperate, angry plea. Quickly, she turned from her old home and walked away from the evil, for now.

# CHARLOTTE

CHARLOTTE AWOKE THE next morning and headed to a small café near her hotel. After eating pancakes and drinking two cups of coffee, she headed to the library to begin that day's research. She entered the library and wove her way back to the computer room. She sat at the same computer as yesterday, logged in, and began her day's research.

She started that day with Susan's family. Within a few hours, she had completed Susan's family tree and started Nathan's. Charlotte was growing weary and hungry, so she left the library and returned to the café for some lunch. While eating she used her phone to send Susan a message: "I have finished my family tree, your tree, and most of Nathan's. I'm taking a lunch break right now and then will finish Nathan's family and will begin on Annie's. Can you get the birthdates and places for the coven members? It helps with the trees. Thanks." Charlotte finished her lunch, paid for her food, and headed back to the library.

She spent another six hours in front of the computer screen, gathering the familial information for Nathan and Annie. She went back several generations before printing out copies of each file. She gathered up her information and headed out for dinner. She decided to go someplace new for dinner and walked aimlessly through the town, window shopping, finding great pleasure in the freedom and peacefulness she now knew.

She checked her phone, but there were no messages from Susan. Charlotte continued walking through the town, looking for a place to eat her dinner. She came upon a small pizza place, walked through the door, and ordered her dinner. She sat at a small round table covered with a red-and-white-checkered tablecloth, and took out her research. She realized that the information was too extensive and would be difficult to compare. She decided that she would make a chart of each family, so she could accurately compare each family member.

She finished her pizza and headed back to her hotel. Once she entered her room, she put on her pajamas, and climbed onto the bed. She then put a movie on the TV, took out her research, and began to compile the information. She decided that the best approach would be to make a chart, listing the family members in columns. That way she would be able to find any common ancestor that may exist among them. She smiled contentedly, remembering how much she enjoyed organization.

She opened a notebook and began building the chart, but she quickly realized that she needed a larger piece of paper, like a poster board. She would have to find a store first thing in the morning and try to find something that would be large enough to contain all the information that she would be gathering.

She put the papers away, checked her phone one last time, and then fell asleep with the TV still playing.

When she woke the next morning, she turned the TV off, stretched out of bed, and got ready for her day. Once again, she left her room and headed into town.

She found a store that sold office supplies and looked for the best tool for the job. When she came upon a poster board-size piece of chart paper. She looked at it more closely and decided that it would do the job. She picked up a few pieces, some new pens, and notebooks and went to the checkout to pay for her supplies.

She left the store and headed to the library for another day of research. She was going to finish Annie's tree and then start organizing the information that she had obtained thus far. It was time to try to find a connection between all the people involved. Before she compiled the information, she checked her phone and found a message from Nathan. It contained the names and birthdates of the women from Lori Elizabeth's coven.

She quickly put her chart paper away and logged on to the computer. She had become very adept at using the search engine and quickly began to put in the names and dates. By lunch, she had finished researching Barbara and was halfway done researching Judy's family. She hoped to be done by the end of the evening. When she returned from lunch, she finished Judy and Edith's families. By the time she was done for the day, she was exhausted. She stopped for takeout and brought it back to her hotel room. Turning on the TV, she mindlessly ate her dinner and went to sleep.

The next day, she went for breakfast and then returned to her room. She then began to write down the information that she had found on the internet. She started by drawing individual trees for each person, starting with Nathan. She had wanted to start on her own tree but was finding it difficult to do. She had never known any of her family, and now she was hesitant to find out who they were.

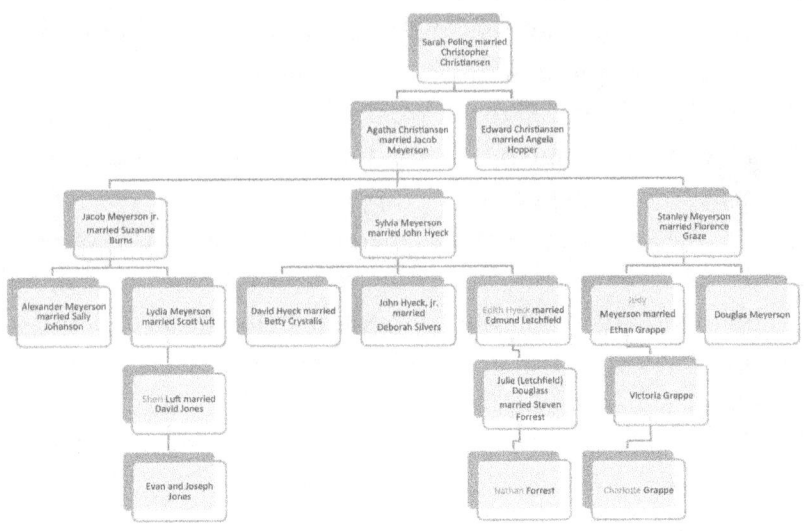

She spent the next hours drawing the rest of the trees.

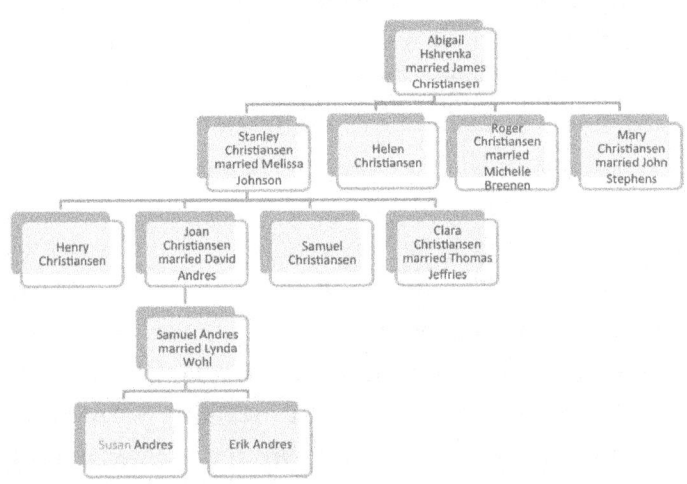

She began to see a connection to the trees and decided

to try to combine them into a singular tree. Could they all be related? Could this be why they could hear it? But what about the women in the coven? Could they hear it too? Charlotte knew that she had to combine the trees into one and then, if her hypothesis was correct, call Susan and Nathan immediately. They had to know.

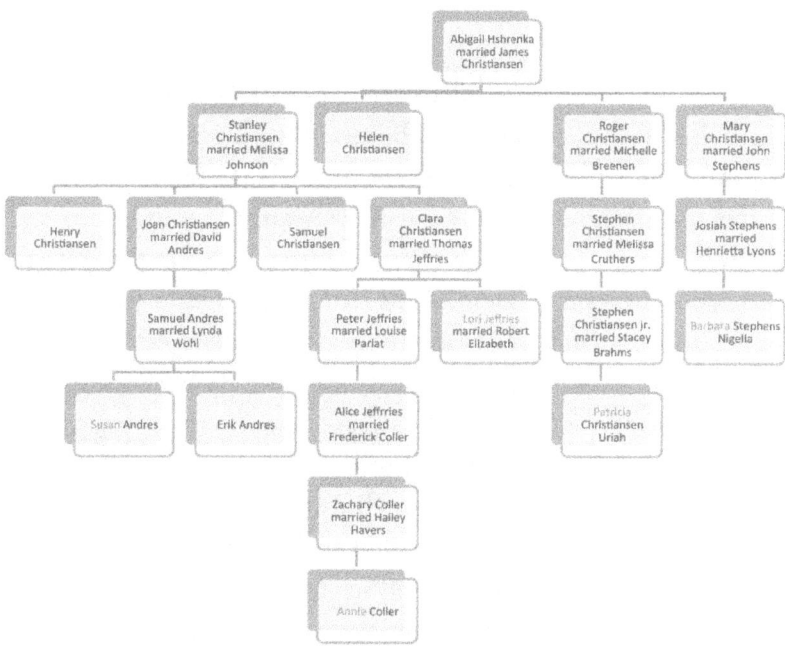

She needed to find out if James Christiansen and Christopher Christiansen were related. She quickly packed up her charts and data and headed back to the library. She went into the computer room and logged on to the computer. She entered the men's names into the search engine and scrolled through her results. Within minutes she learned that they were brothers. So they were all related, going back over many generations. She packed up her papers and left the library. She grabbed takeout again and headed back to the hotel. She quickly ate her dinner and then packed up her belongings. She would be going home tomorrow. It was time for her to rejoin Susan and Nathan; it was time to end this evil.

. . .

CHARLOTTE CLIMBED INTO HER CAR AND DROVE OUT OF THE small town. She headed back home, fully alert for any signs of humming in the back of her head. She was hoping, praying, that the machine would be out of her head. As she drove closer, she became more acutely aware of any sounds, anything that could indicate that the machine had located her again.

When she arrived at the hotel where Susan was staying, she checked in at the front desk and then rode the elevator to her floor. Once in her room she unpacked her bags, sat down, and examined the family trees. She still felt shock over the familial connections they all shared. After a few minutes, she locked her door and headed to the nearby diner. This was the time that Susan always had breakfast. She walked into the diner and scanned the restaurant for either Susan or Nathan.

She saw them sitting together at a back booth. She purposefully walked across the diner and sat down opposite Nathan, next to Susan. She smiled as she laid the family trees down on the table. "Christopher and James were brothers," was all that Charlotte said. She signaled the waitress and asked for a cup of coffee.

Susan and Nathan sat slack-jawed as they read the trees. "Wait, you mean we're related? *Annie* and I are related? Oh

God," Nathan sputtered. His face grew in revulsion the more time he had to digest the new information.

As Charlotte watched Nathan's face contort with repulsion, she realized that Nathan and Annie had been dating and that would mean that they probably had been together intimately. She glanced knowingly at Susan, who was also staring at Nathan with a look of shock on her face.

"It's a distant relation," Susan said, sympathy ringing in her voice. "It's legal and genetically safe. But it is strange that we are all related—some of us distantly, some much closer. This has to mean something."

"What about this psychic you met? Any more information there?" Charlotte asked Susan.

"Well, it was definitely her, the one who was killed. Her throat was slit using a double-edged knife. Why she was killed I don't know, and obviously I don't know who killed her."

"It's just too much of a coincidence. You just spoke to someone who was not only willing to help us but had the necessary skills to help us, and then that person was murdered." Nathan hesitated. "Just, this isn't this demon's method. According to my criminology professor, murderers tend to stick to one method. Why would it change now?" Nathan mused.

"So, what now?" Charlotte asked.

"I'm going to try to get back into Rose's shop. Maybe she left some information for us. Something we could use."

"That sounds not only illegal, but dangerous."

"I know, but we have to find out what she knew. We need her help, even if she isn't here with us. I have to try to find out something; it's the least I can do. What if she's dead because of me—because I went to her, I engaged her in this fight. I'll go tonight and look around. Maybe I won't be able to get in tonight, but at least I can look around and see what I can discover."

Nathan took a sip of his coffee and sighed. "I can't believe this is my life. I go in for a toothache and now I'm planning how to stop an evil demon who resides in a dental straw." He snorted derisively and added, "The dental hygienist I went to as a child called it 'Mr. Thirsty.' Kinda apropos, isn't it?"

They sat in silence, each drinking their coffee. After a few minutes had passed, Susan stood up and said, "I'm going to go and scout out Rose's shop. I'll let you know what I find out." She left the diner and walked to her car. Charlotte and Nathan watched as Susan drove off in the direction of the shop.

"So, what are your plans for today?" Charlotte asked.

"Going to class. Then I really need to study. I have exams coming up."

"Seriously? We have a lot of work to do finding a way to end this. There's no time for studying."

"You want to explain that to my parents? I need to do well in school, keep my grades up, or my parents will flip."

"Okay, sure. But please be available for us, in case we need you."

"You got it. I'll keep my phone charged and on."

Charlotte and Nathan paid for their coffee and then went their separate ways—Nathan headed to campus and Charlotte to her hotel room.

# SUSAN

Susan drove to Rose's shop, parking in the alleyway next door. She exited her car and slowly walked to the side of the shop. She peered through a window into the darkness. She suddenly saw movement in the dark recesses of the shop. The shadow appeared to move throughout the dark shop stealthily, as if the shadowy figure knew the layout by memory. Susan continued to watch through the window, wondering who this person could be.

She glanced around the area, looking for a car that this shadowy figure might have arrived in. She didn't notice when the figure left the shop and approached her.

"Who are you? Why are watching me?" the woman said.

Susan spun around, facing the small, white-haired woman. "I ... I ... " Susan sputtered, " ... wait, who are you? Why are you creeping around Rose's shop?"

"I was her friend. And you?"

"I was a new acquaintance. Rose was helping me with a problem I'm having. Are you also a colleague?"

"Well, yes, I guess so. Only I haven't seen her in many years. She called me and asked me to come in for a consultation for a new client. And you—how long, and why were you seeing her?"

"Not long. I'm having a little possession issue," Susan said half-heartedly.

"Well, good luck with your demon," the woman said as she turned and left the alleyway. Susan watched as she walked away.

The woman went back into the shop as Susan walked back to her car. She would have to return later, deep in the night, so she could look around the shop herself. She climbed into her car and sped away, traveling toward the hotel.

# ROSE

The white-haired woman stood in the doorway of the shop, watching Susan drive away. She still had to find what Rose had called her about; she had to look for anything that would help her understand how and why Rose thought that it was back and killing again.

She looked around the shop again. She opened every book, flipping through the pages. She went through each shelf, moving every piece of furniture, looking at every piece of paraphernalia. How did Rose know?

She sank down at Rose's reading table and stared into the darkness for a time. With a resigned sigh, she gripped the edge of the table to push herself back up. Her fingers, curling under the table, brushed paper. Smiling contentedly, she bent down and peered underneath. There she saw multiple papers taped to the table's underside. She carefully peeled the papers off the table. Once she had removed them, she began the chore of putting the papers in order.

She realized that these were spells and potions to counteract the demon. Rose had started to find ways to fight. Lori reached over and picked up the copy of her journal. She compared the spells, quickly sensing the power that Rose had acquired.

As Lori looked at the rest of her journal entries, she recalled the woman in the alley. Could she be the one who had found the journal? Could her "joke" about possession have been true? If she had somehow released the evil, then Lori would need her to help trap him again. She was going to need a lot of help, as she had grown old and weaker. She was going to need her coven, plus others to garner the strength needed to re-trap the evil.

How was she going to find this woman again? She needed a plan. She sat thinking and then stood to make herself some tea. It was time to contact any remaining members of her old coven. She needed to find out who was still alive, still practicing, and willing to help her after all these years and after what she had willingly unleashed on the world. She had already accepted responsibility for her grief-stricken actions, but would they be able to forgive her?

# NATHAN

AFTER ATTENDING HIS classes, Nathan went back to his apartment so he could study for his exams. As soon as he walked through the door, his roommate gave him a phone message. "Someone named Barbara called for you. Um, she said it was urgent. She sounded kinda old; is she your grandmother?"

"No, just someone who is helping me on a project. Thanks."

"No problem."

Nathan went to his room and called her back. "Hi, Barbara. It's Nathan. My roommate said that you called. What's going on?"

"You must come over tonight. Bring everyone who is working with you. It is paramount that all of you come here tonight. Ten o'clock. I will see you then." Barbara abruptly hung up the phone.

Nathan stood in his room, the phone still pressed to his ear. "Hello? Hello?" He exhaled as he laid his phone on his desk, and then flopped down on his bed. He lay there, staring at his ceiling. He knew that he needed to call Susan and Charlotte, but he just wasn't ready to. After a day in classes, he craved the idea of a normal college existence. He yearned for only being stressed about tests.

He woke up later in the afternoon, shocked at how late

it had gotten. He jumped out of bed and grabbed his phone. He quickly dialed Susan's number.

"Susan, this is Nathan. I got a call from Barbara. She needs all of us at her house tonight at ten. I don't know why, but she seemed, I don't know, insistent. I'll text you the address."

Nathan left the same message on Charlotte's phone. He hoped that they would both receive the message on time. In the meantime, he made himself some dinner and tried to study for his upcoming exams.

As night fell, Nathan left his studies and headed to Barbara's house. As he drove there, he called Charlotte and then Susan. Charlotte was already on her way, but Susan was not answering.

Nathan left another message for her. "Susan, where are you? Charlotte and I will be arriving at Barbara's soon. We'll see you there?"

# SUSAN

Susan was standing outside of Rose's shop. It had grown dark outside as well as inside the shop. Susan breathed deeply as she grabbed the doorknob. As she had suspected, the door was locked. She was going to need to find a way inside. She was desperate to find out if Rose had discovered anything that would help her.

She glanced up and down the alleyway and then began to move empty crates under a closed window. After making sure the alleyway was still clear, she climbed onto the crates and pushed on the window. It opened with ease. She pulled herself in and slid face-first onto the floor. She lifted herself off the floor, turned on her flashlight app, and began to explore the room. She searched through all the paraphernalia, leafing through each book in hopes of finding something, a note or scrap of paper.

After two hours of scouring the shop, Susan had not found anything of value. She looked at her watch and realized that she had to go meet Nathan at Barbara's. She pulled herself up to the window and crawled back out the window and onto the crates. She carefully lowered herself to the ground and walked back to her car.

As she drove to Barbara's house, she wondered if they were going to be capable of stopping the evil. They had lost

Rose and her knowledge. What were they going to do now? Susan began to feel despondent, as a wave of melancholy swept over her. She had never felt so pessimistic before, so desperate with negativity.

# THE COVEN

Susan pulled up in front of Barbara's house and climbed out of her car. She walked up the sidewalk, looking at the immense home before her. She knocked on the front door and waited for someone to open the massive door.

Barbara opened the door. "Susan?"

"Yes, sorry I'm late. I, um, got busy and lost track of the time."

"That's okay. Please come join us in the parlor." She led Susan into the home's interior. As they entered the parlor, Susan froze. Standing in front of the fireplace was the small woman from Rose's shop.

"You? Why are you here?"

"So, you are involved in this. I'm Lori Elizabeth." She reached out her hand in hopes of friendship.

"What?" Susan exclaimed, looking around the room at the other people. Nathan nodded at Susan. "Okay, well, so what have we discussed thus far?"

She looked at the table and saw Charlotte's charts displayed there. She looked around the room, noticing for the first time that everyone in the room was staring at papers in their hands. "What are those papers?"

Barbara handed Susan a copy of the papers. "Our family trees. Here's yours."

. . .

The silence had become deafening. The women in the room looked at each other, "So, in some way, we are all related to each other," Patricia said. "That is interesting. Lori, do you think this will help us in any way? Could we teach them to use any hidden powers?"

"I don't know. There is no guarantee that they have powers to use. It would take years to master the skills necessary to take down an evil this strong."

"But is there anything that we can do? Any way that we can help?"

"No. Powers are not genetic; they are learned over years of practice. I'm sorry, but you three"—Barbara lied, gesturing toward Susan, Charlotte and Nathan—"cannot be involved with this any further. You are a risk. It speaks to you, has already manipulated you into killing for it. It's been in your mind. We can't risk you."

Charlotte interjected, "We have to help somehow. I can't just sit back and wait for this to stop. I need to do something."

Barbara placed her hand on Charlotte's arm. "I know you feel amazing guilt for what you have done, but if it has access to you, it could sense something of us. From now on, we have to be very careful."

"I haven't heard it at all since I returned." Susan said. "I think that leaving severed our link."

Charlotte nodded, "It has disappeared from me too. I haven't heard anything, not even a slight buzz, in days. I think it's gone too."

They all turned and looked at Nathan. "I haven't been near it in a while, so I don't know if I can hear it. Should I find out? I can stop by the office tomorrow and see if I hear it."

"I don't think that is a good idea. So far it hasn't compelled you to kill or be killed. Don't take the chance. Please," Patricia emphatically stated.

They all sat in silence, trying to think of what to do next. Were Susan and Charlotte truly immune now or was it just trying to lure them into a sense of complacency? After thirty minutes, Sheri stood, yawning. "I'm done for tonight. Barb, I am too tired to drive. Mind if I crash here?"

"Of course not; the guest rooms are always ready. Go sleep, darling. We will start researching spells tomorrow. In fact, everyone get some sleep. We can continue tomorrow. Good night everyone." Barbara stood up and escorted everyone to the front door. "I have other guest rooms, if anyone else is too tired to drive," she offered. Susan, Charlotte and Nathan declined and headed out into the night, but Patricia and Lori Elizabeth accepted the offer to stay.

As they walked to their cars, Susan turned to Charlotte and Nathan. "Do you think they are really going to sleep, or are they going to cut us out of this?"

"I don't know. They seem trustworthy, but we may want to check in with them frequently," Nathan replied as he slid into the driver's side of his car.

. . .

CHARLOTTE STARTED TO DRIVE BACK TO THE HOTEL, BUT she felt compelled to turn off the main road and park her car. She climbed out of the driver's side door and walked into a wooded area, deep into the darkness of the trees. Charlotte had never been one to hike in the woods, but she felt the need to be here. She went further into the darkness, listening to the voices of frogs and owls. As she stumbled over roots and shuffled through leaves, her memory showed her the faces of all her victims. Each person whom she had helped to kill haunted her. Tears blurred her vision as she found herself hurtling forward, rolling down a hill. She stopped at the bottom of the incline, next to a riverbed. She sat up and looked at the slivers of moonlight gently rolling on the river's top. She suddenly knew what she had to do. She crawled to the water's edge, tears streaming down her face. She knew that she didn't deserve to live, that she was a murderer; her mother would say that she deserved to die for her crimes. She pitched forward, her face splashing into the water. But then she reversed herself just as quickly, the need to survive overriding her desire for punishment.

She crawled back up the embankment and found her way out of the woods. She then walked down the road until she came to her car, the lights still on.

Charlotte drove back to her hotel, took a hot shower, and went to bed. Tomorrow she would dedicate herself to killing this evil, in hopes that she could redeem herself.

# THE COVEN

AFTER THE THREE left, Barbara, Patricia, Sheri, and Lori returned to the living room. They knew that they had a lot to discuss now that they were alone. They sat, looking at each other, no one speaking for the first five minutes. Then Lori Elizabeth sighed and said, "I'm sorry. For so many things. I never should have made the original deal, I should have kept all of you in the loop as to what I was doing, and I should not have run away. I should have stayed, at least long enough to be certain that he was contained properly. And of course, I should have stayed in touch and let you know that I was safe. I was so incredibly selfish. Every one of these deaths is on me, on my soul. It is a mistake that I shall pay for, for all eternity."

"This is not the time for recriminations. We must banish this evil. We need a plan, and a backup plan. It's time for complete honesty. I have been practicing this whole time. Who else has?" Sheri inquired.

"I haven't, Patricia replied. "Not since, well, not since Lori disappeared. I need to confess I became convinced that we were messing with powers that we could never fully appreciate nor comprehend, so I quit practicing. It's been years since I even thought about it. Now I wish I had kept up. Hopefully this is like riding a bike. Barbara, why did you tell them that witchcraft isn't hereditary? We all know it is; it runs in families."

"They are too much of a risk. What if the machine still talks to them? They are not only vulnerable, they may be more culpable that we know. If we feel that we can trust them, in time, then we can find out if they are at all powerful."

"I disagree," Sheri said. "They came to us; I think that we can believe in them. And we may need their help, their power. It can't hurt to find out. I think that we should take the chance. Start training them as soon as possible. We are going to need their power, if they have any."

Barbara nodded her assent. "We need to go over how all of this happened," she added. "We've read your diary, but I have some questions."

Lori nodded. "I don't know how to begin. Or for that matter, where to begin."

"We know that it started with Robert's death," Sheri said, watching Lori's face for any signs of distress. She thought she might have seen a slight twitch on Lori's face when she heard Robert's name. She had sensed that Lori had still not finished mourning her husband. Fifty years later, she was still suffering his loss. Sheri feared that this could be a liability to their mission. Could they truly trust Lori? What if the demon attempted to make a new deal with her? Would she be able to fight the demon, to potentially sacrifice a reunion with Robert?

Sheri knew that she needed to talk to Barbara alone. They needed to have a plan, in case Lori became dark again. She suddenly realized that the women were talking, reminiscing about the time before Robert's death. She smiled as she joined the conversation.

Over the next few hours, the old friends laughed as they discussed their common past, the friends who were no longer with them, and adventures that they had shared. As the night wore on, the topic became serious again.

"Does anyone have any ideas on how we are going to do this?" Patricia asked, her voice betraying her nervousness.

"I don't know yet, but we are going to have to find a more powerful spell than I used last time. I got that spell from a witch named Rose. She was murdered yesterday. Apparently, she was looking into a new, stronger spell for Susan. Rose called me two nights ago. She told me that the evil was back; that's why I'm back, the only reason I would have ever come back. I explored her shop and her home. I found traces of a spell. But she never finished writing it down. If she found anything more complete, either her killer took it, she hid it somewhere, or she never wrote it down. We have a lot of work to do."

Patricia looked quizzically at Lori. "How strong is this demon?"

Lori pushed all of the air out of her lungs. "Strong. I trapped it in a devil's trap. It's covered in seals and hexes, yet somehow he is able to not only contact the living but manipulate them into killing. Which brings us back to the question, can we trust Susan, Charlotte, or Nathan?"

"They came to us. If they were willingly helping it, they would never have contacted us for help."

"I know that," Lori said. "What I mean is can we trust that the demon is not in their heads? What if—and I posit this as a hypothetical—what if it still resides in them? Is it able to read their thoughts? Can it gain knowledge from them? They may be a liability. I know that they mean well and want to help us, but if it can get into their heads, it will learn all our plans. We will be very vulnerable."

Barbara, Patricia, and Sheri all glanced at each other and then at Lori.

"If that is true, then we are vulnerable. It knows of us already. Let's hope it's completely gone." Sheri replied.

"I think, on that depressing and terrifying thought, I will call it a night. You know your way around my home. 'Til tomorrow, ladies." Barbara stood and left the room. Patricia, Sheri, and Lori all rose and headed off to the other bedrooms, each of them hoping for at least a few hours of uninterrupted sleep.

# LORI ELIZABETH

Lori walked up the marble staircase in Barbara's foyer and headed to the small guest room at the end of the long hallway. She entered the room and gazed upon the room's décor. Barbara hadn't changed this room in all the years that she had been gone. Lori remembered looking at the yellow flowered wallpaper in the week following Robert's death. The week her friends had insisted that she stay with them instead of staying alone in her now-empty house.

She opened the bathroom door and saw a new toothbrush and toothpaste sitting on the granite countertop. She smiled to herself, thinking that it was typical of Barbara to always be prepared for surprise guests. She brushed her teeth and then went over to the clawfoot bathtub, put the rubber stopper in the drain, and began to fill the tub with warm water. She found a green towel and a pink bathrobe in the closet. Carrying them into the bathroom with her, she tested the water temperature and then climbed into the tub.

As she lay in the water, she remembered the last time she bathed in this tub. The night after Robert's death, Barbara had brought Lori Elizabeth back to her home. Barbara had stayed with her until Lori fell asleep, probably fearing that Lori would drown herself in her depression.

Now she was picturing that night again. The pain she had endured that night. She had never allowed herself to suffer like that since. She had spent years locking herself up emotionally, but now all those feeling came rushing back. She found herself crying, not only for her Robert but for all the years she had lost mourning for him.

She left the tub, dried off, and crawled into bed. The activities of the day had left her exhausted and she quickly fell asleep—into a dream-filled nightscape.

*She entered the dark room, to discover it was filled with low-limbed trees, vines cascading onto the moss-covered rocky ground. As she walked through the room, tall weeds grabbed at her clothes. She could hear nocturnal animals chirping all around her. There was something restful yet horrifying about the place. She continued walking into the woods. As she moved deeper into the darkness, a dim light appeared before her. She moved toward the light as it swiftly darted ahead of her. She continued her journey, catching glimpses of the light as she adjusted her course in its direction. She stumbled over something. On the ground, gazing blankly at her, was the boy she had met earlier tonight. He was dead. She let out a gasp but then caught sight of the darting light. She continued on. Soon she came upon a fallen log, mushrooms sprouting from an object lying next to it. She looked at the object and found it was Susan's body, covered with moss.*

*Her heart raced as she continued through the dark woods. Her vision was becoming useless, and she began to feel her way past the trees. As she stumbled through, she felt something brush her arm. She froze and reached over. She felt a hand, a human hand, hanging in midair next to her. She moved closer and peered at the body, which was hanging from a nearby tree. She saw the visage of Charlotte. She, too, was dead.*

*Lori shook. The light once again appeared in front of her, and she moved toward it again. She was unable to catch it, so she continued deeper into the forest. The sounds were getting louder as the light once again dimmed. The sound slowly changed; it began to sound more like words, chanting. She moved closer to it, using her sense of hearing to locate its center. There she saw a fire, around which danced five women. As she moved closer, she recognized her coven as they moved around the fire, chanting. Lori did not understand the language that they were speaking. She moved toward them, as close as she could get before they magically moved away from her. All of a sudden, they stopped and looked at Lori. Recrimination radiated from them; their hatred for her overwhelmed her. They turned in unison, pointing off through the woods. Lori looked and saw the light, once again moving right out of her reach. She again moved toward it.*

*Only now, she was able to get closer, to make progress toward the light. As she got close enough to see it, it turned to look at her. At first, she saw Robert, smiling at her with love. She felt her heart skip, being lifted in joy. She moved to his side, reached out for him. As she touched his skin, she felt it—a leathery feel, snake-like. She recoiled as Robert's face turned into the demon's visage. She screamed and found herself being hurtled back through the woods, past the coven, still dancing, past the corpses of the new recruits, and then finally out of the woods and back into the light.*

She awoke that morning scared but with renewed desire to help stop the evil she had unleashed all those years ago. She decided that first, she would visit her old home. She needed to see if the evil was truly emitting from the old suction straw, that whatever had been controlling Susan and Charlotte was the demon that she had conjured.

Lori walked down the staircase and went to the dining room. There she saw a buffet of breakfast foods, from eggs and bacon to every breakfast pastry Barbara could have delivered. Lori grabbed a plate and put some eggs and a bagel on it. She poured herself some tea, sat down, and began to eat. As she finished her eggs, Patricia came in and joined her for breakfast.

"Have you seen Barbara or Sheri yet?" Patricia ventured.

"No, I haven't. I came in and found all this food waiting for us and started eating. I'm going to head to my old house next. I need to see what exactly is happening there."

"Lori, I don't know if that's a good idea. I mean, what if it recognizes you somehow? We need your knowledge to fight this. Let's wait for Barbara and Sheri so we can check with them. They may have an idea that will make it safe for you to go."

"Okay, I will agree to waiting to confer with them. But I am going to go there today. I need to know exactly what is happening if I am going to come up with a way to vanquish this evil forever."

After finishing their meal, Patricia and Lori set off to find Barbara and Sheri. They walked outside, into Barbara's extensive yard. They strolled past the rosebushes, which had won Barbara many blue-ribbon awards, and headed onto her flagstone path. At the end of the path, they found Sheri and Barbara, deep in conversation.

"Good Morning," Barbara called. "Did you have breakfast? I left you a spread in the dining room."

"Yes, we both did. Thank you," Patricia replied.

"Well, then, I think it's time to start planning. How can we stop this thing?"

The four women stood together, looking out over the

woods. No one spoke for at least ten minutes. Then they all turned and walked back toward the house. Suddenly Barbara veered left and led the women to a large shed in the backyard. She reached into her pocket and withdrew a small key. Unlocking the shed's door, Barbara ushered her friends inside the building.

"What is this? I thought you had stopped practicing," Sheri exclaimed, looking around. The small room was filled with jars of herbs and spices, interspersed with stones, gems, and crystals. "How long have you been collecting all this stuff?"

"Forever," Barbara replied. "I never stopped acquiring materials. I don't practice—I no longer cast spells or charms—but I do believe in being prepared. You never know when you might need protection. Looks like I was right."

"By any chance, do you have an inventory of everything in here?" Patricia asked.

"Not a complete one. I started one a few times, but I got distracted by one thing or another and never finished."

"Well then, I guess it's time to finish," Lori said. "We need to know what other supplies we still need if we hope to beat the demon."

"Let's get started." Barbara said. She went over to a shelf and removed a small notebook and pen. "It looks like I left off at this shelf." She divided up the paper and pens. Sheri and Lori compared the preexisting list with the two shelves that Barbara indicated. Barbara and Patricia began to list all the paraphernalia on the other shelves in the room.

# NATHAN

NATHAN SAT IN his bedroom, books and papers scattered around him. As he reread his notes, he was listening to the lectures. He realized how distracted he had been so far this semester. His notes barely contained any of the information that was on the recordings. He was relieved that he had thought to record the lectures, or he would never have had a chance of passing his midterm exams.

His mind wandered to Annie. He wondered if she was having the same troubles that he was. He shook his head to clear it of wandering thoughts of his ex-girlfriend, so he could focus on preparing for his upcoming midterms.

He stood and went to the kitchen. His roommate had left the coffee maker on day and night for the past week. Nathan poured himself a large cup of coffee and headed back to his room. He had a lot more studying to do before he had to leave for his first exam. He set his alarm to ring one hour before the exam would begin and began to cram as much information as he could.

Nathan was relieved that the coven had taken over; right now, he had too much to do. He didn't think he could fight evil and pass midterms during the same week. He knew that once midterms were over, he would have to rejoin the fight. But for now, he needed to pretend to be a normal college student instead of who he had been forced to become.

Over the next few hours, Nathan focused on his books and got as ready as he could for his exams. When his alarm sounded, he jumped up and headed across campus, listening to the lectures through his headphones. He entered the lecture hall and saw classmates fluttering around, jumping into multiple discussions, trying desperately to cram more information into their brains, hoping to discover that one piece of information that they had forgotten but would need to pass the test.

As soon as the teaching assistant came into the room, everyone put their notes on the back table and moved into their usual seats. They placed pencils on their desks and collectively sighed. The teaching assistant handed out the blue books and waited for each student to fill in their name and the school's honor code.

When Nathan finished his exam, he handed in his test booklet and walked out of the room. As he meandered down the hallway, his brain crying out for rest, he saw Annie leaving her exam. He debated whether he should turn and walk the other direction or continue on his path and risk a run-in with her. He sighed and walked past Annie; he stared straight ahead as if he was thinking about his next exam.

He started down the stairs while he ran through the differences that he had noticed about Annie. She had changed tremendously, yet it was probably imperceptible to anyone who did not know her well. Her eyes had circles under them, as if she had not slept well in a while. She looked disheveled, even more than typical for a college student during midterms.

Nathan knew that Annie was feeding the evil, that she was killing for it. But he still cared for her; he still wanted to help her, wanted to free her from its evil bond. He wanted her to have a chance at a happy life.

He would call the coven later in the day, after his last midterm. Maybe they would know how to get the demon to release her from its grasp.

# THE COVEN

As the four women worked on their task, itemizing the magical items Barbara had collected over the years, they talked about what they would do with Susan, Charlotte and Nathan. They needed to keep them safe, to make sure that the demon could not either coerce them into killing again or influence them to kill themselves.

"What about a talisman? A powerful talisman. We have some of the supplies here to create them. If we can make them strong enough, maybe they will be safe," Sheri said.

"It's not a bad idea, although I still think that we should encourage, not insist, that they stay as far away from it as possible. They are still susceptible to its powers." Barbara replied.

"How do we do it? I haven't practiced in years. We're going to need more supplies. And our old grimoire. Does anyone know where it could be? I haven't seen it since Lori disappeared," Barbara said, looking at Lori inquisitively.

"I left it, wrapped in black silk, hidden in a niche behind a picture in my shop," Lori replied. "Maybe Susan will know where it is."

"I don't think so," Barbara said. "If she had that, she wouldn't have come looking for us. She would have all the information she needed."

Sheri looked at her friends, her first coven. "I have it. After you vanished, Lori, even the police thought you were one of the mummified bodies. I used my key to the shop and removed some important items."

"You stole from me," Lori laughed. "What did you take? Maybe it will be useful."

Looking abashed, Sheri said, "I took some teas and candles, which I have used over the years."

Disappointment showing, Lori said, "Oh. Well. You have the grimoire, right?"

Sheri nodded, "I do. I've added to it over the years. It's quite thick now. I also have some crystals, ones that I found hidden with the grimoire. I'll go home and bring all of it back here." Looking at Barbara, she continued, "I'm assuming that this is going to be our meeting place."

Barbara confirmed that they would not only meet at her house, but that she would prefer that they all stayed together at her house until this evil was defeated.

They decided that Sheri and Patricia would go together to Sheri's house, so they could retrieve not only the items Sheri had taken from Lori's, but any other paraphernalia that they might require. Before they left, Barbara gave each woman a cup of mugwort tea, in hopes of activating their collective power.

On the drive over, Sheri began to reacquaint Patricia with magic, trying to jar her memory. She knew that they would need all the power that they could muster, so she needed to help Patricia recall her power and abilities. She needed to remind Patricia of the powerful witch she used to be; Patricia needed to reclaim her power if they were to defeat the evil.

While driving back to her cottage, Sheri turned onto an

unnamed dirt road. She drove past fields, hoping that this would trigger Patricia's memories. She drove past the grove of trees where they would gather in praise of the goddesses.

Patricia smiled as she realized what Sheri was doing; she looked out the window and exhaled as memories can flooding back to her. She began to recall the words for spells, the powers of crystals and herbs—it all came rushing back, and with it came the feelings of power and dread. What was she doing? How could she be messing with magic, with evil, again? She wanted to run away, to jump out of Sheri's car and flee into the woods, but she knew that was useless. She now knew that evil existed. She could not erase that knowledge; there was no more denying that such things did indeed exist in our world.

She also knew that it was time for her to cast away her fears, rational as they were, and stand with her friends against this evil. She would have to remember the past—the distant, horrifying past. She would have to relive the nightmares that had plagued her for all those years. Patricia was going to have to get ready to fight.

When they arrived at Sheri's, Patricia realized that they had ridden all the way to her friend's house in silence, both lost in their own thoughts. Sheri unlocked her front door and led Patricia into her living room. "Wait here. I'm going to go collect all the things we'll need."

"I'll come with you. I'm sure an extra pair of hands will help." Patricia followed Sheri through the kitchen and down into the basement. She had imagined that the basement would be more of a root cellar, with a dirt floor and shelves against the walls, littered with jars and pots of herbs and potions. She was shocked to see that it was opposite. The basement was finished beautifully with cedar plank floors.

Large wooden cabinets contained artisan jars filled with herbs and potions, each labelled lovingly with calligraphy. In the center of the room was a small round table covered with a green velvet cloth. In the middle of the table, sitting on a silver pedestal, was a crystal ball. A cut stack of tarot cards lay next to the ball, the Moon card showing on top.

"Wow. This is amazing, Sheri! It's so beautiful and organized. I had no idea that you were still practicing so seriously. So, what do you think we need to bring back with us to Barbara's house?"

"I'm going to get the Grimoire. Can you grab some of the boxes from the other room?" Sheri asked, gesturing toward a door on the other side of the room.

"Of course." Patricia walked across the room and entered the back room. She grabbed a few of the smaller boxes and carried them back into the main room. Placing the boxes on a sideboard, she waited for Sheri to return with the grimoire. When Sheri reentered from a back room, she was carrying a large book in her arms.

"Oh my God, it *has* grown. I can't believe how much you have done, Sheri."

"Thanks. I have more to add. I want to add all that we read in Lori's journal. Not only for the new knowledge, but also for as a warning for the next generation. There are some things that you just don't mess with, you know."

"Next generation? What next generation? None of the children of our coven practice, do they?"

"No, but someone will inherit this book, or find it at least. We need to make sure that this does not happen again."

Patricia removed a slip of paper from her pocket and searched Sheri's shelves for the items that Barbara had requested. She hoped that Sheri had the items and they did not need to go to a shop for them. She still found the idea of witchcraft terrifying and was praying that she needn't be too involved with it ever again.

She was relieved to see that Sheri had almost everything that Barbara was lacking. "If you add your supplies to Barbara's, there would be almost everything a witch would need."

"Is there anything that we need from a shop?"

"Yes, we are missing mugwort tea—we finished Barbara's supply. And what about talismans? Should I look for some talisman for all of us? I know that it's best if we each pick out our own, but since this is an emergency of sorts, maybe I should see about buying some. Fourth pentacle of the moon for protection, right? I guess I can go pick some up. Just tell me where I need to go. It's been so long since I've done that kind of shopping."

"Of course, I'll write down the address for you. Now, if only I could remember it." Sheri laughed. "You know how it is; I know how to get there but I'm not sure what the actual address is. I think I have a bag here somewhere, maybe their name is on it." Sheri began to look around her storage room and returned with a balled-up paper bag. Smoothing the wrinkles out, Sheri smiled. "Here it is." She handed the bag to Patricia.

"I'll come back for you when I'm done shopping," Patricia said as she turned to leave the basement. "Then we can go back to Barbara with all the stuff we need."

"Great, I will have everything packed up here soon enough. And definitely pick up any talisman that you see. We can never have too many talismans. Even if we don't pick them ourselves, they will be better than no protection at all. Oh, and some black tourmaline. We cannot be too cautious right now. Drive carefully."

"No fun in that," Patricia quipped as she left Sheri's house and drove away.

. . .

Lori and Barbara sat in Barbara's shed, drinking tea. They had been busy writing spells and making potions since Sheri and Patricia left and now found themselves exhausted. "It still amazes me. I get so tired just completing simple tasks. How did we get so old, so fast?"

Lori smiled. "I don't know. I don't always feel this old, but sometimes when I do too much, I feel ancient."

The two old friends both sighed appreciatively and continued to drink their tea.

# NATHAN AND ANNIE

Nathan stood outside Annie's dorm, trying to decide whether he should go in and talk to Annie or if he should walk away. His mind reeled with the possibilities of either. He vacillated between the chance of saving Annie, maybe even convincing her to join their coven, or running from her, knowing that she had already tried to feed him to the machine once. He needed to decide quickly. So, he stood there, shivering in the cold air.

"Nathan, why are you here? Are you stalking me now?" Annie hissed. "You need to accept it—we are over, done. You must go now." And Nathan knew his answer: Annie was too far in the grasp of the machine. There was no redemption for her.

"How many have you killed?" he whispered to her. "How many have you fed to it?"

Annie looked shocked for a minute but then quickly composed herself, smiled at Nathan, and whispered back, "Too many to count."

"Why, Annie? You can stop; others before you have. You can too. I can help you, please." He stretched out his hand.

Laughing, Annie simply replied, "Why would I want to? I'm finally having fun. Dear Nathan, I am good at this and I like it. I will continue. It needs me; It cannot survive without me." She confidently walked into her dorm. She turned back once, giving Nathan a large smile. Tossing her hair, she wiggled her fingers at him in a playful wave goodbye, closed her dorm door, and disappeared from his view.

Nathan, sighing with defeat, turned and walked away from Annie's dorm. He felt overwhelmingly lost. It was his fault that Annie was lost. If he had chosen a different dentist, she would never have met the machine. He had destroyed her chance at a life, and he was to blame, at least partially, for everyone she had killed. He slowly walked back to his apartment, the cold air searing his lungs.

Nathan sat at his desk, books and notes open. He was going through the motions of studying, but his mind kept wandering to his encounter with Annie. He found his heart was racing. He was scared—scared of Annie and scared for her, for what she had become. She wanted to kill him, to feed him to the machine. He could sense her newfound hatred for him. He wondered if she could sense anything from him. Could she tell that he was as determined to stop the killing as she was to ensure that it continued. He needed to tell Susan, Charlotte, and the other women. They needed to know how serious and dangerous Annie had become.

# THE COVEN

When Sheri and Patricia returned, the women diligently went back to work preparing for the battle. They created potions and wrote spells. Lori and Sheri created rudimentary talismans for all of them to wear for protection against the evil. For all seven they used a seal of the fourth pentacle of the moon. They cleansed the amulets by holding them in a stream of running water found at the edge of Barbara's estate. They then carried them carefully back to the shed and held the amulets in sage smoke while chanting a protection spell over each one.

Barbara called Susan. "Hi Susan, this is Barbara. I need you and the others to come to my home tonight. We have gathered supplies and made the potions. We need to begin to teach you three how to fight this evil."

"I'll let them know. What time?"

"Around eight will be fine. I'm going to nap now so I'm rested for tonight. I'll see you around eight. Oh, and Susan, stay away from It until then. Do not go anywhere near the practice. You are too susceptible to Its power still."

"Believe me, I won't be going anywhere near that place, and I can guarantee Charlotte won't either. I can't speak for Nathan, but I'll call him now. I'll let him know about tonight, and I'll warn him about the machine again. But he is so worried about Annie that I just don't know. I can't make promises for him; I can only try to persuade him to listen to your warning. I'll see you later."

Barbara hung up her phone and looked at her old friends. "I've done what I could. We can only hope that they can resist the pull and come here tonight, before it's too late for them. We should all rest now, together, for there is safety in numbers and we will need to be well rested for what comes next." She stood and headed to the stairs and her bedroom.

. . .

SHE DID NOT RETURN UNTIL SIX THAT EVENING. She appeared in the dining room, dressed in an old frock. It reached the floor and draped over her as if she were a Greek goddess. She stood regally at the head of her table and surveyed the place settings. Everything was set for a dinner party. Barbara turned and entered the kitchen. She walked to the stove, inhaling all the wonderful smells. "Jesse, as soon as dinner is finished being prepared, you may leave for the night. I'll serve the guests."

"Are you sure? I don't mind serving. I have no reason to go home early tonight. This is Barney's bowling night."

"No, no. This is a private affair tonight. Just finish making dinner and I'll take care of the rest. Thank you, Jesse."

"Not a problem. Call me if you need any additional help tonight or if you want me to come back to clean up."

"Of course, but really we should be fine."

"Okay, well, the roast should be done soon. Give me an hour and I'll have everything plated and ready to serve."

Barbara smiled and left the kitchen. "I really should

give him a raise this year," she mumbled to herself. And then went to her parlor to await her guests. Within a few minutes, Lori, Sheri, and Patricia came down the stairs and into the parlor. All three were dressed in silk finery and adorned with jewels.

"We assumed that these were hanging in our rooms for us to wear." Lori said.

"Ah, yes. You all look lovely. If we are to begin our witchy ways again, well, I thought that we should celebrate in style."

Sheri smiled in return. "Yes, back to our witchy ways. I will definitely drink to that." She walked over to the bar and poured herself and the others a snifter of sherry. She handed each a glass, saying, "To us, our coven. May we be blessed by the goddesses."

"For tonight and always," they all said and then drank their sherry.

Promptly at eight, the doorbell rang. Barbara returned to the parlor with Susan and Charlotte in tow. "Sorry, we didn't know the dress code," Susan said looking down at her sweater and jeans abashedly.

"Nonsense. You look fine. Besides, I have something for you both in the bathrooms. Charlotte, go to the one off the living room. Susan, the one next to the office. Come back when you are ready, darlings. We are witches tonight."

Susan and Charlotte left the parlor and followed Barbara's instructions. By the time they returned, Nathan was standing in the doorway, shock playing over his face. "Don't worry, darling boy, I have a tuxedo for you. Just go upstairs and turn left. The third door on your left. We shall see you soon, dressed and in the parlor."

Shaking his head in confusion, Nathan walked up the stairs, looking back down at the women. He quickly changed into the tuxedo, wondering how exactly Barbara knew what size he would need.

Nathan came down the stairs to find the five women, dressed in finery and bejeweled, standing in the parlor, each with a glass of sherry in her hand. He wondered when his life had become this. Costumed, with women of varying ages, drinking sherry, about to embark on his training in witchcraft. This was not what the average college student was doing on the first night after midterms. But then they also weren't about to enter a battle with a demon.

As Nathan entered the parlor, Barbara looked over at him, smiling. "Well, aren't you handsome."

The other women turned and looked as Nathan entered. "Hi, how is everyone?"

"We are all as well as can be expected, under these strange circumstances." Sheri answered. Turning to Barbara, she asked, "What first, dinner or witchcraft?"

"Dinner. I don't want the delicious meal that Jesse prepared to go cold. He is a wonderful chef. Let us go to the dining room and enjoy." They all followed her into the large room and sat around the table. Barbara excused herself and went into the kitchen. There she found their meal, set up on wheeled trays, ready to be served. She rolled the first cart into the dining room and proceeded to serve each guest a bowl of butternut squash soup with homemade croutons floating on the top. Each also had a sprig of parsley resting between the two croutons. As soon as Barbara sat down, they all picked up their spoons and began to eat.

As they ate their soup, they discussed their plans for the battle. "Most importantly, we have purchased talismans for each of us. They must be worn at all times. Anytime it is not on you, you are vulnerable to attack," Barbara informed the group.

Susan swallowed a mouthful of soup and then said, "A talisman? Is that really necessary? And what does it do exactly?"

"Well, yes. It is important." Sheri replied. "In fact, I insist that the three of you wear yours always—when sleeping, eating, showering, having sex. Never take it off. Even after we vanquish this demon. You may be susceptible to further demonic possessions after this experience."

"Wait, what? You're kidding, right?" Nathan sputtered.

"We don't know. But lore tells us that certain people tend to attract the supernatural. That could be you. After this fight, decide what you will, but for now—wear it. It could save all of us. If the demon gets into your head, he can access your knowledge. That could very well kill all of us."

"Oh, okay."

"But what is a talisman?" Susan reiterated.

"Ah, a talisman is a magical item that has a purpose to its owner. In our case, protection. These talismans," Sheri explained while Patricia handed out the items, "are charged with protecting our bodies and souls from evil. They should be successful."

They all placed their talismans around their necks. "What are they?" Charlotte asked, looking at the symbol and stones.

"The symbol is the fourth pentacle of the moon from the Solomon Seals. The stones are black tourmaline, agate, bloodstone, and black onyx. We tried to make them as powerful as possible."

Nathan looked at the necklace in his hands, "I ... you want me to wear this… always. Seriously?"

The women looked at each other. "You don't wear jewelry?"

"Well, no. I don't. Is there any other way to protect me?"

"You could get the symbol tattooed and then just wear the stones in a pouch." Patricia said, wincing with the words.

Nathan looked at the women and then placed the talisman around his neck.

"Is there a talisman for protecting you from people?" Susan asked, looking sideways at Nathan.

"Yes, the sixth pentacle of Jupiter protects from earthly dangers. Why?"

"Nathan needs that also."

"No, no more jewelry."

Susan looked at Nathan. "You need to be protected from Annie. This could help."

"Who is Annie?" Barbara asked.

Nathan cleared his throat before answering, "She was my girlfriend. She's the one who is feeding the machine, the demon. It's my fault."

Nathan's throat caught as he spoke those words. He hoped he could blink away the tears that he could feel rising.

"How is it your fault?"

"After my appointment with Dr. Andres, Susan here, Annie grew curious as to why I was having such vivid nightmares. I went there because I had a tooth infection. So then she went there to investigate. It's my fault that she is ... is a killer."

"She's not a killer," Susan said, "at least not more than I am or Charlotte is."

Everyone in the room froze, spoons in the air. They all glanced around the room at each other, each one trying to access the others' reaction to Susan's comment.

Finally, Lori responded, "No, you are not a killer—at least not in the classic sense. You are as much a victim as anyone. You didn't welcome this into your lives; you didn't call a demon in. That is on me, and only on me. I am the only one in this room who could be called a killer." She put her hand up to stop the protest that she knew was coming, "I called it in, I signed my soul to its doings, I allowed it to work. I alone am the cause of this tragedy. I will not argue the point."

Barbara stood and cleared the table. She rolled the cart back into the kitchen and left it on the side, near the sink. She then pushed the next cart into the room and handed out the next course. "No more shop talk. At least for now. Let's get to know each other instead. Learn about our strengths and weaknesses. You never know what will come in handy during this fight. Maybe one of us has a hidden skill that we can harness and use."

"I'll start," Charlotte said. "Although I don't know where to begin. I really have no special talents. I am organized and methodical, but nothing that qualifies as a talent."

"That is surprising. You are Judy's granddaughter, and she was so amazingly talented."

"Maybe so, but I am Victoria's daughter and she didn't allow for any art in our house. Life was organized and disciplined, not creative."

"I'm sorry to hear that. Judy would be devastated."

"But you are creative," Susan said. "Just not in the arts. You found creative ways around insurance company protocols, creative filing solutions. Creativity takes different forms."

"Still, there isn't a real use for those skills right now," Charlotte said.

"That's not entirely true," Sheri said. "You are tasked, stating tonight, with organizing all the potions, chants, spells and other paraphernalia that we have. We need it catalogued so we know exactly what we have and what we still need to get or do. It's going to be a lot of work. Are you up for it?"

Charlotte smiled, glad to be useful again. "Of course. Give me whatever you have, and I'll get to work on it right away."

"Now you, Susan. We know that you are a dentist, so that means you have some skills, but how can we use these to help us fight?"

"I don't know, but I do know Latin. I went to medical school before dentistry. Maybe I could help with any spells translated into Latin. If that's a thing?"

"Actually, it is. And mispronunciations can cause problems. You can also help us with your knowledge. You were the one to unearth it, and you were the first feeder, right?"

"Yes, but how will that help?"

"You may know something that you don't realize is important. We will sit together later, just us, so I can hear your story."

Barbara smiled as Sheri took the lead in gathering information. Watching her friend back in her true element brought joy to Barbara, even in such horrible circumstances.

"I'm sorry, but I bring nothing to the table," Nathan said. "I have no talents; I'm just an average guy who had a toothache. I'm related to you all, but I think I may be useless here."

"You're not," Charlotte interrupted. "First off, you resisted it. Somehow you can ignore its pull. That could prove to be very useful." Clearing her throat, she continued, looking away from Nathan, "You are also, well, knowledgeable about Annie. She's the new feeder. You know her personality. Is she going to fight to protect it, or will she walk away? What can we expect from her?"

"Um, wow, I'm not sure. She is very maternal, loves to take care of others. I hate to admit this but the needier one is, the more she likes it. If this machine sounds … "

"Pitiful enough?" Susan interjected. "It does. It starts like a mewling kitten and quickly escalates into an injured animal in great distress. You would have to be heartless to ignore it. It sounds so desperate, so … you just can't resist its screams of agony."

"Yes, that would convince Annie to take care of it. To nurture it. To feed it, even if that means hurting another. She grew up on a farm and, well, values life a little differently than I do."

"Nathan, you have to tell them what happened the other day." Susan said.

Nathan looked away from the group for a few seconds. Turning back to them, he said, "Annie tried to kill me, to feed me to the machine. She now knows that I know something is happening, that I suspect that her roommate, Lyra, didn't just go home. We went for a walk to talk about, well, us when I realized that she had led me to the practice. As soon as I recognized where we were going, I made an excuse and left the area."

"Is that the last time that you saw her?" Patricia asked.

"No, I ran into her this past week, in the hallway after finishing a midterm. She looked tired, more tired than anyone else during midterms. She also looked haphazard, disheveled. I don't think she has slept in a while. She also gave me a look of disdain, of pure hatred. It just didn't seem like the Annie that I knew." Looking at his lap, Nathan continued, "I went to her dorm room last night. I pleaded with her to join us, to fight the machine. She won't. She is determined to help it, to feed it. She is dangerous now."

"What?" exclaimed Charlotte, "Oh my God, Nathan. I—I am so sorry."

Nathan nodded, hanging his head. "I don't think I will ever be able to forgive myself for what happened to Annie." Patricia patted Nathan's hand as she shook her head sadly.

They all continued eating their dinner as they thought on the new information about Annie. She might pose a larger threat than they had imagined. They definitely needed to protect Nathan from her. A new talisman would have to be made, that night. Nathan might not understand his value to them, but they were beginning to, and they needed to protect him from harm.

After they had all finished eating, Barbara cleared the table and again wheeled the dishes back into the kitchen. She returned with another cart, this time covered with small dessert plates. She handed out the plates and then poured a cup of coffee for each guest.

Everyone ate their tarts while drinking coffee. Once they had finished, Barbara cleared the room and met everyone at her back door. Passing out lanterns, Barbara led the group to her shed.

"Please, come in all, and join me in a circle." They entered the building, putting their lanterns on a table. Barbara crossed the room and lit seven cinnamon candles. They joined in a circle and Barbara began to chant, "We welcome Susan, Charlotte, and Nathan into our coven. Please bless them, goddesses, protect them and help guide them through the trials that they are about to enter. Look over all of us, empower us so that we can prevail against this evil."

They looked at each other, then Sheri said, "Well, let's get to work. It's time to teach you how to do some magic." She smiled at them as she walked over to a table. She picked up a collection of spells and handed them to the three. "You need to learn these—I mean old-fashioned memorization. You need to know these forward and backward. They should be ingrained."

"Yeah, okay," Nathan replied.

"I'm serious; if you are being tortured, supernaturally, these could save not only your life but your soul."

"Tortured?"

"Yes. This demon is evil, true evil. He will do anything to survive, to feed. That includes torturing or even killing you. Know these spells, know how to use them and when. This is no joke."

"I had a toothache and now I'm fighting a demon? What the fuck happened to my life?" Nathan mumbled as he took the package of papers from Sheri. Lori stood silently in the corner, watching the three reading the rudimentary spells. She walked over to the potions table and began to organize the herbs and spices. "We are going to need some other items," she called.

"I have more in my car," Sheri said. "Could you three help me get them?" she asked Nathan, Susan, and Charlotte.

"Absolutely," Charlotte replied as she, Nathan, and Susan walked toward the door. "I'll show them," Patricia said as she led them to Sheri's jeep. Boxes of jars, bags, and books filled the back of the jeep. They each lifted a box out and carried it back to the shed. They made four similar trips before the jeep was empty. Lori was busy organizing the supplies.

Looking at the clock, Barbara saw that it was already after midnight. "Okay, it's late. Let's get together again tomorrow. You three," motioning to Susan, Charlotte, and Nathan, "please, study those spells until we meet again. If you have any questions or need any help, please call either myself or Sheri. We can assist you in any way."

"You can call me also," Lori interjected. "I've been keeping up on my magic also. Just in case I ever needed it again."

Barbara looked at her shocked, "But you said … "

Holding up her hand, Lori interrupted, "I said that I wasn't practicing, and I didn't. I haven't cast a spell since that night. But I have continued to read spells and make potions, just to keep in shape." Looking at the three she reiterated, "I can help you also."

Patricia laughed, "I might call on you guys also. I haven't practiced since then either. I am definitely rusty with the whole magic thing."

"We are here for each other. If anyone needs help, call on each other. Whether it is for an unearthly problem or an earthly one." Barbara said, saying the last part looking at Nathan. "We must rely on one another's strength now."

"Yes, now go and get some rest. We start training tomorrow." Sheri stated as the group dispersed. As Lori and Barbara headed back to the main house, the rest of the coven each headed back to their homes. Susan, Nathan and Charlotte had decided against staying at Barbara's, for they feared that the demon might be able to find the coven through them. Patricia drove home with Sheri, who had already warded her home against evil.

The next morning was the official first day of Nathan's autumn break and his first day of witchcraft training. He had convinced his parents that he would be unable to come because of his course load; he promised to be home for Thanksgiving day. He sat at his kitchen table, attempting to drink a cup of mugwort tea (Sheri's insistence) while perusing the booklet of spells. He had gotten an early-morning text to meet at Barbara's for their first day of training.

"Hey, Nathan, what are you doing today? We haven't hung out in a while, let's do something," Nathan's roommate, Kevin, said.

"I can't today. I thought you were going to Mexico this week?"

"Nah, couldn't get the funds together for Mexico or for going home. I'm staying here. So, can I join you for your plans?"

"No," Nathan said, too quickly, "I mean, I can't ... you can't join me. Sorry. Maybe we can catch a movie tonight?"

"Um, okay," Kevin replied. "I'll check what's playing and send you a text. See you later." Kevin left the apartment for his morning run.

Nathan picked up his packet and continued to read the spells and their accompanying potions. He finished drinking his tea, looked at the clock, and got up to go to Barbara's. With his roommate here for the week, Nathan didn't have full access to his car. He grabbed his phone, called Susan, and arranged for her to pick him up.

Once they arrived at Barbara's, they found the others in the shed already discussing the spells and potions.

"I really don't want to do that, Lori," Sheri said. "It isn't Wiccan. It's, well, evil, and it's why we are in this mess to begin with."

Lori responded, "I know, Sheri, I know. But we will be fighting an evil that you cannot fathom. We must use dark magic to fight, or at least we must be prepared to do so."

"I don't know either," Patricia said. "It seems awfully risky. I mean, what if it doesn't work and we accidentally conjure more demons?"

"You can't accidentally conjure a demon. You have to want it to happen."

"But you said earlier, Lori, that you didn't mean for this to happen," Patricia pointed out. "Which is it?"

Lori shook her head, "I don't know. I didn't mean for all this to happen. I was in such grief, I was so stricken and beside myself, I didn't recognize what I was doing. Now I do. We need to use dark magic if we are to defeat it."

The others in the coven glanced between Lori and Patricia; the look of worry plagued their faces. "Okay, look, I will make a deal with you. I will be the one to use dark magic. None of you have to use it, just me. That way, we still have the power if necessary. Before you object, hear me out. I am already doomed; I started this mess and will pay for my indiscretions. You are still clean; I will do everything I can to keep you that way."

Susan and Charlotte looked at each other and then at the group. "We are not clean. We are also doomed. Maybe we can help you with the dark side stuff."

The coven nodded with assent. "Okay, that is settled then, Barbara said. "Susan and Charlotte will train with Lori. Nathan, Patricia, and of course, myself, we will train with Sheri."

"Let's split up, then, and begin," Nathan said.

"Susan, you and Charlotte come with me," Lori said. "We're going to Rose's shop. She dabbled in the dark arts from time to time and might have the supplies that we need." The three women walked back through Barbara's yard, climbed into Susan's car and headed to Rose's shop.

Sheri went over the spells with Nathan and Patricia, teaching them how to pronounce the Latin words contained within. They needed to practice the syntax and rhythm of each spell and understand when each was to be used. After repeating the spells for two hours, they felt proficient with each one. They then went into the shed and mixed potions, using various herbs and spices, and gathered crystals for power enhancements.

Over the next week they met repeatedly, growing more confident with each visit. Patricia and Barbara quickly regained their lost skills, muscle memory taking the place of doubt and fear. They both felt comfortable saying the spells, making the potions. They were truly beginning to feel like a coven again, like powerful witches. They were beginning to feel that they were ready for the fight ahead.

Nathan did not feel as confident or relaxed with magic as the women did. He spent his evenings studying the spells and potions, practicing the chants. He struggled with the idea that he might have to use magic against Annie. He shuddered when he thought about how Annie tried to kill him, to feed him to the machine. He knew that he had to fight. He had to defeat—or at least try to defeat—this evil.

After the sixth day of practice, Nathan felt that he needed a break from witchcraft and evil doings. He sent a text to his roommate, Kevin, and arranged to meet him at the movies for a show that night. He knew that he needed time to relax and regroup his thoughts, and this was the best way.

Nathan left Barbara's house later than he had expected. Lori, Susan, and Charlotte had reconvened with the coven, ready to share and explain the spells and potions that they planned on using during the upcoming fight. Nathan left, shaken by the information, and headed straight to the movie theater. He arrived, purchased his ticket, and headed to the section where he always sat with Kevin. Kevin wasn't there yet.

Nathan took out his phone and sent a text: "I'm here. Saving you a seat in our usual spot."

# KEVIN

KEVIN HAD JUST returned from a run when he received a text from Nathan. He missed hanging out with his roommate; he had to admit to himself that he thought of Nathan as a brother rather than just a friend or even a college roommate. They had met their first week of freshman year and had remained close friends ever since.

They helped each other through breakups, failures, and bad weeks. Kevin was shocked when Annie and Nathan had broken up. He had imagined himself as best man at their wedding, an honorary uncle to their children. He hoped that maybe they would figure things out and get back together again.

As he climbed into the shower, he decided to work on Nathan that night at the movies. After pulling on a pair of jeans and a tee shirt, he went into the kitchen to make himself some dinner. As he was cleaning up his food, the doorbell rang. Kevin opened the door. There stood Annie.

"Hi, Annie. Nathan isn't here right now."

"I know. I'm actually here to see you," Annie panted, drawing breaths into her lungs slowly and painfully.

"What's wrong? Are you okay? Come in, have some water." Kevin opened the door and led Annie into the kitchen. He grabbed a glass and gave her some water. Annie sat down at their table and drank deeply.

"I need your help. I got a phone call from the dentist—I guess I'm still Nathan's emergency contact. Apparently, Nathan had another tooth issue and went back to that dentist's office. He needs a ride home and my car isn't working right now. Can you drive me over, so we can pick him up? I need to go since I'm the emergency person."

"Of course, that is so strange though. I'm supposed to meet him tonight at the movies. I wonder why he didn't tell me."

Annie stood and waited for Kevin to get his wallet and car keys. They left the apartment complex and headed to Kevin's car. Kevin glanced at Annie as they drove to the practice. They parked in the back lot and walked toward the front door.

"It doesn't look open; are you sure he came back here?" Kevin asked.

"Yes, they said that they stayed open late for him." She opened the front door and led Kevin into the front lobby.

Kevin began to feel uneasy. He recalled how Nathan had told him about the place, about the nightmares and the dread that he felt after the appointment. "Annie, they aren't open. Let's get out of here." Kevin turned to leave.

"Wait, they said they were leaving the door open for me. The receptionist said that she would be back soon. She was heading out for dinner. He is in room 5."

"I don't know."

"Let's go look." Annie walked through the lobby, hoping that Kevin was walking behind her. She led him down the back hallway and into room 5. She closed the door behind them.

"Where is Nathan, Annie?" Kevin started backing

toward the door, attempting to exit. Annie moved into his path. "Annie, what is going on? What are you doing?"

"Kevin, we need to talk. I'm worried about Nathan; he should be here. Something is happening with him." Annie sat down on the hygienist's stool and motioned for Kevin to sit on the examination seat. Kevin hesitantly sat down, exhaling, "So what is it, Annie? Look, I like you, and I liked you with Nathan."

"He has just seemed different, and I don't know why. I am afraid that he may be messing around with drugs or something."

Rolling his eyes, Kevin said, "He is not using drugs, Annie. I mean seriously, I am his roommate." Kevin quit talking and looked around the room. "What is that sound? Do you hear it?"

"What sound?" Annie responded.

"I don't know. I hear a strange hum. Let's get out of here. It's weird." Kevin began to stand up but found that his desire to leave was waning. Annie just sat, watching, as Kevin became confused.

"Annie, what's happening?"

"Just sit back, Kevin. Accept it; maybe even enjoy it."

Kevin reached over and picked up the suction straw. He moved it toward his mouth, his eyes pleading with Annie.

# NATHAN

Nathan wondered why Kevin had not arrived yet. The movie was supposed to start soon. He texted Kevin again. When Kevin didn't respond, Nathan became worried and left the theater. He looked down the street, but Kevin was nowhere in sight. Nathan was confused. It was not like Kevin to not show up when they had planned something. He decided to head home and find him.

Nathan arrived back at his apartment around eight in the evening. When he arrived at his door, he unlocked it. Nathan's heart began to beat faster. He slowly entered his unit and reached over to turn on a light. Kevin was not home, but he was not at the movies either. Nathan was worried.

He went into the kitchen and saw Annie's phone sitting on the floor under the table. He panicked. Annie had Kevin. Nathan grabbed his phone and quickly dialed Barbara's number.

"Barbara, it's me, Nathan? We have an emergency. I think—I'm pretty sure—positive that Annie is going to feed my roommate to It. I'm in our apartment, he was supposed to meet me at the movies, he didn't show. I found Annie's phone on the floor of my kitchen. We have to stop her, now!"

"Okay, Nathan, first I need you to breathe. I'll call Lori, Sheri, and Patricia. You call Susan and Charlotte. We will meet at the dental practice as soon as possible. Nathan, *do not go in alone.* You are not powerful enough to stop it. Wait for us, please."

"Right," Nathan replied. He hung up the phone and then called Susan. He filled her in on the details of the night. Then he ran out of his apartment, down the stairs, and into the night. He was gasping for breath as he turned the final corner. He arrived at the dental practice. The front door was ajar.

He looked up and down the streets, hoping for a glimpse of his coven. He shook his head. The ease with which he now referred to "his coven" disturbed him. He saw no one coming. Against Barbara's wishes, Nathan entered the practice. He could hear voices, as quiet as whispers, coming from down the hallway. He moved closer to the sound, slowly making his way down the back hallway toward room 5. As he moved closer, he recognized the speakers as Annie and Kevin. Kevin's voice sounded strained, scared. Nathan began to move closer when he felt a hand press on his arm.

Jumping back, Nathan turned his head and saw Charlotte standing next to him. "What are you doing? You were supposed to meet us outside." She mouthed to him.

Placing a finger to his lips, he pointed down to room 5. Charlotte heard two voices. She gestured for Nathan to follow her and they silently left the building. The rest of the women were arriving when Nathan and Charlotte were exiting the building.

"Just a little recon mission." Charlotte said as they joined the other witches. "There are two people in room 5 right now."

"Annie and Kevin," Nathan interrupted. "I know their voices."

"Yes," said Charlotte. "On a good note ... Kevin?" she said, looking for confirmation from Nathan. He nodded in assent. "Kevin has not yet put the straw in his mouth. We may be able to rescue him. What's our plan?"

The coven looked at Barbara first and then Lori, who in turn looked at each other. "I think we should take a two-front approach," Lori started. "Susan, Charlotte, and I will go on the attack. You guys will lend us spiritual support with chanting and potions. We are going to need your strength and power if we hope to win this battle."

Barbara nodded in agreement. "Okay then. Patricia, you and Sheri prepare the potions. It's time to begin."

The women removed vials of colorful liquids from boxes, each labeled with its purpose. They divided the vials among them, making sure that Nathan received any extra that they had. Lori did the same, dividing potions among herself, Susan, and Charlotte.

"Remember your spells. They are as important as the potions. If we hope to send this demon back to hell, we must use everything in our arsenal." She removed an athame from her bag and held it up in the fading sunlight. "This athame has been anointed with certain potions and, thanks to Susan, carved with seals that will destroy the demon's power. But it must be thrust into his chest if it is to fully work. I will do my best to kill him, but if I fail, get this knife and end this. He won't hesitate to kill any of us; we can't falter either," Lori said.

The seven walked into the dental practice and down the long hallway. Room 5 seemed far away. They continued down the hall, chanting, "Linquere hic mundus malus, nam malus comere non attigere huc apud Emmanuel." They each held a black candle, its fire flickering in the unlit hallway, causing shadows to play tricks on their eyes.

# ANNIE

Annie turned as she heard the chanting. The machine began to shriek in her head, *Stop them! Stop them now!* She walked to the door, glancing at Kevin as he held the suction straw. She reached into her pocketbook, retrieved a knife, and locked the door. She moved away from the door and stood by the window. "How do I stop them?" she asked the machine. "How do I save you?"

The machine sent Its message into her mind. *You must kill them. You've done it before; do it now.*

"I don't know how. How do I feed them all to you? There are too many of them. They won't just sit and wait for their turn."

*No, foolish child. I do not mean to feast on these witches. You need to kill them and then dispose of their bodies.*

"I can't kill them. Not if you aren't feeding on them."

*Yes, you can, and you have.* It showed Annie the images of her as she killed Rose. *Do this or they will destroy me.* The humming grew more intense, blocking out all reason from her mind.

"Destroy you? No, that I will not allow." She closed her eyes as the thrumming of the machine enveloped her. She felt the warmth of it surround her body, making her feel safe and somehow loved.

"Yes, I will kill them. I will not only kill each of them, I will enjoy it. I will relish their warm blood running through my hands. They will not destroy you."

*Hold your knife up and repeat after me: Devovere hic cultri ob mortis ea creatricis.*

Annie did as she was instructed, putting the curse on her knife.

She returned to the door, hearing the chanting continuing. She inhaled deeply, preparing herself, as the door began to open. *Of course, they had a key*, Annie thought as she raised her hand. Charlotte began to enter the room, potions in her hand. She was ready to make the first assault on the demon. Annie smiled at Charlotte and then thrust her knife downward into Charlotte's shoulder.

Charlotte let out a primal scream and recoiled out of the room, blood running out of her wound. Susan grabbed her elbow to help her regain her balance, continuing the chant. Charlotte stumbled back to Barbara, who caught her and began to clean her wound. "Keep chanting, Charlotte. Try to keep chanting." Charlotte gritted her teeth and continued to say the chant.

Susan kicked the door open again and looked at Annie. "Move out of the way, child," she yelled at Annie as she moved to Kevin's prone body. She pulled the suction straw out of his mouth and lifted him out of the examination chair, carrying him to the hallway, never letting her eyes leave Annie.

Annie just stood, frozen, as Susan left the room with Kevin's unconscious body in her arms. She listened as the machine gave her instructions, telling her exactly what she would need to finally release Him. He felt that He was at last strong enough to escape His imprisonment.

*Now, child, say the words. Smash the seals as you say the words, and I will be no longer bound.*

Annie walked to the suction straw, lifting it so she could see the base. There it was—the seal. Annie looked around the room, trying to find something she could use to render the seal useless. She walked toward the cabinets and picked up her knife. Using the hilt, she began hitting the base of the suction straw, saying "Solvere atque portare contra mea" repeatedly. The seal would not break. She knew that the others would be back soon to continue their attack. She slammed the base against the floor, cracking the seal. Annie watched as black-red ash came circling out of the base.

Before her stood a small man. He was dressed in old-fashioned clothing, holding a diamond-topped walking stick in one hand.

Outside the room, the chanting intensified. Annie dropped to her knees in reverence. "What should I do now? How can I serve you?"

"Ah, my child, you must slay the witches. I shall help with the more powerful ones. But they all must die, tonight."

Annie smiled. "Yes. They will." She turned and headed toward the door.

. . .

NATHAN HELD CHARLOTTE IN HIS ARMS. THE SPOT WHERE the knife had entered her skin had grown black, and a putrid smell emanated from it. "Something is wrong. She's dying! You can't die from a shoulder wound. Why is she dying?" Nathan yelled. He cradled Charlotte as she gasped for air, the blackness spreading through her. She could feel it creeping into her lungs. She shuddered as she fought for her final breath. Charlotte died in Nathan's arms. He gently laid her down, stood, and slowly walked back to the witches. "Charlotte," he choked, "She ... she's gone. Oh God, she died!" His eyes brimmed with tears.

We will mourn her later," said Barbara. "For now, we fight." She handed Nathan the new demon trap. "Hold this. You are in charge of it now. Hold it tight. Let nothing damage it while we perform the ritual."

Nathan held it. Charlotte's blood covered his hands and clothes. He moved forward with his coven.

As Lori and Susan entered the room, Lori gasped when she saw him, standing there as if he had not been vanquished at all. "How are you here? How have you been released?" Lori demanded, holding her amulet in her hand.

Coming out of the shadows, Annie said, "I did it. And now you will pay the dearest price for your betrayal." Annie raised her knife, swinging the blade down toward Lori. Lori moved with an agility belying her age, the blade just missing her.

Lori raised a potion, chanting over it. "Expello tergi contra infernum." As she tried to throw the vial at the demon, she felt her arm forced backwards by an unseen power. The crack of her bones echoed in the small room. "Nooo!" she screamed in pain. But she still fought. She raised her other hand, armed with a similar vial. And again, she felt her arm thrust backwards, searing pain careening throughout her body. "Expello tergi contra infernum," she continued. Before she could react, she once again felt her body attacked. Her upper torso bent back, her head touching her feet; her spine snapped. Her body lifted into the air, spinning, and slammed against the far wall. Lori Elizabeth's body crumpled into a pile.

Susan backed up, the only one left who had learned the dark arts. She knew that she could not beat the demon using magic; she needed another way. She left the room, saying to the others, "Lori is gone. Keep chanting; I'll be back." She ran down the hall, entering one of the other examination rooms. She quickly opened a drawer, withdrawing a large syringe. She froze for a minute, the deaths of Charlotte and Lori overwhelming her. How was she supposed to win this if a witch as powerful as Lori Elizabeth couldn't? She shook her head and blinked back tears. She couldn't let anyone else die; she had to defeat them—she had to win.

Retrieving a vial from her pocket, she filled the syringe with the potion. She then did the same with as many syringes as she could find in the room. She could hear the coven chanting "Expello tergi contra infernum" repeatedly. She hoped that they could hold him long enough for her to finish filling the syringes. Once she was done, she left the examination room and headed back down the hallway to room 5. She passed Barbara, Patricia, and Sheri, standing in a circle, holding hands, chanting. They each stared up at the ceiling, their eyes unblinking, as if in a trance. Susan could smell the scent of cinnamon emanating from them. She quickly drank a gulp of mugwort tea, which Barbara had prepared in a thermos, and steeled herself to re-enter the room.

Holding a syringe in her hand, she said an enchantment, "Mea sic genae caecus." Nathan gasped as Susan disappeared before him. "How did—" Nathan began.

Barbara interrupted, "Keep chanting, darling, keep chanting. We cannot stop or break."

Nathan continued to chant as he held the demon trap in his hands. His mind wandered to Susan, hoping that she would be successful in whatever she was doing. He wished that he had learned about the dark magic, about what the three had planned.

Susan slipped into the room. She looked at Lori's broken body, crumpled on the floor. Breathing deeply through her nose, she continued moving, inching toward the strange little man. She reached his side and moved into position. Holding the syringe against his skin she began to slide the needle in when her arm was stopped. A voice hissed in her ear, "I see you."

Susan gasped and tried to move away. "Oh no, Susan. You are mine now. He turned his face to her and smiled. Susan wanted to scream, she could feel it rise in her throat, but no sound came out.

She saw her skin becoming visible again and his talons digging into her flesh, droplets of blood pooling around each spot he touched. He opened his mouth, his teeth sharpened into fangs. He smiled, the horrifying smile of a shark, and lunged toward her. Without thinking, she plunged the syringe into him and pushed down on the plunger. The fluid flowed into his body. He bit down on her, puncturing her flesh. Severing her blood vessels, he began to feel the effects of the potion.

He felt as if fire ran through his body. Releasing Susan, he let out a scream that echoed through the building. Susan, laying in a pool of her own blood, smiled upon hearing his scream. She had hurt him.

He turned to her and hissed, "You bitch cunt, now you will die slowly and painfully. Much more so than I had originally planned." He lunged at her, his teeth shining with her blood. She reached into her pocket, retrieved another syringe. "You won't stab me again," he hissed as he waved his hand, causing the syringe to fly out of her hands.

Susan could only watch as he bit her again, ripping a large piece of her torso off. Shrieking in pain, she gathered all her willpower and again reached into her pocket. She angled the syringe and plunged it into her own thigh. Pushing down the plunger, she felt the potion enter her own body. She did it three times more with the last of the syringes. She lost consciousness as her body began to convulse. The demon continued to feast on her.

Annie stood in the corner of the room, watching as her master ate Susan's body, a smile playing on her face.

Barbara, Patricia and Sheri continued to chant. They heard Susan scream in pain, but then they heard a different sound. "Nathan, be ready. It's almost time."

"What? How do you know?"

"That sound, that shriek. It wasn't human. Somehow, she hurt him. We need to attack now."

The three women and Nathan walked together, hand in hand. Nathan held the demon trap in front of them. As they moved, they chanted, "Qu eccere incesta revertere utu bi nasci."

The strange little man looked over at them and laughed. "None of you are powerful enough to defeat me, to send me back. You can only hope that I will kill you quickly."

Nathan looked around the room and saw something silver gleaming next to Lori's body. He quickly moved toward it and grabbed the knife. Before he could think, he lunged at the demon and plunged the knife into his chest. He then held up the trap and yelled, "Incesta immanitas eo foras in tua inauditus ara."

The demon threw Nathan across the room, slamming him into the countertop. Nathan lay on the floor, gripping the demon trap in his hands, thrusting it into the air. The demon glowered at Nathan with a look of shock and anger playing on his face. He could feel the pull of the trap. Looking at Susan's desecrated body, he screamed, "What did you do?" He could feel himself weaken from the potions and the knife. He started to dissolve into dust, swirling through the air.

He turned to look at Annie, who let out a primal scream. The strange little man reached his hands out to Annie as she ran to him, trying to stop the process. "No!" she cried. "No!"

She grabbed his hands as they disintegrated. His corporeal body was no more as he floated through Annie, burning her skin, and was summoned into the trap in Nathan's hands.

"I have him. He's inside." For the first time since entering the building, the witches stopped chanting. They left the small confines of the examination room and regrouped in the hallway.

"It is done," Sheri declared. "Now what do we do with that?" she asked, pointing at the trap in Nathan's hands.

Nathan looked down at the trap. "Well, I don't want it." Then he remembered Annie.

"Annie," he said. He walked back into the examination room. There on the floor lay what was left of Susan. Feeling sick, he looked around the room. There stood Annie. "Annie, are—are you okay?"

Annie turned to face Nathan. A handprint of blisters, with a blackened center, displayed on her left cheek, as if she had been burned. "Oh God, Annie," Nathan whispered. "We have to get you to the hospital. We will get you help. I promise."

"Fuck you, Nathan," she hissed. "You destroyed Him.

You will pay for this, one day. I will make you suffer." Grabbing her knife, she climbed out the window and ran off into the night.

Barbara placed a hand on Nathan's shoulder. "We will figure out what to do about her, Nathan. But right now, we need to, well, to clean up here. What happened here tonight cannot be known to anyone."

"How do we do that?"

"Sheri, gather up any evidence of witchcraft. Patricia, you, me, and Nathan will carry the bodies to our cars. We'll bring them to my house for now." Patricia looked at Barbara, horrified. "Now Patricia, we don't have time for second-guessing. Let's go. Nathan, in my car is a bag of shower curtain liners. Bring them in; we'll use them to carry the bodies."

Nathan went outside to Barbara's car, finding the packages of liners in the back seat. Carrying them inside, he looked for any signs of Annie. He saw nothing. She was gone. He brought the liners inside and helped lay the bodies on each one. Then Patricia and Barbara carried Lori Elizabeth to the trunk of Barbara's car. Laying her inside the trunk, they returned to the building.

They found Nathan sitting next to Susan's body, tears glistening on his cheeks. Barbara touched Nathan's shoulder, saying, "We will give all three a proper burial. I promise." Nathan nodded and folded the plastic over Susan's body. He then carefully lifted her in his arms and carried her to Susan's car. He placed her in the trunk and then re-entered the building as Patricia and Barbara were carrying Charlotte out to place beside Lori.

"We have a problem. What about Kevin? How do I explain this to Kevin?"

"Did he see you here? Did he stay?"

"I don't think so, why?"

"Then you have no explanation; you know nothing about it."

"Right, okay. Now what do we do?"

"Bring the bodies to my house. We need to bless them and then bury them properly."

They each got into their cars and caravanned to Barbara's house. They drove behind the house, parking outside the shed. Climbing out of the cars, they opened their trunks and lifted the bodies out of the cars. They carried them into the shed, laying them on the floor.

"Tomorrow, we will meet here at midnight. We will then say our goodbyes to our fellow witches. Go home now and sleep. We had a tiring night."

Patricia, Sheri, and Nathan left Barbara's house and headed back to their own homes, each wondering if sleep would be possible after that night.

Barbara went to her storeroom and retrieved what they would need for the blessings. She would need three altars built and graves dug in the morning. She looked at the demon trap Nathan had left on the counter. She knew that she had to bury that also—a steel box and some cement. She laid the demon trap within the steel box and then locked the box. She had etched seals over the box and then consecrated it with oils and spices. She wrapped a strong chain around the box, locking it into place. She then placed the box into her wheelbarrow, along with a long-handled shovel, jugs of water, a lantern, and a bag of cement. She pushed the wheelbarrow into the woods, along a dark path.

Barbara had lived in this house for many years and knew her woods from memory. She knew when to turn, which path would bring her to the demon's final resting place.

As she neared the spot, she had to leave the wheelbarrow behind and carry the items by hand. When she had finally brought all that she needed to the spot, she lit her lantern and located the hole she had dug earlier. She emptied the bag of cement into the hole, pouring the water over it. She then mixed it together until it thickened. She dropped the steel box into the cement, pushing it down into the liquid until all of it was submerged. She then refilled the hole with dirt and placed a metal seal over the spot, which she also covered with dirt, hiding it from view. She uttered a prayer to the goddesses to look over the spot, packed up all her belongings, and headed home. She knew she had a busy day tomorrow and had much to plan.

But first she needed to sleep.

# NATHAN

NATHAN ARRIVED HOME to find Kevin sitting in their kitchen, drinking a glass of whiskey.

"Hey, Kevin. What happened to you? You didn't show up to the movie."

Looking up, glassy-eyed, Kevin responded, "Your ex-girlfriend is crazy. I mean certifiably insane. Man, I am tempted to call the police."

Feigning shock, Nathan sat down, replying "What? What do you mean?"

"She came by here, claiming that she needed me to take her to that dentist's office, the one where you had that surgery. She said that you were there and needed a ride home. Anyway, I went with her and somehow, well, she must have drugged me, because I was in a dental chair and for some unknown reason, I was putting that sucking thing, Mr. Thirsty, in my mouth. I don't know why. But it felt like she wanted to kill me."

"Kill you with a suction straw? That's not even possible. Where is she now?"

"I don't know. I was suddenly outside and really thirsty. I think I have drunk a gallon of water since I got home." Chuckling, he added, "and this," waving a half-empty bottle of whiskey.

"I don't even know what to say, man. Look, I'm beat. Let's talk this over in the morning, when I am better rested and you are, well, sober." Nathan left the kitchen and went to his room to sleep.

When he awoke the next morning, Nathan dragged himself out of bed and brewed some coffee. He then jumped into the shower, changed into clean clothes, and reentered the kitchen. Kevin was sitting at the table. A cup of coffee steamed in front of him; his head, hovering over the coffee, rested in his hands. "Just speak quietly," he muttered to Nathan. "Really, really quietly."

"Okay," Nathan whispered. "How are you feeling, besides hung over?"

"I don't know. I am still incredibly thirsty. It's like I can't drink enough. I feel like last night was a nightmare, but it was so vivid, so real. But why would Annie try to kill me? It must have been a dream. Sorry, bud. I didn't mean to scare you."

"It's okay. Just get some rest. Sleep off the hangover. We have classes on Monday."

"Right. I'm going to drink this coffee and crash again."

"Cool. I think I'm going to go for a run. It's been a while, thought it would be cathartic. Hey, by the way, do you know of any tattoo parlors around here? I'm thinking of maybe getting one." He touched the two talismans, which hung around his neck, out of sight.

"No, man, but Charlie should."

"Thanks, I'll ask him. See you later, then."

Nathan left the apartment and began his run. He soon found himself at Annie's dorm. He slipped inside and went to her room, using Lyra's old key. Annie wasn't there. He looked around the room. Most of her stuff was still there, but some of her clothes and photos were gone. Nathan knew that Annie was gone, at least for now. He left her room and continued to run. He rounded the psychology building and headed into the wooded area at the edge of the campus. He entered the trees and began to weave through them. He could hear leaves crunching under his feet as he took each gliding step. Birds were singing in the treetops. He suddenly felt a pressure in his chest, as if a vise tightened around him. He stopped running as he tried to catch his breath. The trees began to move around him, circling him. He sat down on a bed of moss, drawing his knees up. He placed his head on his knees and began to breathe slowly, attempting to control each intake of air. Tears burned down his cheeks. He sat in the woods and cried; he cried for Susan, and Charlotte. He cried for Annie, for who she had become—because of him. When he realized the sun was going down, that he had spent the entire day crying in the woods, he ran back to his apartment. He showered again and then laid down on his bed. He slept.

# THE COVEN

BARBARA AWOKE THE following morning, came downstairs and ordered her breakfast. She then went into the garden and walked to her shed. She glanced around; seeing no one, she unlocked the door and entered the room. *It wasn't a dream*, she thought, looking at the three bodies on her floor. *Well then, I need to have three altars built and three graves dug.* She sat down at her table and began to plan. She knew that the altars would be easy; her gardener could build them. She would just tell him they were display stands for plants. The graves were going to be harder to explain. She stood up and left the shed to find the gardener; she needed him to get started immediately.

She found him in the rose garden and gave him the instructions for the three altars. She then asked him to have three holes dug in the back grove.

"I am going to begin cultivating a garden and need to prepare the soil." He gave her an odd look but nodded. "It's a Wiccan thing," she explained. "I want to begin growing my own herbs to use in potions, so I need to prepare the earth. If you have any questions, I shall be in the dining room." Barbara walked back to the house, praying to the goddesses that he believed her story.

. . .

When midnight, the witching hour, came, the four members of the coven met in the shed. Carefully carrying the bodies, which had been adorned with flowers, frankincense, and myrrh, they brought them to their altars. Each altar was covered in rich velvet. They laid the bodies on the velvet and placed a white memorial candle for each woman. They placed other white candles around the altars. A single crystal lay on the chest of each woman.

Lighting the candles, Sheri began the blessing ceremony, paving the way from the world of the living to that of the dead. They each told stories about the three, celebrating their lives. And then they wheeled them to the graves. Laying their fellow witches—for after all that they had done, Susan and Charlotte were now witches, part of their coven—in their freshly dug graves, the witches sprinkled herbs on their bodies and then covered them with dirt, saying their final goodbyes.

www.ingramcontent.com/pod-product-compliance
Lightning Source LLC
LaVergne TN
LVHW091123090725
815713LV00001B/63